a
Speck of
Coal Dust

Praise for *A Speck of Coal Dust*

'Manchanda writes with a mock-gravity and gracious lightness of touch that are rare among present-day Indian English novelists ... this remarkably accomplished and occasionally very funny first novel brings a small mining town in Eastern India to life, a world to which he has given an unforgettable incarnation.'

— AMIT CHAUDHURI

'A finely paced novel about growing up in a small mining town, richly observant, its satire never cynical, its stories poignant, its effect far-reaching.'

— ADIL JUSSAWALLA

'A spectacular debut ... keen observation of detail, lyrical prose ... Manchanda manages to make the incidents narrated of absorbing interest.'

— KHUSHWANT SINGH, *Hindustan Times*

'Perhaps the most striking thing about Rohit Manchanda's novel is that it feels like a Bildungsroman with none of the genre's progressive temporality ... The book's focus on the provincial intriguingly anticipates the English popular novels from India of the following decade ... This deeply personal novel is also profoundly historical, achieving the verisimilitude of historical thought that can only belong to a child.'

— SAIKAT MAJUMDAR, *Los Angeles Review of Books*

'Wonderful eye and ear for detail ... poetic charm ... words have been employed for their sheer shape and sound and sensuous feel. Exciting flashes of experience are rendered by Manchanda in such painstaking detail that they often bring a painful lump in the throat.'

— *Biblio*

'Manchanda is exceptionally aware of the virtues of precision in a descriptive novel [and] portrays the idiosyncrasies of his characters with brilliant flourish ... A beautifully told story ... invariably witty ... immensely enjoyable.'

– *Outlook*

'Engaging and memorable ... a leisurely, unburdened style ... everything is seen minutely, steadfastly, tenderly.'

– *The Pioneer*

'A living and moving book ... exciting excursions into the recesses of a child's eagerly receptive mind ... throbbing with the spirit of childish abandon.'

– *Sunday Observer*

'Manchanda is able to capture the magic of childhood enduringly. Very few contemporary Indian writers can be said to have accomplished this feat. Warm and funny ... keeps you smiling all through the book.'

– *The Week*

a Speck of Coal Dust

ROHIT MANCHANDA

FOURTH ESTATE · *New Delhi*

First published in India in 1996 by Penguin Books
This edition published by Fourth Estate 2024
An imprint of HarperCollins *Publishers*
4th Floor, Tower A, Building No. 10, Phase II, DLF Cyber City,
Gurugram, Haryana – 122002
www.harpercollins.co.in

2 4 6 8 10 9 7 5 3 1

Copyright © Rohit Manchanda 1996, 2024

P-ISBN: 978-93-5489-885-3
E-ISBN: 978-93-5489-993-5

This is a work of fiction and all characters and incidents described in this book are the product of the author's imagination. Any resemblance to actual persons, living or dead, is entirely coincidental.

Rohit Manchanda asserts the moral right
to be identified as the author of this work.

For sale in the Indian subcontinent only

All rights reserved. No part of this publication may be reproduced, stored in a retrieval system, or transmitted, in any form or by any means, electronic, mechanical, photocopying, recording or otherwise, without the prior permission of the publishers.

Typeset in 11.5/15 Arno Pro at
Manipal Technologies Limited, Manipal

Printed and bound at
Manipal Technologies Limited, Manipal

This book is produced from independently certified FSC® paper to ensure responsible forest management.

*To the Jharia and Raniganj coalfields of eastern India.
Where marvels abounded, and went largely unrecognized
for what they were.*

AN EVENING IN THE DARK

In a room at one end of a bungalow overlooking scrubland that sloped down the side of a valley carved out by a river, of which, when it was in flood, a beige flowing tongue could be seen from the window, two boys darted about in random directions, hunting mosquitoes.

One clapped his hands below and behind his right thigh, which made him look momentarily like a folk dancer keeping time to his steps. Then he held up his hands and inspected the palms. 'One hundred twenty-nine,' he said.

Soon after, the other, younger boy threw out his arm and squeezed the air with his fist, at a point a little beyond his natural reach, so that he lunged maladroitly as he did so. He kneaded the air inside his fist for a moment, then held up his palm. 'One hundred thirty!' he said.

The boys wore tight dog-eared half-buttoned shirts and crumpled shiny gaberdine shorts whose contours changed fluidly with every movement they made for lack of underwear. They were fresh from their evening bath and their necks and torsos were clownishly white with prickly heat powder which had the feel and smell of crushed chalk, a rough and refreshing sensation.

Their movements were rapid and instinctive, as of mountain goats familiar with their terrain. Going wherever the mosquitoes flew, and in running on to the beds or jumping on to a table, or circumnavigating the chairs and stools that stood about the room, they needed never to pause to look around for bearing or for footing.

The younger boy opened a fist out of which an injured but not dead mosquito emerged, at first yawing and tumbling and pitching gently in the air, as though stupidly intoxicated or caught in a small storm; then, recovering its senses, and regaining direction, velocity and height, it made urgently for the ceiling. There it landed, calmly and immaculately, upside down.

'Escaped!' the boy said. 'My hands must have gone dry – I'll just wet them and come.'

It was a ruse they had discovered recently. Wetting one's hands gave a great fillip to mosquito-hunting, as the insects either got glued to the moistened hands or became catatonic after contact, leaden winged, easy to kill.

In the bathroom, the boy gave his hands an appraising look. Each palm had become an abstract fawn-coloured batik, fishbone-lined where the destinies on his palm ran, and patchily smudged grey here and crimson there with mosquito debris. At places, where mosquitoes had been flattened by slaps, there were lifelike imprints left by their corpses, clear as well-preserved fossils in rock. He sniffed at his palms a few times in an intrigued way. His reaction hung undecided between distaste and bemusement at the faint ammoniacal whiffs that issued from his hands. Giving up on classifying the smell, he opened the tap and washed his hands, leaving them dripping wet.

Meanwhile, 'One fifty-six, one fifty-seven,' came his brother's tally from the room. 'Come here, Vipul, I'm going to sweep the ceiling.'

Vipul went in to find Sameer standing on tiptoe, stretched to full height, on a table, trying to reach the ceiling with a coconut-fibre broom. The ceiling was speckled with twin blotches of mosquitoes and their giant oblique shadows. There on the ceiling the mosquitoes would normally rest until, on a sanguine whim, they would again descend, like frogs from the surface of water. Vipul wished he had a blanket that he could cause to gravitate upward and smother them all at once. What a large and instant difference it would make to the score: like hitting a six at cricket.

Sameer said, 'Vipul, be ready down there. I'll disturb them and you get them.'

'Ready,' Vipul said.

Sameer jumped a little, the tips of the broom's fibres scratched the ceiling, and dozens of the blotches got flicked off their lofty perches and wafted down. Vipul went on the chase again. Sameer changed position and shook off more mosquitoes from other parts of the ceiling. He then drove them out from their best-favoured hiding places, behind curtains and tablecloths. The room was alive again with game.

Again the boys scurried here and there, up and down, in an agitated murine way, puncturing the air with sharp claps and with shallowly reverberating slaps on the walls and furniture, and with silent fist-clenches. Vipul was becoming especially adept at the last manoeuvre, and took pride in it: it was technically the trickiest.

His hand had just been thrown, and was halfway to its target, when the lights went off. There was a brief, blank after-image, yellow as egg yolk, in Vipul's eyes for a second, and then a thick, viscid darkness fell over the room. Arrested in mid-motion, the boys turned for a fleeting moment into ill-postured mannequins, their joints flexed at unnatural angles.

But for the eternal undulating chant of the crickets and the frogs outside, it seemed to Vipul that the world had suddenly shrunk to a point, to the small space which his senses told him his body occupied. And he felt strangely exposed and vulnerable, as though the lamplight had served in fact to conceal him in a shroud of light which the hand of darkness had now lifted. He felt a little afraid. In light he was visible to those who lived by it, known familiar entities, but now he was visible only to the creatures of darkness, unknown, unseeable, and reputedly malevolent.

'The nnn ... night is full of EVIL,' Sameer said, in the low voice that he employed in order to sound sinister.

'Shut up!' Vipul said loudly, trying to drive out his dread with his own voice.

A droning sound approached Vipul's ear, low at first, then gradually becoming loud and piercing and threatening, then receding again, a microscopic fighter aircraft on reconnaissance. All that Vipul could do was to slap himself by the ear when the pitch of the drone appeared to peak, a measure that more often than not resulted only in stinging temples and aching ears, while the drone smartly, tauntingly, ebbed away to safety.

It was the mosquitoes' turn to hunt.

'Let's go out,' Vipul said.

To get to the veranda they had to negotiate two rooms, first their parents' bedroom, then the large high-ceilinged drawing room. They traversed the rooms cockroach-wise, in small blind zigzags, their arms put out before them making the swift feeling movements of antennae. As they emerged into the veranda, the darkness seemed to ooze out from behind them, from the interior of the house, and thin away rapidly in the open, as does smoke from a chimney, and finally get dissipated in the drizzling starlight by which Vipul could once again make out the contours and silhouettes of a familiar world: trees, walls, the gravelled driveway leading in from the gate; and on the terrace fronting the veranda, four cots and two motionless human forms reposed in wicker chairs, from which two voices issued: their mother animatedly telling their father of the effrontery of Thapa, the sweeper, who had broken yet another piece of precious bone china that day and remained as unrepentant and callous as ever; their father listening to this and humming a neutral uncommitted hum now and then, as to a story that did not concern him at all; Vipul could sense the distant attentive look on his face, as if he were engaged in picturing, on an invisible screen ahead, the incidents that their mother was describing, her words the restless rays of a movie projector.

'Why do the lights go off *every* day?' Sameer asked his father in some exasperation. He had been relishing the hunt. Today's tally was promising to be one of the highest ever. In an unclear way he held his father responsible for the failure of the power supply system; electric power, he knew, came from coal, and his father managed a coal mine; he was one of the links in an unreliable chain.

'It's load-shedding, son,' their father said. That was his stock reply, and made it appear that the power cut was somehow a necessary measure, even a virtue, and that after a period of light there needed to be one of darkness in order to maintain some cosmic balance, as in being cautious with money after an indulgent expense.

'What were you two doing?' their mother asked.

'We were studying, ma,' Sameer said.

'Good children,' their mother said. 'Live long, my diamonds.'

'What were you studying?' said their father, in a singing, casual way; he might well have been saying, 'What a lovely night.'

'Maths,' Sameer said.

'I was practising my handwriting,' Vipul said, feeling this to be a smaller lie.

'My gems and my hearts, Bitty and Bittu,' their mother said.

'Uff, ma, stop saying that,' Sameer and Vipul said. They were comfortable with the nicknames, but being called diamonds or gems or hearts made them feel cossetted and feminine.

Their mother said, laughing, 'My diamonds, my gems, my hearts. Bitty, Bittu, Buttu, Bitta.'

And when she said this their nicknames also sounded bizarre. As indeed they were: they had no provenance but for a poetic stroke of the imagination; no meaning. Almost every child in India has a gloriously nonsensical nickname: Kuku or Kiki or Kaka; Baby or Baba or Bubby; Happy or Jolly or Lucky; and most sublimely, yearningly, Lovely or Sweety or Beauty. Their 'real' names are meant only for official consumption: for schools, hospitals, railway reservations. At home using a real name is like calling the sky 'firmament': wasteful and pompous and cold.

They sat on one of the cots, and the strapping made of coarse jute rope pricked their thighs for a while before the sensation faded, considerately accommodating. From the scrubland beyond the compound wall, there came the sound of jackals wailing. And from the direction of the lawn to one side of the terrace, whenever a slight breeze brought it over, there came a smell both sweet and cool, of the white spindly blossoms of raat ki rani, the queen of the night, a shrub which lay low by day, its flowers closed and drooping, meditating on a course of action, and which at a stroke burst into a song of fragrance and of white rays at night.

They lay down on their backs, and looked up. There was no moon. The air had been cleansed of coaldust and made transparent, in the same way, it seemed, as is a windscreen by a wiper. Now the clouds had gone, and the sky was intensely and endlessly blue-black, as water deep in a dark well.

Sameer said, 'What was the score?'

Vipul said, 'Wasn't it two hundred eighteen?'

Their father said, 'What score?'

'The cricket match at school, pa,' Sameer said, and then whispered to Vipul, 'Good. That beats yesterday's score by thirty. Tomorrow we'll make it two hundred fifty. Then three hundred – imagine getting five hundred one day!'

Vipul, less ambitious on this front, said, 'Instead of this, why don't you teach me how to drive the jeep in the evenings? We'll never be able to kill all the mosquitoes.'

'You can't drive the jeep.'
'Why?'
'You *can't*. You're not big enough.'
'You promised me you would teach me this year.'
'But you haven't grown.'
'But you promised me.'
'Okay. But listen. You'll also have to promise me something.'
'What?'
'I'll tell you tomorrow. Ma, what's for dinner?'

Their mother was now talking about what had happened at the Ladies' Club where she had gone during the day to play rummy. Apparently Mrs R.K. Prasad, Auntie Prasad to the boys, had brazenly cheated...

'Moong dal and nenua tori, son,' she said.
'Which one is moong, yellow or black?'
'Yellow.'
'Why didn't you make the black one?' Sameer's voice whined with disappointment. 'It's much tastier.'
'You'll get it tomorrow.'
'I want it every day.'

Their mother ignored this and continued talking about Auntie Prasad. 'So childish and excitable, cheating for a few small points at her age...'

Vipul, thinking of the taste of the nenua tori, the slender gourd, sweet as peas and soft as papaya, continued to gaze at the stars. The longer he gazed, the more intricate and three-dimensional the sky seemed to become, its depth ascending into an ever-darker interior with each passing minute, its margins ceaselessly receding. Now it was a clear bottomless lake with lights submerged in it to various degrees. And those points of light which earlier had appeared adjacent to one another could be seen to be separated in fact by great depths, and no star really had a close neighbour; it was a cold companionless universe, deceptively gregarious, like a large family that on first encounter appears cohesive but on closer examination will quickly reveal its countless internal strains and distances. But the constellations had acquired a new kind of beauty: they no longer corresponded to the flat diagrammatic figures that appeared one day at the beginning of every month on the third page of *The Statesman*; they had now moulded themselves into dynamic forms, thrusting from the sky or diving into it, acquiring curves and warps and weaves. And on the surface of the lake above, adding to it a trace of warmth, floated the serpentine muslin veil of the Milky Way, cloudy and translucent.

Vipul thought of the names of the stars in the constellations that he had got to know from a booklet by Patrick Moore: Spica in Virgo, Arcturus in Boötes, Betelgeuse in the Orion: the names as quirky as the boys' nicknames. And perhaps they were indeed nicknames; perhaps the real names of the stars were in fact the standard humdrum ones – Laxmi and Jaya, Abhishek and Bhanu.

'Sameer! Look! Isn't that a satellite?'

Sameer looked to where Vipul's finger pointed.

'Yes it is. Ma, pa, I can see a satellite.'

'*I* saw it,' Vipul said. 'What is its name?'

Sameer said, 'Sputnik.'

'It's Russian, isn't it?'

'Yes. Isn't Russia bigger than America, pa?' Sameer said.

'Yes, it's very big.'

'America is smaller, and it also doesn't have a satellite,' Vipul said. 'If Russia and America wrestled, Russia would throw America on its back, wouldn't it?'

'What nonsense you talk,' Sameer said. 'Are these countries or people, that they can wrestle?'

To Vipul this mattered little. He pictured the maps of the USSR and the USA rising from the atlas and having a terrific tussle, in which the map of the USSR won easily, pinning down the American map with a deft, powerful pick-up and throw, leaving it bruised and distorted, looking like Argentina. There was also news of a 'cold war' going on between the two nations, and Vipul imagined their armies having been sent out to the glacial solitudes of the Arctic to fight their forlorn battles there.

The squat figure of Ayah appeared soundlessly from the drawing room, the folds of her teak-brown face and dark green sari thrown into sharp relief by the shadows cast by the candle that she carried, stuck into the mouth of a Coca-Cola bottle. Although she looked sixty, she was only about thirty-five years old; eleven children in eighteen years had transported her in a time machine to somewhere in the future.

When she saw the boys, anger and astonishment moved the shadows on her face.

'Ey,' she said, her voice hoarse, masculinized by beedi smoke, 'children-folk lying on the bed at this time! How will you build your appetites for dinner this way? Come on, get up and run about. Go, play. Up, up!'

She started tickling their bellies. Laughing, asphyxiated, helpless, they got to their feet. Then she said, to their mother, 'Namaste memsaab, I'm going. The food is ready, warm it up later. Chapatis are in the box.' And she said to the boys, in English, 'Good night, baba.' The boys laughed at her, as they always did when she used one of the few English phrases she knew: 'good night', 'good morning', or 'how are you'. They laughed at her raw accent, and at her intonation which made her sound gravely insinuating. She said these things with a broad smile, knowing that she would be laughed at, and apparently relishing the laughter when it came; it was an act of mild clowning.

She put the candled bottle on the floor, pinched the sari over her head and moved her head a little to adjust the hood, then made her way down the terrace and round the side of the house, the green flashes of her sari weakening as she walked away, dissolving finally in the dark.

And then, a jackal wailed very loudly, from the bush just beyond the boundary wall, and then another, and another. The jackals sent up their siren calls at about this time every evening, like a summons to the faithful for prayer, or as though a member of their tribe died every evening and whose passing they lamented, addressing the moon. But then one must have been born into their tribe every day, too, else the immemorial wailing would have dwindled quickly to extinction.

And the jackals were a nuisance.

Sameer said, 'These jackals. They eat up all our bhuttas. One day we'll go and kill jackals, okay, Vipul?'

'How?'

'I'll take the airgun.'

'You'll kill a whole jackal with only an airgun?'

'I can. You'll see. What you have to do is to get very close to the jackal and take good aim right between its eyes.'

'As if he's going to stand there and just watch you do that.'

'We'll go to the entrance of their lairs. Then as soon as one's face looks out – phat!'

That night Vipul said to his mother, 'Mummy, I'll sleep with you.'

Occasionally, once or twice a month, Vipul would ask to sleep with her. It was one of the greatest pleasures that he knew, ranking alongside the eating of a ripe litchi or watching and listening to the rain fall. Often he slept with her for reasons other than just the pleasure it gave him: at times he did so to ward off the oppressively frightening sense, which came on unpredictably now and then, of being watched and waited for by a ghost, and at times to feel her protective cover after some unpleasant incident involving the children of the driver or the gardeners, with whom he sometimes played. On such occasions he would draw up to her, and to feel her arm lying over his body would suffice to dispel fear and render him secure once again.

But when he lay with her for pleasure, he would talk to her, asking her about her parents and her childhood, and while listening to her he would transport himself to Delhi, where he went for his winter holidays, and then try to picture the Delhi of the 1940s and '50s, the Delhi of his mother's childhood and youth. This activity he found to be qualitatively the opposite of trying to construct an image based upon a narration: by default he imagined Delhi as he knew it, and then he would have to take away particular elements from the scene as his mother went on: for instance she would mention that she went to school in a tonga, and then he would remember that his mother had told him earlier, too, that then there were mostly tongas and cycle-rickshas on the roads, and almost no cars, and he would suddenly have to pluck out one of the elements of the image of Delhi that enthralled him the most – the roads full of cars, many of them sleek and foreign – and replace them with horses and carts, and horse dung on uncongested roads, and trotting hooves making clipped music. Or his mother would tell him that at such and such time, Balram mamaji, her younger brother, had been away in Bombay trying out a job, and he would then have to think of his grandfather's house in Delhi without Balram mamaji in it, which was a strain on the imagination because now he was there like a fixture, as essential to the aura of the edifice as the forever peeling paint on its walls.

And Vipul would ask his mother, as he did today, to make his back itch. She would then scratch his back very lightly with her fingernails, running her fingers in a variety of directions and patterns: up and down, or across, or in circles; in large sweeps or in a local strum. Much of the thrill lay in not being able to guess what her nails would do next, and where. And although it was his back that was scratched, Vipul would feel as though small sparks of itch were being touched off in his brain, making him dizzy and dreamy, and small cold shivers would run along his spine.

FOREIGNERS

ONE

The next morning, while Sameer and Vipul waited for the jeep to arrive to take them to the riverbank, they took a walk upon the parapet of the well.

They walked slowly and meditatingly, keeping to the parapet's outer edge, avoiding the vertiginous sight of the dark diving centre. Each walked with hands held behind his back, head bowed, reminding an onlooker of an entranced bridegroom and his bride circling the marital fire.

Vipul's senses were yet to recover from a tumult of recent sensation. Breakfast, the purpose of which appeared to be medication and therapy rather than to cater to taste, continued to be a rankling memory on his tongue and in his nose. It had started with an egg and a glass of hot milk. The egg left a gummy, cloying, stale coat on his tongue and made his mouth feel befouled for hours. And the milk went straight to his head, dizzying him, particularly if on its surface there formed that silky crinkled film of milk fat as it cooled. Then there were skinned almond kernels (to improve his eyesight with) that warmed his mouth, hardened his stomach; and then the raspingly sour amla:

amla, the myrobalan with the highest content of vitamin C, they said, of all fruits in the world, an acid distinction. And finally, there was that demon among tonics, the unqualifiably harsh 'blood purifier' called Safi, a green-black, sludgy liquid distilled from the bark and leaves of the neem tree, that, no matter how speedily he swallowed it, made the back of his mouth ache with bitterness.

After the very healthy breakfast, Vipul looked forward very much to having his uncomplicated tiffin in school.

Sameer said, 'I want to tell you about the promise you'll have to make if you want to learn the jeep.'

'What?'

'The first thing is that we should stop behaving like children now.'

'How?' Vipul said.

'The thing is, we complain too much.'

'What about?'

'Just about each other. We should stop this.'

Vipul was silent.

'I'm not asking you to promise alone. I'll also promise if you do.'

Vipul remained silent. It was always he who got beaten in their fights, and only he needed ever to complain to their mother or father. But the jeep – he had to learn the jeep.

Sameer continued, 'We shouldn't be like the others, Bitty. Look at the kinds of boys that complain. Like the Mosquito. He behaves like a girl, running to his mother if you so much as touch him. We shouldn't behave like girls. Now look at Fatty and William. Do they ever complain? Should we not be like them rather than like Mosquito?'

Reminded of his storybook heroes, Vipul gave his promise, and extracted one from Sameer about the jeep.

The jeep arrived. It was a squat open-sided American Ford, left hand driven, a survivor of the Second World War, still in its martial olive-green uniform. It had a tarpaulin hood and side-flaps. When the weather wasn't too hot or too rainy, as now, the side-flaps were rolled up, and the jeep was a girl with her hair in curlers; and in summer and in the rainy season, they hung down and flapped wavily about like an elephant's ears. Vipul liked the jeep most for its running board. When he sat at the side he put one foot on the running board, so that half of him, lengthwise, was in the jeep and half out; and then he thought he might be looking a little like a pioneer, an explorer, because he had seen pictures of men in safari apparel, armed with binoculars and intrepidity and slaves, sitting thus in jeeps, surveying primordial African wildernesses.

Every day the jeep, starting from their bungalow, took the boys around Khajoori, picking up other schoolgoers from their homes on its way to the river. It was a straightforward drive, for there were but two roads in Khajoori. One started from a point further up in the valley, and went past Vipul's home directly down to the river. The other branched off from the first just near their home and ran parallel to the river for a kilometre or so before turning into the valley. The roads were untarred, stony and gutted, no more than strips of clearing over which only jeeps and dumpers could run; and when you drove over them, the earth underneath seemed to pass into disquiet, thrusting up its surface here, and there sucking it back down, in jolting tossing lunges. Of Khajoori's roads the wits said that they saved you having butter: you just ate milk fat and drove on them, and butter got churned within.

As with its roads, so with Khajoori: it had not yet arrived at a steady state, a consistency; it was as yet in the way of an unintended artifact, something in the process of becoming. It was neither village nor town nor suburb, nor indeed that most inclusive of appellations, a settlement: for no one had settled in Khajoori; everyone was impermanent, a guest in the place for a time, just doing the jobs that the business of the mining of coal entailed.

Khajoori was, in fact, nameless. Its name had been borrowed from that of a village, some kilometres distant from the colliery, that no one remembered or visited. The town nearest Khajoori was Jadugoda, across the river Damodar and some twenty coarse kilometres away. And Khajoori, like the original village whose name it had fraudulently assumed, had either been forgotten by the world across the river or had never been noticed at all. No milestone anywhere told the distance to it, and no board marked its bearings with an arrow. On maps, even on the most detailed ones of Bihar, in which state it lay, there was only a patch of indeterminate buff in the region where, instead, its name ought to have stood next to its own self-important dot.

And as anonymous as Khajoori was everything in it. The houses, scattered here and there, had neither numbers, nor names, nor addresses. The roads had no names. Even the biggest shop – owned by the Marwari trader Badri, on whose earlobes hair sprouted in whiskery profusion (a sure sign of great wealth already there and great wealth further to come, it was said) and who was (it was said) presently on the lookout for a second-hand car – even this shop did not have a board or a name.

And yet a magazine published in Australia called *Hemisphere*, made of paper that smelt of varnish and that reflected light like a sheet of mica and on the skin was as flawlessly smooth as a bathroom tile, once arrived at Vipul's home bearing the address:

>   Shri J.N. Uberoi,
>   Khajoori,
>   India

(Vipul was struck by the use of the Hindi honorific for his father; he imagined the Australians to be an extremely solicitous people indeed.) It arrived many months after its issue date, but the marvel was that it arrived at all; and Vipul thought of the many places where it might have been rebuffed and disowned before falling into the hands of, no doubt, a postman with a sense of mission.

So indifferent, though, the world to Khajoori: it would not even send news of itself in time. Today's newspaper would arrive tomorrow afternoon, carrying yesterday's news – and, like a hardened, stupid liar, pretend to be current, carrying *tomorrow's* date, excusing itself by stating, in the top right-hand corner, that it was a 'Late City Edition', three asterisks printed next to the phrase, to lend it occult weight.

An old sardarji, Jarnail Singh, delivered the paper and the mail around lunchtime. He would shout at the gate when he arrived, so that Rover, who took objection to only one man in the whole world, to wit, old Jarnail Singh, should be restrained from chivvying him about and nipping at his calves – and Jarnail Singh saved the ignominy of hopping and shrieking as one possessed. It was not clear why Rover should victimize, of all people, Jarnail Singh, for the old man was harmless and truthful, and even looked so. He had the face of a large-cheeked boy underneath his white whiskers and beard; his boyishness was accentuated by the ill-fitting khaki shorts that he wore, and by his unexpectedly thin and hairless legs below; and like all old boyish sardarjis, he looked a mixture of unknowingness and acute wisdom.

He had learnt to distrust the papers he delivered. 'News is lies, and lies is news,' he would say.

It began the day the papers carried photographs of American men walking, floatingly, on the moon. Jarnail Singh was outraged. He said to Vipul's mother, showing her the picture, 'What is this I'm hearing from everybody? Some man has reached the moon?'

Vipul's mother said yes, some Americans had landed there.

'You believe it too. The Americans have convinced everyone.'

'Why do you say that?'

'How can a man reach the moon?'

'They went in a rocket,' Vipul's mother said. 'Its picture was also there in the papers.'

'No, no. Whatever they went in. What I'm asking is, how can anyone reach the moon? It's not in this world.'

'In a rocket, I told you. A rocket can go to the moon.'

'Such a terrible lie.'

'How else do you think they got the picture?'

'This?' Jarnail Singh said. 'Anyone can take a picture like this. Tell someone to put on these strange clothes and make up a set of rocks like for the cinema.'

'But it is true. Ask anyone.'

'Terrible, terrible. They'll pay a big price, the Americans, for trying to fool the whole world like this. The moon is God's own land. No mortal can put foot on it. It's a bad joke they are making. And even educated people are fooled.'

On the way up-valley the jeep went past the coal stockyards and the functionless unclaimed land around the pithead. There were hillocks here, and mounds, and small pits and neat piles, all sculpted of coal. Sunshine turned black here and shone with carbon's blunt intensity from the glossy surface of impure coal, and was absorbed entirely by the purer mineral.

And all about, wherever the coal was not, there lay, settled in all-anointing profusion, its dust. Khajoori's transcendent feature, its soul and its advertisement, was its coaldust. Coaldust hung upon the air, made it heavy and indistinct and – on winter evenings – sinister. It lay thick on all surfaces, like an extra skin – on roads, leaves, walls, lawns, clothes. It crept; it did not look dark at first, but on collecting sufficiently, endowed on everything a grey-black, sorrily gleaming sheen. It invaded and settled on and in bodies, so that when Vipul picked his nose granular black flakes emerged, and when, in the late afternoon, after school, he wiped the film of sweat off his face with his shirtsleeve, the cloth was smeared black, smeared like his father's face when he returned from an inspection of the mine, looking fatigued for battle. And his mother's days were one long war against the dust. It bedevilled all her efforts at keeping house: her white and pastel drapes – curtains, bedcovers, lampshades, antimacassars – turned to uncertain grimy hues within *minutes* (she said, when especially aggrieved) of dry cleaning. Thapa, the sweeper, swept and swept, and swept, driving the dust off the floor every morning and afternoon, casting it out by the panful; but the dust did not wish to go anywhere else, and floated in again even as he expelled it, so that Thapa's function on earth seemed to have been reduced to fuelling this perpetual circulation of dust, in and out, out and in, in and out, this ceaseless rearrangement of Nature. The ungoing dust was, then, the coal's revenge for having been mined.

In the morning the jeep went up-valley along the first road, collecting some girls from the houses near the colliery; on the way back it turned into the other road, parallel to the river, collecting some more girls. Other than Vipul and Sameer, no boys went from Khajoori to their school, St Francis, in Bansidih. But the fact that Vipul was surrounded by girls was devoid of any supposable merit, for they were all older than him, each one a didi, an elder sister, who seemed to be interested only in being kind to him or in teasing him.

Of these girls Vipul liked Pinki didi the most. She too, like Jarnail Singh, was Sikh, and so her hair had never known a cut; it hung in two thick black braids along her back and down to her hips, ending there in a rubber-banded constriction beyond which hung small pendulous ponytails in their unlikely places. To school she wore pleated blue skirts that covered her legs almost to her ankles, and she was forever levelling her skirt with her palms or rearranging its pleats with her fingertips; but her skirt required neither levelling nor rearrangement, so perfectly ironed and draped it always was. It was her face that was the sweetest part of her. It was perfectly ovate and oily, and her thin voice and its shape combined to give her the aura of a weak edible thing, a lollipop. Her shape of face she shared with everybody in her family: her parents, and her six brothers and sisters who middled on her. For some reason, of the seven siblings, only Pinki didi was kept at Khajoori and sent to St Agnes school, the 'sister school' to Vipul's. The others studied in Punjab, and came to Khajoori only for their holidays, and then they were like inspectors on patrol, looking about for signs of change since their last visit.

Vipul went often to Pinki didi's home in the evenings because her father, Uncle Gurbir Singh, would ask his wife, Auntie Gurbir Singh, to give Vipul freshly fried pakoras to eat, which she never failed to be equipped for. Lying in a sparse vest and pyjamas on his bed in his sparsely appointed bedroom, uncle would talk to Vipul in stories and riddles. And when his other children were there Vipul and Sameer went there more frequently, for one of them, Harpreet, a wiry and strong boy with the air of a farmer, was fond of the same things as they: cricket, playing in and around the river, chasing jackals, talking about the pictures.

Eggs, and reminders of eggs, overran Pinki didi's home. The family kept poultry; there was an incubator in their home which, unlike the now untenanted one in Vipul's home, teemed with hens; and the courtyard often had yellow neurotic ragged balls of fluff skittering about. Harpreet was particularly rapacious on the eggs. He would steal, in contravention of his mother's standing ban, into the incubator, scare off the hens, select two or three prime eggs, wash them, break them at their tips, and pour their contents raw into his open uplifted mouth. It astounded Vipul to see him to do this. Even the thought of the cooked egg he had for breakfast made him queasy; to see Harpreet drink raw eggs with such aplomb was to witness a minor precocity, a rare talent.

And in the sitting room of their home, on the mantelpiece, there stood a rotund plastic hen. Its legs connected to springs inside its belly;

when you pressed on the hen, its body sank and its legs receded up into its belly, and then when you released it, it laid, in an act of creation consummately easy and immaculate, a spherical pink plastic egg that bounced like a ball.

When they had come on to the second road, Vipul said, 'Nizam, can I drive?'

Nizam, saying nothing, shifted to his left, and Vipul slid into the space so vacated. Nizam took his hands off the steering wheel; Vipul gripped it fiercely, as though it meant to fly away. He steered, while Nizam controlled the pedals and the gears. This was as far as 'driving' went for Vipul; it was dissatisfying, and he wanted to learn the other trappings of the art too; he wished Sameer would keep his promise.

But even steering the jeep was not easy. Much of what Vipul saw through the windscreen was blue sky and treetops; no matter how he craned his neck, no more than a faint stretch of road, many metres distant, became visible. Furthermore, what Sameer had said about the jeep was true. Its play had prodigious depths. When you moved the steering wheel it swung free, frictionless, through some unforecastable degree of rotation – but only the steering wheel swung, and not the jeep's tyres; the jeep travelled on in its initial direction; and then when, in fright, you gave an urgent twist, the tyres turned abruptly through a large, equally capricious arc. Unless you knew this steering wheel like your own child, as Nizam said he did, you went in petulant zigzags. In the circumstances, Vipul's navigation was an implicit act of faith; faith in the jeep, and faith in the course it would take.

But the relationship between Nizam and the jeep was unreciprocal, as it is between many parents and their children. Nizam did all he could for the jeep, cared for it and tended it and spoilt it; and the jeep was thankless. It kept letting him down, kept breaking down, kept him busy and dismayed. Nizam would often be seen engaged in probing the mysteries of its workings. Near his home there was a ramp on to which the jeep could be driven and, from underneath, diagnosed and repaired. Nizam was frequently in the groove of that ramp, poking and jabbing at the jeep's underside with parental absorption. And in the afternoons, when Vipul returned from school, while he was still on the bank opposite, he would see, on the river's far shore, standing in the sand, the jeep and Nizam. The jeep's bonnet would be raised, resting against its windscreen in a big-hearted insolent salute, and Nizam, one foot on a running board, would be bent and gazing down into the engine, exploring a nostril with a little finger to aid his analysis. And he would seem to be saying to the carburettor, 'What a mystery, what a puzzle. But I'll work you out. One day I'll work you out, you'll see, even if it takes me another birth to do so.' And the jeep, still saluting, would resolve to remain unfathomable.

Near Krishna's shop, the Ford went nearly off the road.

Everybody shouted, 'Ey!'

Nizam's hand jumped to the steering wheel and brought the jeep back on course.

'*Don't* touch!' Vipul said.

'Baba...' Nizam said.

'I can *drive*.'

Again the jeep careered, this time to the side opposite.

The didis at the back shrieked, 'Vipul!'

Nizam yanked the jeep back on track again.

'Don't *touch!*'

'Baba, you can *not* manage on your own,' Nizam said.

'Here, then, take your jeep and keep it,' Vipul said, letting go of the steering wheel, throwing his arms out in the way one does in unfurling a bedcover, tiring of this crazily indirigible shimmying machine.

The jeep went halfway into a ditch and after a few touch-and-go, heaving moments, staggered back.

When they were at the end of the road, about to move into the river's sandbank, Nizam said, 'You can drive here.'

Ahead, in the dun sand, ran a pair of deep furrows, meandering like two snakes frozen in the course of a synchronous twist. Once the jeep's tyres entered these furrows, you could take your hands off the steering wheel; the furrows then led the tyres as if by the hand, so that the act of driving was reversed. Nizam had created these furrows himself by repeatedly driving over the same pair of tracks until they deepened sufficiently. But being offered a chance to drive here was like being offered, when you were interested in advanced mathematics, problems in percentages to solve for practice.

'Keep your jeep to yourself,' Vipul said.

They got down from the jeep to climb into the boat. Here in its valley, the river Damodar flowed sedately along. This was the time of year when it appeared drowsy; in summer it would go quite to sleep, and Vipul would be able to cross it wading; then, in the rainy season, it would quite abruptly wake up, as though from a bad dream, and throw an almighty tantrum.

In the boat, a small dinghy made of welding-scarred, knobbly cast iron which on a matter of principle harboured, at all times, an infinitesimal, worrying leak in its floor, Sushma didi did her usual thing. She rocked it violently. She seemed quite unafraid of toppling into the water, and, standing with her legs wide apart, shifted her weight to this side and to that until the boat's gunwales kissed – just kissed – the river's surface. She wore skirts that were much shorter than Pinki didi's, clear above her knees, and when she swayed, hands on hips, her skirt went first a little up one leg and then a little up the other, so that her dark thickening thighs showed. All through this she laughed a wild loud laugh, her face eyeless and plastic in merriment. At such times Vipul thought that Sushma didi was really quite shameless, making everybody nervous with the rocking of the boat and with the exhibition of her thighs and her indecent laughter.

The boatman, Hari, muttered his protests but could do little about Sushma didi's destabilizing spirits except to struggle to keep the boat on course, just as Nizam had struggled with the jeep in the face of Vipul's efforts. To see Hari powerless was odd, because he was a young man with a boxer's body, his chest flashing and his arms bulging at many places. He rowed the boat with a solemn intentness and a ferocity that suggested he viewed his job as just another set of exercises with which to develop his muscles. He was a very quiet and disciplined boatman, always on time, accurate in his landings; he was also very shy, which explained his reluctance to take issue with Sushma didi, Vipul thought, as shy people tended not to confront brazen ones like her.

In the afternoons another boatman, Govardhan, took over. He was not shy, and he shouted at Sushma didi to keep still, but because Sushma didi was shameless and impossible, his shouts seemed only to encourage her so that now she made the boat tilt enough – just enough – for slithers of the river to actually pour into it. But physically, Govardhan was an example of how you could be weak to the limit and still manage to row a boat. His weakness was forgivable, though: he was an old man, and Vipul liked to imagine that he had once been as spectacular as Hari, and that he had dissipated himself on tobacco since. His unpunctuality, however, was neither forgivable nor unforgivable; it was simply absurd. He was never there at the bank when you arrived to be rowed across. He was either on the bank opposite, or in the middle of the river somewhere (often without a passenger, heading nowhere, a picture of watery aimlessness and complacence), or, with the boat moored on your bank, missing, nowhere to be found. He never rowed straight across. He probably did not have the strength to do so, and in any case never tried. He would instead haul the boat some way upstream of his target on the other side and, it would seem, let the river do most of the work, he only nudging its currents with gentle pats of the oars, which when he rowed made their wood-and-water music –

Chop-click, groan-gurgle,
splash!
Chop-click, groan-gurgle,
splash!

– giving one to fancy that the oars' paddles were slurping the water at each stroke, then swilling it samplingly about in their mouths, then squirting it out in surprised distaste.

On the other side of the river, they covered the three kilometres to the bus stop on a cycle-ricksha. The Imperial Coal Company had for years been promising them a jeep on the other side, but none had arrived. Rekhai, the rickshawala, was as strong in his legs as Hari was in his arms: his calf muscles seemed to have been struck by mild elephantiasis. When he pedalled the ricksha it creaked pleasingly, like just-rusty hinges; but the creaks seemed to come not from the ricksha but from the propulsive machinery inside those enlarged glistening calves of Rekhai's, from the gears and springs and cogwheels of his flesh. Vipul could almost feel Rekhai's muscles ache – but Rekhai never complained of pain. When he pedalled he did not sit in the saddle; instead he stood by turn on each pedal, and imperiously thumped. Every now and then, when he wanted a rest, he would haul himself backwards and upwards and sit, and stop pedalling, and wipe his neck with his shoulder cloth. There were only two points, at the top and at the base of a very steep incline that fell on the way, where he stalled and asked the children to get down and walk, for he could neither pedal hard enough to keep the ricksha going uphill nor brake hard enough to prevent it from cartwheeling when they came down.

In the Imperial Coal Company's school bus, which they boarded next, there was relief for Vipul from the girls, and it was complete. The boys sat to the left of the bus's gangway, and the girls to the right, the segregation absolute: even brothers did not talk to their sisters once aboard the bus. It was sudden, too, this apartness, and inexplicable, for the moment the boys and girls had alighted from the bus they would talk, and sister would rag brother or be ragged by him. The bus had its own unsparing quarantining spirit.

And in the bus, there was the company for Vipul of Koyala, whose real name was K.S.R.S. Balasubramaniam, and who boarded the bus from where it started, two hours' drive away, so that he had to get up very early indeed to go to school. Balasubramaniam had been endowed the epithet for the colour, coal-like, of his skin. Sometimes he was also called 'Southie', sometimes 'Keralite', at others the Crow. He did not mind. Koyala had hair that never sat, and his eyes and teeth shone in his face. He believed in the use of terrifyingly foul language, and it was a joy to listen to him. In this Vipul could never emulate him, for he was sure that his tongue, were it to utter the delicacies that Koyala did, would precipitously wither and fall.

TWO

One morning, two new faces appeared in the jeep, and some mornings after this, a third.

The first two were girls; and Vipul's desolation grew.

They were called Ratna and Chetna. Their father, Mr Agarwal, was a Marwari. In contrast to all other Marwari men, who took to business in the same predestined, sensual way that a Punjabi takes to non-vegetarian food, he had deviated in instinct somewhere along the line and made a mining engineer of himself. His daughters had faces of a kind that Vipul was not accustomed to, and they so bewitched him that he kept staring at them, making them uncomfortable on their very first journey from Khajoori to school. They had inherited – he saw later – the very thick eyebrows of their father which met in the middle without thinning, a frank headband of hair over the eyes. Their foreheads were low, their heads of hair starting right above their eyebrows. Their eyes were deep-set, lips wide, and chins bold. Vipul thought of them as men in the process of turning into girls. The beauty in their faces was as yet ineffable; but there was some promise of it diminishing into the conventional kind in years to come.

Vipul did not talk to the girls on the way to and from school. He was too shy, because the girls were younger than he and from that very fact there arose possibilities; and the girls, perhaps for the very same reason, seemed to be shyer still. Sameer, bolder than Vipul, did try to talk to them. To everything he said, the girls first winced, in pain from embarrassment. They glanced at each other; they glanced away. Their lips and cheeks twitched in confusion. They looked so at bay and friable that if you touched them, they might crumble into heaps of coalfine. Then one mumbled her reply, looking again at the other as she did so, measuring the other's reaction, and giving the impression that it was her sister who had asked the question. In this way any external attempt at conversing with them was, by virtue of their shyness, engulfed and made into a conversation of their own, and even Sameer sometimes gave up, looking beleaguered.

Then the new boy joined the schoolgoers. He was tall and gangly, and wore spectacles. He sat in the back of the jeep, with all the girls, since Sameer and Vipul occupied the front seat in the mornings. There, in the back, he read a book. At the girls he would just not look. When they got into the boat, he continued to read the book, and Sushma didi's gyrations did not affect his concentration. And then when they were on the ricksha, he read the book. The book was wrapped in the kind of dull brown paper, run through with fine stripes, that the teachers at school insisted the boys should use: covers in colour, or with pictures on them, were off-limits, looked upon as frivolous, unscholarly.

But the new boy was not reading a textbook. In the ricksha, Vipul saw that the pages of the book were ochre, and thick; the kind of pages that smell sweetly of roasted peanuts; and when Vipul saw the typeface, he was certain: it was a Kenneth Anderson book.

So he said, 'Are you reading *The Tiger Roars*?'

The new boy replied, '*The Black Panther of Sivanipalli.*'

'Great book,' Vipul said. 'Have you read the story about the wasps in the tiger's den?'

'No.'

'Or about the maned tiger of Chordi?'

'No.'

'You know, I wish I was Kenneth Anderson's son.'

'How could you be?'

'I said I wish I was. His name is Donald. He shot forty panthers and fifteen bears before he was twenty-three years old. Imagine!'

The new boy imagined. And from the wistfulness that overtook his face it looked as though he, too, wished now that he had been Kenneth Anderson's son Donald.

Vipul said, 'What's your name?'

'Pawan,' the new boy said.

'Class?'

'Seventh.'

'Mine's the same! Section?'

'A.'

'Mine's the same! What a thing! Good that you're joining the same class. We can be friends.'

'Yes,' Pawan said, unmoved, and bent his head again to the realm of impenetrable liana-and-teak jungles, wounded hunted tigers shattering the ravines with their swansong oo-oonghs, moonlit mountain streams flowing silver – all suffused with the sweet ochre smell of roasted peanuts.

*

Vipul and Koyala tried to get to know Pawan better in the way that boys have, of inciting an acquaintance. In the bus, one of them would clip him on the head while walking past, then turn his head about and smirk and wink in silent challenge: 'What do you say to that?' Or they would pull his shirt out from inside his shorts, again and again, so that he was condemned forever to the motions of dressing. Or they would snatch from his hands the book he was reading, or whip off his spectacles, and scamper to a small distance, taunting him to give chase.

Pawan did not react to the overtures. He just looked befuddled, as if even in his imagination he might never have conceived that he could be harassed in such pestilent ways. In spite of his height and apparent strength, he did not protest.

'The treatment has to be stronger,' Koyala said.

So they started using more persuasive methods of striking up a friendship: their hockey sticks, boots and compasses. They whacked him on his buttocks, kicked him on his shins, and pricked him here and there, at first politely, as a notification of their intent, and then, of course, in all solemnness. Pawan was still not shaken.

'He is quite a bull,' Koyala said, adding that since he was so thick-skinned, he should be able to withstand higher grades of disciplining still.

Once, after school, while they waited for the bus, they held him by his arms and dragged him to the football field. There they twisted his arm, so that to avoid the pain he had to swivel and his arm swung over to behind his back, but in that position, from which there was no escape, they twisted it further. They lashed him with switches that they wrenched off young trees. They threw him to the ground, and lashed him there, mocking his mute helplessness.

Vipul felt a current of thrill when he tyrannized the Bull. It gave him a sense of acute power. For the Bull was much stronger than he, yet was felled so easily when Vipul yanked him; yet his arm could be twisted at will, acquiescent as a tube of rubber.

His confidence rising, Vipul felt he should impress Ratna and Chetna by demonstrating his newly discovered strength. One afternoon while the others climbed into the bus at the school's gates, and while from the bus the girls threw elsewhere-looking glances at the crowd of boys below, Vipul and Koyala attacked Pawan. This time they tied his hands behind his back, like a slave, and beat him in front of the girls, guffawing all the time as if in thrashing him, with each slap or punch or kick, they were both cracking and savouring a joke.

At short intervals, Vipul looked up to catch the admiration in Ratna's and Chetna's eyes.

But, just seconds after the show had begun, the girls' eyes had become regretful, and their heads had turned slowly away; there was not a flicker even of curiosity in those eyes.

Yet Vipul did not beat the Bull because he disliked him; in fact he was getting to be quite fond of him, partly through sheer intrigue at his placidity, and partly because of what Vipul was discovering to be a considerable shared interest in foreign books and comics; and the Bull, on his part, seemed not to develop – intriguingly, again – any antipathy towards Vipul; the summons that Vipul expected each day to result, from the Bull finally complaining to his parents or to a teacher, never materialized.

School had just ended. The usual torture was going on. Koyala had had another brainwave. A bull, by the very nature of its being, should be yoked and led by a rope. So they yoked a hockey stick on him and roped his neck, and led him to the playground for another round of thrashing. As they led him they held tufts of grass to his face and cried, 'Bull! Bull! Ahh! Tsu, tsu.'

He submitted even to this.

And in the playground they started on him again. This time, as the enchanted drubbing was being dealt, Vipul noticed that the Bull's eyes, behind his spectacles, were becoming obscure and that his lower lip was fibrillously twitching.

Vipul and Koyala were each holding one of the Bull's arms, by the hand and wrist, and twisting it, when there was a jerk. The Bull's arms drew together, and Vipul's head collided with Koyala's with a stony thud. Then the Bull's arms flung outward, and Vipul and Koyala fell to the ground on either side, as in a fight scene in a film. Their heads rang and quickly swelled, and there were bruises over their legs and arms, smarting saltily. The Bull stood there, bewildered still, but now at what he himself had done. He seemed almost apologetic.

Vipul got up and said, massaging his temple, 'You're strong!' Then he added, 'I always knew you were strong.'

Koyala said, 'How you sent us flying.'

Vipul said, 'Look, Pawan' – for once he felt he should call him by his name – 'you must fight like this every time.'

Koyala said, 'It will be fun.'

Vipul said, 'Don't mind how we treated you over the past few weeks. We were in fact trying to prove that you were actually strong.'

'But you never reacted.'

'So we continued.'

'But today you did.'

'And with such style.'

They shook his hands to congratulate him, and patted him on his back. When they walked back to the bus stop, the Bull strode in the middle, and Vipul and Koyala each draped a far-upraised hand over his shoulders.

Beyond Khajoori – on its side of the river – lay the unknown. Nobody from Khajoori ever traversed those miles and horizonless miles of land – mixed land, neither all agricultural nor all forested nor all arid nor all hilly – that led into the heart of nowhere. Everyone's sights were trained on things the other side of the river: on towns; passages to cities; civilization; where the newer life was lived; where life really, it would seem, mattered.

Now and then Vipul and Sameer took walks into the unknown. On the way they came across the natives – sometimes across wild-looking men, very tall and broad and with axes on their shoulders, autochthons who seemed to have sprung out from the illustrations in the Mahabharata; sometimes across very small very dark people, the women accidentally naked-breasted, the men ruefully emaciated.

Khajoori's settlers – its guests – called these people the 'locals'. It was not an unreciprocated point of view, for the 'locals' called them the 'pardesi', or 'foreigners'. The locals, to Vipul and his friends, were a curiosity and an amusement. Most of them knew less English than Ayah did – that is, none at all. In Khajoori, where they felt emboldened, Vipul and the Bull, who had now become friends, had stopped a local boy and started asking him questions in English. The local looked troubled, as though charged with a crime. Vipul and the Bull laughed. The local, relieved, joined in their mirth. Then the boys asked in Hindi, 'How far is the sun from the earth?'

The local, after overcoming his surprise at the question, said, 'Four miles.'

Again the boys chortled. The Bull demanded, 'How old are you?'

The local said, 'I don't know.'

Another snigger, and then Vipul said, 'Fifty years old. You are fifty years old.'

'It must be, if you say so.'

'Have you heard of Delhi?'

'Yes.'

'Where is it?'

'In a foreign place.'

'He knows no Geography!' Vipul said.

'He doesn't know his own country!' the Bull said.

So Vipul asked, 'Have you heard of Bihar?'
'No,' said the local.
'Arey! But you live there – here.'
'I live in the village of Chanchi.'
'Doesn't even know his state!'
'Do you know who we are?'
'You are foreigners.'
'Foreigners! But we are Indians. Or do you think that you are an Englishman, that you call us foreigners?'
'No, sahib, no, I'm not an Englishman.'
'We are Indians. *You* are Indian.'
'You are foreigners.'
'We are Indians!'
'It must be,' said the local boy, 'if you say so.'

THE MISSIONARY

ONE

At Khajoori, too, there was a school. Or at least there was a school building. It was the sort of building where you would expect bats to live quite reposefully. It was a single large block of brickwork, and the facets that you saw from the road had no feature but for rows and columns of small rectangular black eyes, shutterless and paneless. As with everything else in Khajoori, no signboard introduced the building's name or function. At its front there stretched a barren clearing that sloped and bounced; here, in the afternoons, local boys played games that bore pronounced resemblances to cricket and football. It was said that the school ran without teachers.

There was a school in Dudhiya, too, across the river, near the spot where Vipul and the others boarded their school bus. The Dudhiya School was grander in structure than Khajoori's – it stood on an expansive plinth, giving it an imposing air, and a wide short important flight of steps led up to it. It was also more notorious. The boys who enrolled here were not seen on its premises for months astretch; and yearly they were promoted to the next class, 'by God's grace', they said. They were the sort of boys who would proceed and adjust effortlessly to Jadugoda's only college, Macaulay College, where students stuck knifepoints into desks at examination time, dutifully beat up recalcitrant lecturers, and generously waived their right to education in order to make space for the matinee shows in the town's talkies.

Vipul's school, St Francis, situated in Bansidih some five miles off, was a missionary school. It occupied grounds that had been donated to the missionaries by one of Jadugoda's rare philanthropic businessmen. The grounds sprawled amidst a somewhat desolate area, there being no coal presumably to be mined underneath it. The school's main building was eagle-like, with a central chunky administrative body, on either side of which radiated long slim wings abounding in classrooms. It was painted white and lined red, like many big buildings of the coalfields, at once cool and passionate in the sun.

Among the men and the women who taught in St Francis there were the missionaries and the non-missionaries. Only the non-missionary women seemed to have a licence to exhibition, and dressed and made themselves up with purpose and vigour (and sometimes grace), lending sporadic colour to the school. In the afternoons, when everybody made for the homeward buses, these ladies, gladioli-like in their saris and dazzling goggles, were intermittent screams of colour cleaving a khaki-and-white uniformed monotony.

While the non-missionary women taught to supplement their husbands' earnings, the non-missionary men did so to alone support their families, and looked needy; they wore their shirts hanging out, in order to cover the numerous lines left in the seats of their trousers by alterations made in deference to their slowly swelling girths, as also to their constrained finances which stretched out into long years the intervals at which new clothes could be acquired.

The missionaries – sisters, brothers, mothers and fathers – were mostly of European stock, except for the occasional Indian convert, and in their white cotton cassocks and black leather shoes, an attire which made them look like overgrown boys and girls play-acting noble ecumenical parts, seemed to operate quite beyond the compass of finance. On rare days – on a Sunday or a public holiday – a brother or a father would do away with the cassock, and appear in public in a shirt and trousers, and he would then look liberated, a little iconoclastic, and rakishly smart – for a day, a man about town – before reinserting into his robes and inclosing himself in his holy shell.

Many of the children who went to St Francis did so because their parents adored Father Armand, the principal. He was a large man with narrow eyes and a nose so snubbed that he seemed to be ceaselessly sampling the air, as does an alert predator, and he stood and walked with mildly convergent feet. He was a gentle, kind man; the way he spoke, and his narrow eyes, and his inpointing feet, were all redolent of his gentleness and kindness.

By way of contrast there was Father Vane-Pearce. He carried, at all times, in one hand a cane and in the other the clasp of a leash, at the far end of which a bald box-faced terrier strained and puffed through a hot, red mouth.

Father Vane-Pearce was the drill master for Junior School, and Vipul had passed through his hands two years ago. A big hall, empty but for pillars and a desk and chair in one corner, occupied a large part of the third floor of the Junior School building. Father Vane-Pearce used it for the drills; he did not like the open, hot air. And then there was the advantage for him that in the closed hall his voice, amplified by its own multiple reflections, resounded like the engine of a twelve-tonne dumper. He would tether the murderous terrier, whom (perhaps to bait the world) he called Daisy, to one leg of the desk. During the Drill he would pace between the rows of boys, shouting his orders, looking down at the boys' legs for a delayed or a clumsy movement. But for some cryptic shouting followed by strokes of the cane, sincerely delivered, he offered no corrective suggestion. Daisy looked on from the corner, impassive and alert, ready to drag the table after her if the ever-craved need arose to attack.

The boys did not dislike Father Vane-Pearce; you cannot dislike a ghost or a terrorist; you are just insensibly terrified of it. Vipul's mind would go numb in the Drill class, his faculties straining only to execute each command correctly and smartly: 'Attenn ... shun!' 'Sta ... annd ... Ateese!' (Such a sardonic directive it seemed, 'stand at ease', when every muscle tensed and trembled from the very effort to remain still and from heart-stopped panic.) 'Abaa ... out *TURN!*'

Often in these periods the most untimely thing that can ever happen to anyone in public happened to the boys: their bladders relaxed, there in the Drill class, and little patches of wetness appeared, like divine materializations, on their knickers and on the floor.

There were several other fathers in the school, each with his own trait of irregularity; but there was one father who was quite proper. He wore spittingly polished shoes whose soles drummed when he walked; his hair was set so firmly and so irrevocably in its appointed place that it seemed to have been painted on to his head; and his face took on the nicest expressions: his lips just so, the eyeballs just so, the smiles perfectly demure. He was an Indian father; and in the matter of graces he quite outshone his foreign peers. His name was Father Kendal; not his primogenital name, of course – that might have been Mr Nair or Mr Annamathaiah before he became Father Kendal – for it was obvious from his physiognomy that he was from Kerala or thereabouts. Yet he emulated the other fathers in his accent of English, which was more sinuous, more curlicued, than theirs. Once he had said, 'You cannot hold a candle to the way the British govern themselves' (for he taught them Civics, in which the issue of governance, which to Vipul seemed as diffuse as mist and possessed of the most nonplussing vocabulary, arose again and again). And from the way he pronounced 'candle' he came to be known to the boys as Father Cane-Dull.

One or two school buses could always be trusted to be out of sorts on any given day; and one afternoon, the boys of Vipul's bus were stranded after school.

Vipul, the Bull, and Koyala were playing tops – playing the vicious version of the sport in which one boy's top (that boy's who cannot throw it twirling in the air and catch it spinning on the palm of his hand) is tamped into a small hollow in the ground and the others try to split it asunder, in three tries each, with the whetted nails of theirs; at the end of which the tops look as chipped and bruised and honourable as soldiers returned from action.

As they played, the Lizard – a loafer known thus because of his transfixing, arch eyes – ran up to them and said, 'Come, come, I have something for you to see.'

'There are many things to see in this world,' Koyala said with grave wisdom, wrapping the twine around his top, making an Egyptian relic of it, mummified and embalmed.

'But you won't see every day what I have seen. By God, promise.'

This was earnestness indismissible.

'Where?'

'In the 6B classroom.'

'But the classrooms are empty.'

'That's what you think. But this one isn't.'

'You're talking as though you've seen the god of lizards in person.'

'Lizard's son yourself. Anyway, it's better than seeing any god even.'

'Look, don't waste our time.'

'Listen. I'm going back to see it. Come if you want.'

'And if it isn't any good?'

'Didn't I say, by God, promise?'

So when he ran back towards the school building, they ran after him, full-tilt. Class 6B was on the top floor of the school, at the central end of a corridor. When they reached the stairs, the Lizard said, 'No sound now, or *we'll* get caught instead of *them*.'

When he reached the corridor, the Lizard rose on tiptoe, and so did the others after him, but their shoes still sounded a perilous whisper. And they could hear, from the end of the corridor, soft strains of music.

'Take off your shoes,' the Lizard said, stopping and unlacing his own.

'There's no need.'

'I don't want to be caught. Do you?'

They took off their shoes and, holding one in each hand, walked gingerly along, as on a pebbly beach.

The music grew louder. Whoever was inside that room could not have heard footfalls in any case. Yet the Lizard kept turning about, putting a finger to his lips.

They reached the back of the classroom. The door was very slightly ajar, forming a hair-wide slit through which one could see a narrow column of space within the room.

The Lizard pointed at the slit, put an eye to it, then turned around triumphantly, excitedly, and moved out of the way. Vipul took his place.

The room was wrong. Where there should have stood the boys' desks and chairs, there was just clear space. He held his gaze. The music continued to waltz. There was nothing to see. He turned around and addressed the Lizard, twirling his hand in peeved inquiry.

The Lizard pointed a trembling urgent finger at the slit.

So Vipul looked again. And there it was. Something flitting past, in a swirl of bright red and flashing white. Two human forms. He kept watching: there they were again, visible for a split second as they whipped across the slit.

Despite the brevity of the glimpse, he thought he could make one of them out. Was it ... could it be ... Father Kendal in his white robe? And the other, a woman in a red dress, who was she?

But there they were, dancing to the music.

Dancing – and holding each other.

Vipul turned around and looked at the Lizard gratefully, then he turned to watch again.

For a goodish while he had a steady view. The couple danced along the line of his vision, and his guess was confirmed: Father Kendal it was. And the woman in red: ah yes, ah yes. It was that new Anglo-Indian school secretary, Miss Margaret, she who dressed always in the brightest ever colours, brighter even than those of the non-missionary lady teachers. He saw that they were dancing in each other's arms: Father Kendal's hands on her waist, hers on his shoulders, but neither looking at the other, looking instead at the air in the classroom where the notes of the music wrote themselves out. The music was a sad waltz, a gently marching waltz, the kind that Vipul heard sometimes on Radio Moscow.

How desolate and happy these dancers seemed; mute expressionless dolls sprung into motion. There was this austere beauty about the dancers; and there was also the crime.

Father Kendal! And the new secretary Miss Margaret! Dancing! *Holding* each other! All alone!

And Vipul left his place, which was taken by the Bull and then by Koyala, and each looked anxiously for a while and then with a quiver turned about with that same thrilled thankful smile, the kind that must come to the lips of a naturalist on sighting out of the blue a highly rare and secretive species.

The music continued, but the dancers did not reappear. The boys crept along to the shuttered windows, finding similar, but horizontal, slivers through which slices of the classroom were visible. The Bull spotted something and waved to the others. Through his sliver they could see the teacher's large desk and chair at the head of the room; the secretary sat in the chair, and Father Kendal leaned on the table; they were talking; and between them, on the table, stood a dark red bottle, and in their hands were goblets full of a deep red liquid of whose identity there could be no doubt.

The boys could not catch the couple's conversation for the music, but they were sure that it was full of ardour and of sin.

Father Rocqueforte was the most aberrant of the missionaries. There was only one class that he taught; the seventh, every year. At the beginning of the year, when he entered the class and the boys rose and said, 'Good morning, father,' he did not respond, not even with so much as a glance at them; instead he turned, seemingly in disgust, to the blackboard and wrote on it in a rambling, cursive hand:

WILLIAM CLARENCE ROCQUEFORTE
LITHUANIAN JEW TURNED CATHOLIC

Then he turned and said, 'That's me, and that's where I come from, and that's what I am. And anybody who says I'm American because of my accent is a dead Indian.' And that was his epiphany.

Then he wrote a word jumble on the board, and said, 'Now do it. First one to get it right gets a magazine.'

Father Rocqueforte was old, not short, and wore spectacles of such power that they gouged his eyes out of their sockets and placed them in a plane just before his face. He walked fast. When he walked he was erect from his feet to his waist; upward, his body leaned forward at a teeter, until his neck and face jutted with the pryingness of a cartoon detective's. He was a worried man. His face was tattered with worry. It was not the kind of worry that arises from apprehension, but the kind that tells of restlessness, of too little time and too much to do in it. His voice, too, was frayed: it fluttered nervously in the way that abuse of coffee brings about. The worry made his eyebrows twitch incessantly, and his cheeks to hang low, so that they jiggled when he talked. It made his words flow in a torrid flood. And the worry made him pinch between his fingers the free end of the sash of his cassock and compulsively run his fingers along its length, as though the sash, and not he, were the anxious one, and he its succour, soothing it with these poultice caresses.

Father Rocqueforte's periods were not classes; they were condensed disquisitions. He would take up some issue or the other – quite at random, it seemed – and lecture on it, after he had given away the prize to the winner of the jumble. His choice of subject was inapprehensibly eclectic: the political situation in India or in Vietnam; Shakespeare; Catholics and Protestants; sport; the Emergency; Western classical music; English grammar; but dearest of all, Lithuania's subjugation by Russia and its prospects, remote, of independence.

He used very long and very uncommon words, and Vipul, whenever he caught them correctly, would look them up in the dictionary later, and be surprised by their meanings: words such as 'ecclesiastical', 'desideratum', 'infructuous'. And while Father Rocqueforte expounded, the boys, understanding nothing, listened enthralled. What he said did not matter; what mattered was that he talked to them in this way. They felt adult; they even felt fifty years old, older than their parents, for nobody ever talked to their parents about such momentous things in such an adult way either. It was as though he took them into confidence in each class and admitted them to a patch of an esoteric, limitless world.

But a few things that he dwelt upon were local and quite accessible, and he would revert to them often. One was what he thought of the other fathers in the school, another his liking for the coalfields.

He did not like the other fathers. In Father Vane-Pearce's case that was understandable – for who in their right mind could actually like Father Vane-Pearce? – but he rarely mentioned him. He did not like the fathers whom everybody thought it was impossible not to exalt as minor deities. He did not like the kind and gentle Father Armand. Father Armand, discharging gravely his principal's duties, would move along the school's corridors on cat's pads, often to present himself abruptly at the back of a classroom and from there watch, like an apparition, the proceedings. Other teachers had trained themselves to kill all signs of astonishment when he appeared. And so boys who rose from their seats while the teacher's back was turned and executed lurid pelvic thrusts or some other such bodily pleasantry, would have a miserable ensuing week, having to explain and lie profusely first to Father Armand ('Father, I have a condition, and it itches very much, and sometimes I have to get up and move my hips about and scratch') and then to their parents, and to write out a thousand numbered times, 'I shall not do mischief in class', and to kneel on the floor throughout the day for a week. And so even though the teachers, too, had to remain watchful not to be hauled up themselves by Father Armand for some ill-advised wisdom they'd thought fit to dispense or for being caught napping – literally napping, that is, during the spells over which they gave the boys exercises to do, working out sets of nasty five-digit divisions or learning by heart the definitions and examples of all forms of participles – they generally appreciated his practice of the cat-padded haunt.

But Father Rocqueforte said, 'I don't know what he thinks he is. If he thinks he's a ghost, let him go turn into one. Just comes and stands there at the back, spying on me like a wife on her husband. He's got no right to. What I say in my classes is entirely my business.'

Of the coalfields, he said it was a hot place sometimes, but he liked it there. 'You know, boys, you're lucky,' he said. 'You're independent, not like us Lithuanians, and yet you're not quite loose, not like the Americans, not corrupt and frivolous,' he said. He also liked the monsoons, and the way people visited one another without alarm.

But he gave American magazines as prizes to the boys – old issues of *Sports Illustrated* and *National Geographic* and *Life* and *The Plain Truth* – and even as he extolled the place he lived in, he purveyed beckoning dreams, beautifully and seducingly photographed, of a faraway other.

TWO

Father Rocqueforte was supposed to be teaching them Moral Science. That he seemed to have forgotten entirely.

The Moral Science books prescribed by the school contained essays, parables, and incidents from the lives of saintly women and men. At the end of each such piece there was a section called 'Lesson to Learn', four or five noble-minded lines printed in letters so thick and bold that they throbbed upon the page with blackness and rectitude, punishing the eyes. The previous year's Moral Science teacher, Sir Dubey, a man rendered globular and narcoleptic by an uncomplicated fondness for food and rest, and handicapped further by the slotting of his periods for the forty minutes immediately after lunch, had treated literally the words, 'Lesson to Learn', and compelled the boys to memorize each one of them. Meanwhile, in the tradition of the best teachers, he dozed off, the better to savour the passage through his stomach of his lunch. He was thus apt, more than any other teacher, to be roused from his dreams by a voice murmuring, with an odd mix of softness and austereness, 'Mr Dubey?', and by the sight of a slimly cassocked six-footer looming at his side.

The boys for their part learnt their lessons without learning anything from them. Sir Dubey, on the strength of his own peremptory evaluation, ranked the Lessons, as each arose, on a scale of relative merit. When they came to the jewel of the pack he announced, 'Mark it: bhery bhery bhery bhery bhery bhery *bhery* important'. The next best was, of course, to be marked 'bhery bhery bhery bhery bhery *bhery* important'. Such Lessons were certain to be founts of questions for the tests. And a Lesson that was rated very important was lowly and base, and you did not take it to heart.

One Lesson said:

'Work is the foremost Religion; for God is gladdened by no Practice so much as that of Industry. Work gives Livelihood, and

Work sustains the Mind and provides Occupation; above all, Work lends Dignity. By Working Honestly and Diligently we approach the Almighty closer than we ever may by the Selfish Act of Prayer. For Prayer is but an Appeal; Work is Communion, Work is true Worship.'

And Sir Dubey directed that they should mark it a very important lesson.

Vipul discovered that he was good at solving Father Rocqueforte's jumbles. The scrambled letters seemed to jump out from the board into the air, and permute and repermute themselves there until they congealed again into a legal word. In this way Vipul steadily built up a substantial, variegated collection of American magazines, and Father Rocqueforte began to notice him.

One day outside the classroom he bid Vipul come over and asked him if he would mind missing football in the Games period and climb up to his room instead.

Father Rocqueforte's room was on the top – the second – floor of the building, in its central chunky section. Vipul felt privileged to have been asked to come there, to that cloister where the fathers lived their Christian lives of occultness and celibacy, where boys normally never had cause, or invitation, to go. But he was disappointed by Father Rocqueforte's room, for it was small and indigent. Vipul had expected the fathers to live in some splendour, at least those of them who were white; furthermore it was a room in torment, one in which man fought for domination against paper, the paper threatening to take over. There was paper all over, loose and bound, dictating what space was available and what was not; paper filling the room with smells of sweet heartwood and of sawdust; paper multiplying and proliferating, and giving rise to its own ecological niches, with silverfish and spiders and geckoes going about their subsurface pursuits, strewing everywhere their webs and droppings and young; paper lay everywhere, and through the gaps in its profusion you saw a wooden chair and shelf here, a desk and typewriter there, and on the floor, against the skirting, erroneous like a scream in a temple, a bottle of rum. Were all fathers like this, Vipul wondered, did they all have wondrous undercover existences?

Father Rocqueforte said, 'I've called you up because I've noticed you're doing well on the jumbles.'

'It's a good game, father,' Vipul said. He vaguely recalled Sir Joseph having taught his class just recently that when someone said you were doing well, or gave you something, you were to say 'Thank you, sir' or 'Thank you, auntie' while slightly stooping and shuffling, but he hadn't had sufficient practice at the art.

'You seem to like English.'

'I like reading English stories.'

'Which ones?'

'Books of Enid Blyton and Kenneth Anderson and Richmal Crompton, and comics, father.'

'That's all right to get started. But I reckon you should start reading better stuff now.'

'I will, father.'

'Look, to begin with, read Dickens. Read *David Copperfield*. It's in the school library. Or have you read it?'

'No, father, I will.'

'And the best way for you, out here in the coalfields, to get a feel of spoken English might be to listen to the radio. Listen to the BBC. Got a radio at home?'

'A Murphy radio.'

'Then take this and use it,' Father Rocqueforte said, and handed him a piece of paper.

On the paper was typed, not written:

BBC World Service
Metres: 16, 19, 25, 31, 49.
Broadcast: 2.30 p.m. to 0.30 a.m. local time (0900 hours to 2000 hours GMT).
Note: 19m best for early evening, 31m best for late.

In the course of one of his classes Father Rocqueforte happened to stumble upon morality, and took up the matter. This was the first time he had touched upon the subject, and Vipul thought that Moral Science lessons were at length to begin. Presently, father started speaking of American morality. 'Degeneration,' he said, 'absolute degeneration is what is happening to America. Leave aside everything else, they don't even spare the women, though they call themselves civilized. Christ, the pornography they produce. The girlie magazines – they have just no limits. They show everything. Everything, right down to the venereal hair. It might be somebody's daughter, somebody's sister, somebody's wife or mother or aunt – but no matter, nudity, stark and complete, is all they want. In big centrespreads you can cover walls with. The moral fabric of society has gone – like that.' And he clicked his fingers. His words were flowing at tripping speed and his fingers swept over his sash, over and over, in mute mobile fury.

He went on, but he had already said enough to make the boys numb with consternation. They knew that they should expect him to talk about almost anything, but they had not thought he would bring up anything quite so irreligious as naked women and their sin-wrapped parts. After the period there was turmoil. 'What magazines they must be.' 'But what do they show?' 'Idiot. Didn't you get it? That hair.' 'Which?' '*That!*' 'But what's it called?' 'Ven ... verel ... something. We'll have to look it up.'

The next morning many of them had looked it up. One said, 'Venerable. Means something I should respect.' He was laughed at, and silenced. Another said, 'Vernal. Like spring. Youthful, fresh and young. What is he talking about?' Somebody said, 'Venereal. Related to...' here he paused, in fright, 'sexual love or intercourse.' 'Oh my God. That's it.' 'He's talking even about that!' 'What a father.' 'These Europeans are something.' 'Do you think he has these magazines?' 'Maybe he also dances with Miss Margaret.' And so the fever grew.

But Father Rocqueforte never spoke on sex again, and the boys kept waiting, through the following months, for a second enlightening, heart-stopping, period on morals.

One afternoon, when it was beginning to get summery, Father Rocqueforte asked Vipul to stay back after school, and come with him for a drive. He had requisitioned the school's car, and when they were some way from the school, in the depth of the surrounding wilderness, he directed the driver to turn off the tarred road into one of the dirt tracks that Vipul saw on his way to school, the kind of track that made him wonder where it led, for there appeared to be no reason for it to exist. In fact the path went on and on, and there was nothing on either side except flat scrubland and quarries. Quarries dotted the coalfields, and many of them were full of muddy opaque water, so that they looked solid yet bottomless. Father Rocqueforte asked the driver to stop by one. He led Vipul to its edge. And there they sat, in the late afternoon, on dusty rocks, looking at the water thick and caramel-brown with mud, in the midst of shrubby barrenness all about, everything in sight touched with yellow and beige, in a sombre and peaceful and despondent time and place.

'You know, people drown themselves in these quarries,' the father said. 'Like Sinha's son.'

Sinha sir was one of the few teachers in the school upon whom the boys hadn't conferred a sobriquet. Vipul said, 'But he has nine children, father.'

'And how does that matter, my boy?'

'No, father, but his younger son Abhijit was saying.'

'Like what?'

'One day he asked me, "Do you know the story of the pig and the she-pig?" I said no. He said, "The story is that one of the children of the pig and the she-pig died. But because they were pigs and couldn't think, they had another."'

Father Rocqueforte said, 'So they're having another, are they?'

'Father, it's what Abhijit said.'

'Look, son, remember one thing. Respect your parents. No matter what.'

'But they are very poor, father, that is why Abhijit said.'

'I know. But regardless. Parents are parents. Otherwise you'll become like those Americans. It's already happened there. No love lost between parents and children.'

Vipul was quiet.

'Anyway. I brought you down here to talk about myself. Want to know my history? My country's history?'

'Yes, father.'

'You know, Vipul, I think I like being in India because I feel sort of at home here. I feel I am part of a history that is as much mine as it is yours. I mean, Lithuania's gone through phases that are very similar to those that your country's gone through. Did you ever know that?'

'We never study Lithuania's history, father.'

'No, of course not. Well, consider this.' And the father told Vipul of how, up until the thirteenth century, there had not been a city in his land, and nothing written, no script; and Lithuania, feudal, no more than a collection of warring tribes; that medieval Lithuanians had been nature worshippers, with numerous gods ('We have eighty-eight crore gods,' Vipul broke in to say; and, 'Sure you do,' the father said); and how his ancestors moved to Lithuania in the sixteenth century, when the nation was subjugated by Poland:

'Now because at that time Polish culture was more modern, all successful Lithuanians began to ape the Poles, and then naturally the

Poles and the Pole-like Lithuanians came to dominate everything, so much so that Polish became the fashionable language and Lithuanian was relegated to a peasants' tongue which everybody scorned. Like your Bhojpuri in Bihar. Or like Hindi is becoming in the cities. Have you heard of the word "anglicization"?'

'Becoming English, father.'

'So you'll understand what polonization means. Well, the polonization of Lithuania made it a complete subjugate of Poland, just as the anglicization of India subjected her all the deeper, for a while, to Britain.'

Then father described how for a whole century Lithuania, after a brief unsuccessful independence – during which the father as a boy and his family led a level, agrarian, god-fearing existence, on the banks of the river Nemunas, farming dairy and poultry – how after this it was tossed like a ball between Poland and Russia and Germany, each keen to cash in on the milk and eggs that the land produced to abundance. And how, eventually, Russia and Germany decided between themselves that Lithuania should belong to the former; following which came the deportation of those who did not agree with this; and Father Rocqueforte's family thus came to America where, in course of time, the father was to become a Roman Catholic, and a missionary.

'At the time, of course, we were furious with the Russians, but just a few months later we were to become in fact very thankful to them. Because a few months later the Germans took over again, and they simply killed ninety-five per cent of the Jews in Lithuania. If you ever come across the word "holocaust", Vipul, that is what it means. And had the Russians not deported us, there's a ninety-five per cent chance that I wouldn't be talking to you today, by this quarry this moment. And when the Germans had finished, the Russians took over *again* – can you believe it? – but since then there's been no change, and we are the Lithuanian Soviet Socialist Republic. That is, my country is. I only hope Lithuania becomes independent during my lifetime, so I can go back and visit again the farm I grew up in, paddle once more my feet in the cold clear water of the Nemunas.'

'I'm sure you will, father.'

'I'm not so sure, my boy.'

Afterwards, the father dropped Vipul off at the riverbank, where they stood for a while looking across, waiting for the boat. The early summer evening gave to the river a coat of aluminous light, intense and unnatural. Father Rocqueforte said, 'So is that your home over there?', pointing to where Pinki didi lived.

'No, father, you can't see it, there on the side it is, and much bigger than that one,' Vipul said.

Father kept looking across, as if wondering what might be going on in those homes, in those families. Vipul felt that he should this very evening ask his mother to invite the father to dinner one day, or even to stay.

When he was home, he did not do so. He could not imagine a comfortable evening at home with Father Rocqueforte there. His parents might not approve of his candour, his language. He might not approve of the curried food. He might miss having his daily bit of beef. Vipul's parents might not have much to say to him. So Vipul simply wondered what father would do of an evening – that evening perhaps, when, had he been invited, he could have been at Vipul's home and created some discomfort – what would he do, in his room, without family, in the company of his flood of paper and his typewriter and his bottle of rum?

THREE

They were in Father Rocqueforte's room, the father sitting on his study chair and Vipul on a small clearing on the bed. Vipul was glancing through a magazine that concerned itself exclusively with the American state of Maine and its impossibly gorgeous landscapes and equally gorgeous properties which, for some twisted reason, their owners wanted to sell.

Father Rocqueforte said, 'You know, Vipul, I may not be amongst you guys much longer.'

Vipul looked at him with a question. He wondered if Father Rocqueforte meant what all ageing people did by such statements, which were as common, surprisingly, in real life as in films; but the father was not the sort of person who made such statements; he was not a stock person at all.

Recognizing Vipul's question, father said, 'No, not what you're thinking. It's just that I'll soon be flying to the States. To America, as we call it. Whoosh – once and for all.'

'Oh.'

'Now get this clear. I may be going, but it's not because I *want* to go. I'm being sent.'

'Oh. Why, father?'

'For being me.'

In Vipul's eyes there was again a question.

'Listen, my boy. It's no big mystery. I talk too much and on too many things. You know I'm not appreciated around here.'

'Father, you are.'

Father laughed. 'Would you say so?'

'We like you very much,' Vipul said.

'But you, Vipul, and whoever else is "we", don't matter. Not the least bit. Those who do matter don't like me and they are sending me away.'

'Yes, father,' Vipul said. 'But why?'

'Ostensibly because I have diabetes. Know what that is?'

'No, father.'

'Sweet blood. Sickeningly sweet. Lots of sugar in it. Now you'd tend to think that sugar should be good for me, wouldn't you?'

'Yes.'

'Funny thing is, it isn't. It's terrible for me, and terrible for anyone who has it. Vipul, pray to God no one in your family gets diabetes.'

'I will, father.'

'And these dolts say – they think – they like to believe – that I can't look after myself. That I need better medical care, the best medical care, American medical care.'

'Yes, father. It must be the best in the world.'

'But don't you see, Vipul, what it is that would kill me?'

'Yes, father.'

'Go on.'

'Sugar in the blood.'

'Ah, dear Vipul, after all my classes and after all our talk, you say, "Sugar in the blood." Come now, son, come on. You're smart enough to know. What is it that would kill me?'

'America.'

'Say it again.'

'America, father?'

'A – ME – RI – CA!'

'Yes, father.'

'They're killing me, Vipul. Do you realize that? They're as good as murdering me.'

Vipul kept silent. It was difficult to think of Father Armand, or even Father Vane-Pearce, for all his bluster, plotting a murder.

'They know that sending me away from Jadugoda would kill me; they know that not sending me back to Lithuania would kill me; they know that God-blessed America would kill me. But they're doing it to me all the same – on medical grounds. Doesn't it make you laugh, Vipul?'

'No, father, surely not.'

'I see what you mean. They're getting rid of me. Getting rid of me, Vipul. Because they can't abide me.'

The father's eyes were burning into his; his spectacles had turned crimson with those huge eyes, now weak with anger.

And his trembling and his twitching, and the tremor in his voice, had become pathological.

He gazed in impatience at Vipul, clearly waiting on a judgement.

Vipul made a mental note that he would look up 'abide', and that word he had heard a minute ago, 'ostensibly', in the dictionary that evening. And, not knowing what judgement to pass, he said, 'Father, I'll miss the bus. Good afternoon, father.'

'Good afternoon, my boy,' the father said, and for the first time in the months that Vipul had known him, his voice sounded punctured and limp.

And as Vipul was leaving, Father Rocqueforte called him back and said, 'Now, Vipul, have you read any more books of Dickens's?'

'Yes, father. *Oliver Twist.*'

'There's an excellent book. What did you like most about it?'

'The smell of the pages.'

'I mean in the text.'

'When his mother dies.'

'Ah yes, that's a good passage. Good. Now, after I'm gone, I'd like you to start reading the books of Thomas Hardy. Start with *The Mayor of Casterbridge.*'

'I will, father.' Then, Joseph sir's admonition kicking in, 'Thank you, father,' he said. 'Good afternoon.'

FOUR

It was the Friday before the Sunday on which Father Rocqueforte was to leave. Father's room had been cleaned of its cancerous paper; its emptiness had been retrieved; and it looked, strangely, ransacked. Father gave Vipul a pile of magazines that he had set aside for him. Vipul considered the uncertain treasure. He might distribute most of these, he thought, to win obligations; he would however keep, for the purpose of cherishing, one or two of them, and inscribe on their covers: 'Gifted to V. Uberoi, by Father W.C. Rocqueforte, of Lithuania, on his day of departure from India.'

Father Rocqueforte said, 'Well, Vipul, it may be difficult for you to empathize with the feelings of an old man like me in my kind of situation, but let me tell you, I feel sad and betrayed. Do you ever feel sad?'

'No.'

'Brave young man! Well, I wish I could be – what should I say – unsaddenable – like you. But an old man does tend to become maudlin, and you'll find that out for yourself in your own time.'

Vipul noted the words 'empathize' and 'maudlin' for future reference. For the present he thought that 'maudlin' meant musical, or melodious, and thought it odd that Father Rocqueforte should feel so at this time.

'Now, Vipul, I want to ask you one final question before I leave. What do you guys really think of us?'

'How, father?'

'I mean, what do you think we missionaries are doing here? Do you think we're useful?'

'Of course, father.'

'How is that?'

'I don't know, father. Many ways. But boys are saying some bad things about fathers these days.'

'I know, I know. Like we're buying converts. Decimating Hinduism. Evangelist marauders.'

'No, father,' Vipul said, getting the drift of the words. 'But other things.'

'Oh. Yet others. Go on.'

'No, father.'

'Come on, come on. I'm leaving the day after tomorrow. You owe me this much.'

'They talk about the dancing and the bar, father.'

'Dancing and the bar!'

So Vipul told him, after some persuasion, about Father Kendal and Miss Margaret.

Father Rocqueforte said, 'I see. I do suppose he overstepped. But the bar … now what bar is that?'

'Your bar.'

'My bar? *My* bar? Where do you see a bar here?'

'All the fathers' bar, father. The one here,' Vipul said, indicating that he meant the central section of the building.

'But who's been there, that you know?'

'I don't know, I just heard.'

'And you think there is a bar?'

'Yes, father.'

'So there is a bar and all the fathers drink. And that scandalizes you, does it?'

Vipul was quiet.

The father said, 'Do you think that it's bad to drink? That it's immoral?'

Vipul looked down to see a silverfish crawl out of one book and into another.

'Well?'

'For fathers, father.'

'Aha. So it's evil for us to drink, is it? And the boys are angry not because we *drink*, but because *we* drink, eh? Is that right, son?'

Vipul thought the distinction over and said, 'Yes.'

'And how about you? What's your opinion?'

'I don't know.'

'Come *on*.'

'For fathers it must be bad to drink.'

'Ah, well. Well, well. Well, my dear boy Vipul, so be it. You're quite right. And of course you've seen that ... that bottle of evil ... several times in my room. So the boys must think I am a debauch.'

'I haven't told anyone, father, promise.'

'That's fine, my boy, there's no need to promise. I believe you. But. But that's interesting. I'll remember this for a long time – for however much longer that I have.'

'Okay, father,' Vipul said, rising.

'God bless you, and goodbye, son,' the father said.

'Goodbye, father. Thank you for all the magazines.' He struggled for something grandly valedictory to say. 'Enjoy yourself in America, father,' he said.

'Yeah.'

THE GEM SNAKE

The day before Holi, Sameer and Vipul and the Bull foraged the bush for the flowers of the tesu.

A couple of weeks before, soon after a hailstorm had tidied and softened the air, the tesu trees had come into flame. Each hailstone, where it had struck a tree, had left behind an ember, latent and waiting for the sun to breathe on it; and struck by that flaring yellow breath it had blossomed into a flame-shaped, flame-coloured flower.

The boys were on a small hillock, and had before them a view of the valley stretching down in front and climbing up again beyond the river, its watery tongue from this vantage invisible. Vipul considered the tesu trees that haphazardly dotted the landscape. They seemed to be in various stages of dress and undress: no tree had erupted orange all at once. On each, the tips of the branches were the first to bloom, upon which the flowers spread in towards the tree's trunk; the fire then crept steadily along the branches as it might along a length of rope. And as the flowers went on their centripetal march, the leaves – the indelicate leaves of the tesu, large and heavy and prone to collect coaldust and lose their sheen (unlike the leaves of the peepul, fluttery and excitable, quivering at the touch of the slightest breeze, shrugging the dust continually off and looking bathed and brahmin always) – the tesu leaves dropped away to clear the way for the flowers. At this time the trees seemed to be in the act of rolling up one shirtsleeve, dusty green, on each of their limbs, and revealing another, gushing orange, underneath. And after Holi the trees would be dressed, over a brief spell, entirely in orange, and wherever there stood a tesu tree, there would appear to be a bride in regalia, shy, burning with apprehension.

But the flowers, even though so implacable in their conquest of the leaves, did not reign long upon the trees, dropping down, voluntarily, entire and moist, long before they were to wither. The leaves, which had fallen resentfully earlier, lay brown and dry and crinkled on the earth, crackling when the boys stepped on them.

Each boy held a pail, and filled it with flowers. They brought the pails home, and boiled the flowers long and hard, so they had three bucketfuls of home-made saffron-coloured Holi water for use on the following day.

On the morning of Holi, after their prayer on ritually empty stomachs to no god in particular, Vipul's mother opened one of the numerous wooden trunks in which she kept things whose hibernal existence only she remembered. She pulled out old, old clothes for everybody, clothes long jettisoned and forgotten, like outworn acquaintances, so that the sight of each decrepit garment awakened many dormant memories, memories that had gone into hibernation along with the clothes, of the person who had gifted the cloth, of the tailor who had ruined it, of the party to which it had been worn for the first, special, self-important time. And when they changed into these clothes it was like stepping backwards in time. Everyone looked younger and littler and historical, and the boys in particular looked destitute, for they had far outgrown their clothes.

When it started to get warm people came visiting, and from then on until evening the sensation of colour ruled over all others; the melodramatic, primary colours of powders; the vague dark colours, seeping into the skin, difficult to remove, of the moist crystals; the feeble orange of the tesu's flowers; the metallic hues, ghastly on skin, of the pastes that Vipul hated: copper and silver and steel. There was colour and mixing of colour and clashing of colour. Colour played havoc with people's faces. One moment, after someone had applied a streak of magenta to Vipul's father's cheek, he looked childishly manhandled, kissed with violence by somebody large lipped; the next moment, someone had rubbed red into his hair, and he looked auburnly European; a moment later there was a slap of jade on his forehead, which appeared stale, mildewed; and then somebody massaged his cheeks with purple, and he looked bruised. By afternoon, peoples' faces had been repetitively, wantonly assaulted with colour until they were recognizable only by the whites in their faces, by their eyes and their teeth, which gleamed nightmarishly through the encircling masks.

And the spirit of the festival worked upon its celebrants in a rash, rude way. Men tried to lift one another by the waist in unbalanced shows of strength. They had several rounds of tug of war, and on each much money was placed and lost and won. Women played in pairs upon mridangs, one drumming its skin, another tapping a spoon on its wooden shell, creating simple trotting rhythms, and singing bold songs rarely heard. And the men and women, for one day in the year, discovered how exhilarating it could be to be ribald and risqué, and passed salacious innuendoes, and then laughed in embarrassment and confoundment, with the air of a child who has just uttered an expletive for the first time. For Vipul the hues of confoundment and embarrassment became, not pink and crimson, but a motley of interleaved Holi colours.

While the songs and the troubled immodesty were going on, there came from the direction of the gate the swelling shouts of a crowd. Presently Munwa, the day-guard, came along to report that some men wished to see Vipul's father who, along with a few others, went to the gate, followed by the boys. There Vipul saw a snarl of men forming a ragged ring, most of them facing the ring's centre. When they saw Vipul's father, they parted to let him view the core. There stood another man, coloured in streaks of scarlet more vivid, more linear, than those on the faces and bodies of the others. And his scarlet streaks were flowing; they kept issuing from ever newer spots on his head; the others were still stoning him. His eyes were closed. Vipul noticed that he was not standing; he was being held up by two paradoxically sympathetic men. Vipul caught the gist of what they were saying. The man had transgressed while applying colour to a woman, and justice was being done; and they were taking him around Khajoori to show that this was so. And when the festivities of Holi ended that afternoon, streaks of flowing, oozing, festive scarlet kept coursing through Vipul's mind; this the colour of justice.

At dinner that evening, Vipul noticed his father considering him and Sameer with an unwontedly meditative gaze. Finally his father said, 'Can't see their faces properly.'

Vipul knew it wasn't the residues of colour and paint that still washed over his face that had prompted his father to say this, and he said, 'Pa, it's because of the paint.'

'Not the paint,' his father said.

'We'll call Lakhan tomorrow,' his mother said.

'Ma, I *said*, no? It's because of the *paint*,' Vipul said.

'Soon they'll start looking junglee,' his mother said to his father. 'We'll call Lakhan.' The following morning when Lakhan, the barber, arrived with his oblong wooden box that held his tools, Vipul was not to be found.

Sameer, who had had his haircut, said, 'He will be on the roof.'

Sameer had an instinct for guessing correctly, each time, where Vipul might have hidden himself when exigencies such as this arose. The reverse was never true. Sameer had an equal genius for discovering or inventing inscrutable hiding places. Once, when the compounder had come on his annual mission to inject the typhoid-paratyphoid A&B-cholera-hepatitis vaccine, a potent mixture whose stiffening, febrile, and tenderizing consequences the boys dreaded a great deal more than the possibility of contracting any of the diseases, Sameer had frustrated the efforts of four men and two women for an entire morning by secreting himself in one of the poultry incubators, weathering, valiantly, its hair-raising stench.

But these emissaries of nemesis, the compounder and the barber, could never be denied their due. They were timelessly patient, seemed never to have other business to attend to, and seemed to enjoy immensely the entire process of the boys being sniffed out and brought struggling to their punitive mercies. They were as on a hunt, and thrilled as much in the tracking of quarry as in the final kill.

Lakhan was a spare man with a spare face sculpted into bony ridges and fleshless indentations, like a relief of a raw mountainous area. Because of his general air of rigour and grim purpose, these features appeared to have arisen from disciplined self-flagellation rather than from circumstantial malnourishment. But to the boys of Khajoori the most inauspicious thing about Lakhan was his own hairstyle, a minor variation of which he grafted on to every client's head. He seemed to entertain no other possibility in the technique of hairdressing. He was like one of those 'social singers' – people who could just not be dissuaded from singing at get-togethers – whose repertoire was limited to a solitary piece which they proudly rendered identically, dissonantly, every time. It was said that Lakhan dressed his own head, by placing on it an inverted bowl, cutting close all the hair excluded by it, and then trimming what was left under it. Thus he and everyone whom he barbered resembled the tufted Caesarian Romans that Vipul came across in comic books, figures of great ridicule.

*

The bungalow's generous roof, with its rivet-studded rust-encrusted water tanks, its fat hooked ventilation spouts and its many parapets at many levels seemed a satisfactory refuge until Vipul heard the voices of the sweeper Thapa and the gardener Jamuna gaining in altitude and in volume as they came scaling the ladder.

Lakhan had spread out a gunnysack in one corner of the chabutra fronting the house. Placed upon the sack was a squat wooden plinth, and by the plinth a trestle table on which he had stood his mirror and arrayed his implements with all the fastidiousness and care that a jeweller brings to arraying ornaments in a cabinet. There were large snipping and small trimming scissors, a cut-throat razor, a comb with teeth as sharp as thorns, a self-supporting mirror encased in a scalloped aluminium frame. He sat on his haunches, chewing a quid of tobacco. In another corner of the chabutra, Vipul's mother and his father reclined on canvas-slung deckchairs in innocentmost angles of repose. Exactly in the manner in which villains in the pictures became babylike minutes after their foul deeds, thought Vipul. Just last night they had spoilt his enjoyment of the chicken curry; and here they were today, childlike, as though unaware of the proceedings, as though they would really be astonished to see, on opening their eyes, Lakhan squatting there. His father, in holiday shorts and a vest, his albescent upper arms and thighs set off against the light tan of the rest of his body, had nearly dozed off, a newspaper resting on his head, shading his face. His mother was reading, through an academic spectacled frown, a film magazine, critically scoring the smiles that the actors and actresses gave. When she saw Vipul led up (passively, for he had given up the struggle), she said, 'What's the use of hiding on the roof when you know you can't avoid a haircut?' Then she uttered the most dreaded words of all, 'Lakhan, make his face come out.' This, then, was going to be one of the more unsparing of Lakhan's ministrations, and Vipul's qualings mounted.

Vipul sat cross-legged on a low toylike chair. Lakhan tied a flowery blue bedsheet, supplied by Vipul's mother, round his neck, making him hair-tight downward. Vipul felt the blood vessels in his neck stiffen and swell and throb. Lakhan had a bowlful of water ready. Into this he dipped his fingers and moistened Vipul's hair with slow strokes.

As he stroked, Lakhan said, 'Baba, I'll tell you a story while I cut your hair. What kind of story would you like to hear?'

'A ghost story.'

'In this sharp sun? How will it have any effect?'

'Yes.'

'How about a story of love and revenge?'

'Don't talk rubbish.'

'Vipul!' his mother said from the back.

'Then?' Lakhan said.

Vipul thought. 'A *snake* story,' he said.

'I know a few. I'll tell you the best one.'

'What's it about?'

'A snake.'

'Uff. *Apart* from it.'

'You'll have to listen to find out. But there are pearls in it.'

Lakhan picked a comb from his oblong box and plastered down Vipul's hair so that it fell straight over his eyes. From behind the curtain of hair Vipul now saw, indistinctly in the small mirror, that it had indeed grown long: its tips were kissing the tip of his nose. Lakhan continued to run his comb. It hurt. It was crude, made of metal and equipped with, it seemed, whetted teeth. It branded his scalp.

Then Lakhan picked up his bowl. And Vipul said, 'No katori on my head.'

He saw Lakhan throw a glance at his mother.

He said, 'Ma, if he cuts with a katori on my head I'll get up *halfway*.'

His mother, surprisingly conciliatory, granted that Lakhan could leave the katori aside.

Lakhan protested, in resignation and dismay, 'Now *how* do I cut.' Then he said, 'It's a story about my own childhood when I was as big as you – or a little smaller or a little bigger.'

'How many years old?'

'We never count our ages. It is said to bring death early. It's a story of my village Khooni in Gorakhpur…'

'What a name, Khooni. Are you all murderers?'

'Our villages have just such names. Now in Khooni there are more trees than houses.'

'So?'

'It's not so in every village. The reason we have so many trees is that many of them are special. They are not cut down.'

'Like the peepul, the banyan, the neem tree? Or fruit trees like mango?'

'Those there are in every village. But Khooni has a special kind, a rare kind. We call it the motiya, for it bears pearls. And in the rainy season, and for only a few days then, it sheds its pearls.'

'Pearls are in the sea. I saw a picture about a pearl guarded by an octopus. Jeetendra was the hero. He killed the octopus and got the pearl.'

'The sea too has pearls, but I don't know what this octopus is. Jeetendra I think I have seen. But this tree had its own pearls. They were not like sea pearls. They were hollow and very frail, just thin shells. They were small, round like marbles, but smaller than the marbles you play with. And they were white, white as milk. Very light they were; unless you picked up a few dozens you wouldn't feel their weight. They had their own smell. It was like the smell of their leaves, which smelt of lemon.'

'Eggs,' Vipul said. 'Ants' eggs.'

'Many thought so. But didn't I say, they were so small and hollow. No, this tree had its own pearls. And in the rainy season, it shed the pearls. Not one or two, or two or three at a time, not like fruit, but hundreds, thousands together, like heavy rain, like light small hail. Being the rainy season, the pearls fell on green grass. Often bright small red spiders crawled on the grass and the pearls. We used to pick up the pearls and bring them home. We thought they would bring us luck. But they had some other purpose. Despite gathering them I continue to be a barber, after all.'

Vipul thought of this privileged tree, a tree covered in its own precious creation, and it should have been an image of happiness, but it was not, for there was also the image of the rain of pearls, which must make the tree downhearted, mourning its loss even as the pearls fell.

Lakhan brought out his pair of scissors. To limber his fingers, he snipped vigorously at the air. The scissors squeaked and ticked and crunched, bad-jointed from overuse. Vipul had unpleasant memories of these scissors. Before they cut through his hair, they wrenched at it; each clip was accompanied by a stab of pain.

Lakhan lifted with his comb sheets of Vipul's hair above his head. He cropped the hair that overhung the comb. There were those stinging nicks of pain, and then neat rectangular arrays of glistening black hair fell on to the flowery sheet. Vipul looked pensively at the clippings. The effort of weeks of oiling and massage, neutralized. Soon the severed hair dried, and curled a little, and the arrays dispersed. The sheet was now filmed over with fine grey curvelets. Fresh black tassels continued to fall among them.

Lakhan punctuated the hairdressing with his little subroutines. He drew thoughtfully on his beedi, analysing his work. He walked over to the edge of the chabutra and, making dreadful tuberculous noises, spat out the tobacco-provoked phlegm. After each productive expectoration he looked as fulfilled as one might after a cup of strong sugary tea. Periodically he exercised his scissors in the air and sharpened them against his comb. Often he made the minutest adjustments to the angle of Vipul's head, like a jeweller turning a gem through infinitesimal degrees to catch its brightest facet.

And every few moments, or so it seemed, 'Keep still,' or 'Don't twitch,' he demanded, while the hair-ends on Vipul's nose and neck tormented him with their sharp prickles. If ever I catch this man with his back to me and an airgun in my hand, thought Vipul wistfully.

'I too had a dog when I was small,' Lakhan continued. 'Mitthua. A good dog, although obstinate and a total donkey sometimes. I took him along on all my walks. The pearl trees were in a small clump just outside the village. One day, in the rainy season, as we were passing by the trees, Mitthua started barking like a dog gone mad. I ignored him; he was a born barker. But he wasn't coming along. He had stopped by the pearl trees. And he kept barking, looking at something in the bed of pearls. I went to see what it was.'

'The snake, going like *this* through the grass and the pearls,' Vipul said, tracing a rapid sinuous path with his hand under the bedsheet.

'Baba, don't move. The snake it was. But at first I couldn't make it out. It was nearly dark. Above, clouds. Only a pinch of light from the drowning sun remained. That day it had rained with force and a great number of pearls had fallen. So I couldn't make out, for in the grass in the dark there are always snakelike shadows. I thought there was nothing, that Mitthua had really gone mad, the way he was barking. But then it started to move. Like a thin long shadow in the grass, amid the pearls. Slowly, slowly it moved, but still I couldn't see it, I could see only that the pearls kept separating along a twisting path, as though they themselves were alive.'

'So the snake was black.'

'Yes, but I was not sure of that until some days later when the moon was out, and the clouds had scattered. Then I saw that it was black, so very black, like the walls of coal inside Khajoori's mine. How it shone in the moonlight, sparks of blue everywhere on its body. And how beautifully it moved. Calmly, gently swinging, like a girl with a good waist, and as if no one was watching. And I even felt sad seeing it move. The only way you can tell how a snake feels is by its movement. A brisk snake is a happy one. This one, although you could say that it was lazy like a shopkeeper, this one struck you by its gait as being sad, and made you sad. Sad and calm, skylike calm, as though no one was watching. I would go to see it every evening.'

'But you were watching, and Mitthua was barking.'

'If snakes could hear, then Mitthua was barking. But after a few days, even Mitthua stopped barking. It seemed that the snake's air of peace had settled upon him. One day I noticed something strange.'

After Lakhan had lopped Vipul's hair on top of his head, he started on the strands that hung over the eyes. Now came the spell of greatest anxiety. What if Lakhan momentarily lost control of his movements? Or went mad? Suddenly became a mutilator? A blinder? The thought of the point of the scissor-blade piercing his eyes threw Vipul into a rigor of body and mind. All sensation was lost; the external world no longer intruded on him.

When Lakhan's scissors had run their course, Vipul felt a great relief, a deliverance from danger. He opened his eyes. In the mirror he saw with great lucidity his face, the curtain of hair drawn up, the sun lighting it. But could it really be *his* face? It was all mouth, nose, and forehead, the way it appeared when on occasion it was reflected in a convex mirror, flaring and protrusive. With the bedsheet's large pink flowers flowing all about him, with parts of his face still tinged with the residues of Holi colours, dull faded streaks of green and purple and crimson, he looked pitiably ludicrous, almost a Roman. But that snake ... that blue-spangled snake...

'What was the strange thing you saw?'

'I saw a pearl on the snake's forehead.'

'One of the tree's pearls!'

'Not one of those. But a real pearl.'

'On its forehead?'

'There,' Lakhan indicated, tapping his comb between Vipul's eyes.

'It was a real pearl, like the one guarded by the octopus in the picture?'

'A real one, although I don't know about the octopus or the picture.'

'The snake was carrying it?'

'How could it? No, it was embedded in its forehead. A pearl bigger than the tree pearls, and stony, shiny and hard. A white gem in a forehead black as coal, that's how it was.'

'A gem snake!' Vipul said. 'I have heard of these snakes. Mali keeps talking about them. But I've never seen one.'

'They exist. But there are very, very few. Even fewer are the people who ever get a chance to see one. It's an auspicious sight. They say it brings you luck, that it leads you to treasure. More stories in the air. See what I am, see what I do. But I was told all this much later. I kept the snake to myself for a long time – for some rainy seasons. No one in the village knew that I had seen the gem snake. It was easy to keep it to myself. The snake was just an occasional visitor. Only in the rainy season; only when the pearl trees' pearls had fallen on the grass; only on certain days, when the moon was full; only at dusk. Others may even have passed the spot where it used to appear, without noticing it.'

Vipul's sense of peace, which had come over him when the mirror had been removed, was aborted when Lakhan took out his cut-throat. Why did everything he'd do have to be so coarse? The barbers in town had trimmers, delicious on the skin with their light, gnawing creep and the cold flat touch of their metal. While Lakhan ... well Lakhan only had his murderous cut-throat, which he now glanced off his scissors so as to sharpen and smoothen its edge, which was nevertheless always jagged and scrapy.

'Can't we stop now? The haircut is over,' Vipul said.
'The story is not finished, and a razor-shave is a must,' Lakhan said.
'Who says?' Vipul said.

His mother intervened: 'Don't you want a man's sideburns when you grow up? Do you want to grow up with a girl's face? With curls of hair dangling from your temples?'

So Vipul submitted himself to the scraping pain, the redness, the stinging hairline.

'Did you not follow the snake to the treasure?' Vipul said.

'I could not. It was among the pearls. If I tried to follow it, I crushed the pearls, and it got to know. For I did try it once. As soon as I stepped on to the pearls, it looked back, and then it moved swiftly away, fast as a krait, into the bushes. And when it looked at me, baba, in its green eyes there was a glint of warning that said not to follow it. I saw it as clearly as I see the back of your head now. So I satisfied myself after that by just watching it and the pearl on its forehead, admiring its beauty, without thinking about the treasure.

'For what happened eventually I and only I am to blame. I have often pulled my own ears for it. Those days I had a friend who had returned from Patna city after some study. There, I thought, he must have learnt all about snakes in the books. I thought he would be able to recognize the snake correctly – I was sure and yet not sure that it was a true gem snake, for who can go only by what one's own eyes are saying? So I told him, one rainy season, that I could show him this gem snake, if he wanted. He said he wanted to see it.'

'And?'

'I took him along. For a few days the snake did not appear. My friend was beginning to disbelieve me. Then, finally, one evening, I saw the moving shadow, parting the pearls. I pointed it out to him. He bent down to look at it closely. Now the snake did a strange thing, something it had never done with me. I think it sensed that it was being observed by an enemy. Now, instead of sliding away, it turned, and very slowly started moving towards us. It was hissing. The pearl on its forehead glowed like a miner's headlamp.

'My friend ran over to a bush, broke off a fat twig. And he battered the snake dead with it.'

'O.'

'He said that he became suddenly afraid. Some people do. Some simply enjoy killing snakes. But I think he was after the pearl. Because after the snake was dead there was not relief on his face, but disappointment.'

'Did he not get the pearl? Or you?'

'Don't you know, baba? The pearl lives with the snake, and with the snake it dies. When the snake was dead, there was no pearl. Just a plain forehead.'

'How can that happen?'

'God makes these things, He makes these things happen. What do we know? Greed and impatience lead to nothing.'

'And?'

'And what?'

'That is the story?'

'That is all that the story is.'

'A good story but not much in it.'

'You wanted a snake…'

'Not such a snake.'

'It was not an ordinary snake. It was a gem snake.'

'But not such a snake. A more frightening snake, a dangerous, whipping snake, a swift, slim, long, extremely poisonous snake.'

'There are other stories for that kind of snake.'

Now Lakhan administered a scalp massage, his only and significant point of merit; the barbers in town had forsaken this art. His hands gripped Vipul's head, turned it sharp to one side. Vipul, instantly realizing what was about to happen, thought to ask him to stop. It was too late. Just when his head had reached its limit of rotation, Lakhan gave it an extra tug, swift and strong. There was a click, as of bone disengaging from bone; Vipul's neck ached. Immediately Lakhan repeated the procedure on the other side.

Then Lakhan ran thickly oiled fingers through Vipul's hair, tousling it. His hands were big and rough; with each swirl they were able to feed a touch and a rub to every point on Vipul's head. Then his hands drummed: a rain of smart sharp slaps, trills played by the fingers, and soft fisticuffs; joined hands, as in a namaste, brought down on the head lengthways, producing castanet-like claps. All were in erratic sequence, so that you did not know if it was a slap or a fist or a finger that would land next, or where it would land: a shower of pressure pulses, pointillistic like his mother's wandering fingernails on his back when she lulled him to sleep.

And as Lakhan rubbed, massaged, fisted, slapped, drummed, and clapped his head, Vipul felt that his skull had become hollow, breezy inside, as though all internal matter were being pounded out from it.

His senses became sharpened. From the direction of the guava tree there came the warble of bulbuls – liquid, as though emerging after having bubbled through miniature hookahs in their puffed throats, and going:

Tran – quilli – ty, tran – quilli – ty.

And there was the fused rustle of leaves and the coarser rustle of the unread newspaper that guarded his father's face; and his father's gentle snores; and occasionally his mother's deep inhalations and sighs, like moments of suddenly falling, quickly lifting sadness. There was water gurgling close by, irrigating a flower bed. There were waspish drones that approached and withdrew, rose high and dipped low, leaving filamentous trails of sound etched in the air. From high above, kites, the cunning kites that, at school during the lunch break, swooped down from behind and above and snatched away his tiffin, and whom he could now picture gliding in alternately contracting and expanding circles, specks of easy, ordered motion against a clear daylit sky, giving out their ravenous tremolo cries. Vipul smelt in Lakhan's hands a mixture of tobacco and hair oil, at once astringent and cloying. He smelt the patch of soil that received the gurgling water, and it reminded him of rain. And the sun continued to supply the critical amount of heat that kept things warm but did not heat them up, and his skin felt at peace, in perfect equilibrium with the air.

Now Lakhan's hands moved to flesh, where they felt grainy as a coarse blanket. They pinched Vipul's shoulders; pressed on his nape; kneaded his arm's muscles like putty; crushed his hands; pulled at his joints; wrung his skin. Vipul's hands, when Lakhan worked on them, felt recreated. Each joint felt loose and soft; his skin burned. Small electric discharges snaked along his spine. And a chill current flew down and through, most sensationally, his penis, which felt curiously vivid – its existence seemed to possess the half physical, half vaporous quality of a sensation experienced in a dream. And when thus thrilled it seemed to detach itself from Vipul's body so that the sensation was then located somewhere in the air, an inch adrift of the flesh; the somaesthetic equivalent of ventriloquism. Vipul knew this feeling well. It occurred also when he swung down from a height, or when he was in a car that, speeding over a low elevation, was airborne and falling for a brief instant. But just now it seemed an illicit pleasure, for the reason that it was being fed by touch, and that too by the sandpaperish local hands of Lakhan's; the crude and the erotic in concurrence.

Eyes shut, dissolved in sensation, the sun's warmth upon him and the various murmurs around, Vipul's head started to nod.

Just then he heard his father's voice directly in front: 'It still seems too long to me.'

Startled, he woke to see his father standing there, gazing at his hair in dissatisfaction.

'It's still standing tall on top. Lakhan, you should have cut it down more.'

Vipul said, 'Uff, pa, it's short enough.'

Lakhan said, 'I'll see to it now, sahib.'

'No,' said Vipul, rising.

'Keep sitting!' his father said.

Lakhan, standing behind him, gently pushed him down.

Vipul struggled. He was nearly in tears. 'Then I'll keep moving. Then you won't be able to cut it.'

'Vipul!' his father said.

'Vipul, Vipul!' Vipul said, his voice thin. 'What Vipul! I don't want it shorter.'

'Sahib, should I let go?' Lakhan said.

'No. Make his face come out.'

Vipul started to cry. His tears were full and oily and warm. The thought of his parents' pig-headedness enraged him. He squirmed again. Lakhan held him down easily. He started to kick the air.

His mother had also risen from her chair, and he heard her say, 'Ayah! Thapa!'

While he continued to struggle, Ayah and Thapa arrived. 'Hold him down,' his mother said.

Thapa gripped his ankles; Ayah pinned down his wrists. They kept saying, 'Bitty baba! Quiet, Bitty baba.'

Restrained all about, he swung his head manically. His ears filled with his own screams. He wished death on Ayah and Thapa. They laughed.

Presently, exhausted, he slumped. The struggle had so numbed his senses that he did not properly feel the teeth of Lakhan's comb or the tug of his scissors. Lakhan went on and on. And when Lakhan had finished and held the mirror up to him, Vipul saw that he was as good as clean shaven. Parts of his pate reflected the sunlight.

Bald! But he was so tired that he no longer cared. Lakhan said, 'I'll give you another rub now.' And again Vipul shut his eyes and gave himself up to the massage. This time he did doze off. He started to dream. He was on the banks of the Damodar, riding a tiger. The tiger was the shape of a buffalo and as friendly as Rover, and had a sheen of warm silk. Vipul tugged at the tiger's neck, and the tiger turned his head and licked him with a sodden red tongue, smiling in its tigerish way. The next moment Vipul was down on the ground, on his back, with the tiger above him. The tiger's face was shot with hatred, barbed with fangs. Vipul felt hot, clammy. The tiger's face changed, and its body changed; the tiger was Lakhan. Lakhan, gloating over his bald victim. Yet Lakhan was kind. He held his fingers gently, and massaged them. He started to feel a great affection for Lakhan. But then his mother's voice came, anxious and urgent, 'Lakhan, leave him! Vipul, come back! Vipul! Get up!' Vipul was terrified. Why did his mother speak as though Lakhan were dangerous? A miasma of wickedness enveloped Lakhan. He was a blood-eyed killer armed with a cut-throat. He had a tiger's dripping fangs.

'Come, Vipul, get up. Lakhan, he's had enough.' This time the voice was sharper, cleaner. It was a voice of the waking world. He opened his eyes to see his mother standing in front of him again, as she had done when insisting that his hair be cropped shorter. But this time she was not looking at him sternly. She had a musing, satisfied look on her face.

Lakhan stopped the massage. Vipul rose slowly. 'Go and have a bath now,' his mother said. And she called out to his father to come up for his haircut.

Vipul walked past his father, who had gone back to sleep in the same angle of repose as before. Odd to think that just a few minutes ago he had made him cry.

In the bathroom, he avoided looking into the mirror over the sink for fear of catching sight of his baldness. But as he was getting undressed, as he swivelled to take off his vest, a glimpse presented itself.

His hair was still there. It was short, but he was not bald; not even short cropped, just moderately shorn.

He pondered for a moment.

Then, to celebrate, he executed three whippy somersaults on the bathroom floor.

DAYS OF SUMMER

ONE

At summer's onset, school's timings were changed. Classes began at seven in the morning and ended at twelve, leaving for Vipul entire afternoons to battle, or enjoy, the removedness of home. 'Morning School' was the name given to the new schedule. The change was made purely out of respect for the zeal of the summer sun. A regular nine-to-four day in April or May would incur too large a dose of heat for anybody to buffer; the students would become refractory, the teachers irascible, everybody dehydrated. During the lunch break at twelve-thirty or during the Games period at three, there would be the constant promise of somebody fainting from sunstroke. So the day at school was folded in half.

For school to now occupy fewer hours, subsidiary adjustments were made: each period was shortened; the Games period was done away with, and so, to the delight of all except, one imagined, Father Vane-Pearce, was the Drill. And although the curtailment in the duration of each period was but five minutes, the periods went skippingly by; classes were over before the teachers had had time to settle into a good harangue. Perhaps it was the general sense of starchiness and crispness, brought on in the teachers as well as the boys by the early morning air, that rendered the classes palatable.

Vipul liked Morning School all the more for its incidentals. He liked getting up at four-thirty in the morning, when it was still dark, and getting ready for school as it inapparently grew light. Every day it made him feel at the threshold of a long and irreversible journey.

When he was younger, his mother used to bathe him. He missed that indulgence. She used to bathe him only during the months of Morning School, feeling perhaps that he would be unreliable, at five in the morning, in cleaning himself properly. While she bathed him she would sing devotional songs, and he would stumble after her, his sense of tone still nascent, the meanings of the bhajans' words still unclear to him. She bathed him gently; so much more gently than he bathed himself. Yet she seemed to be so much more efficient in degriming him. On his own, he would rub the soap almost into his bones to try and get a lather to form, and afterwards he would splash himself lustily with mugs of water from a bucket. But his mother would no more than slide the soap over his skin and with a slight skimming massage work effervescent clouds of lather out of, it seemed, nothing. She'd would pour on him smooth continuous tapers of water, like a balm, swabbing away the soap with a sponge, and finally dry him with a towel so lightly it made him feel as brittle as a piece of china.

And as she sang, a koel would start its predawn koohooing outside in the garden, joining in the prayer, addressing some bird god of its own. Then Vipul would be dressed and readied by Ayah, whose timings also changed with those of the boys. She would pour a small pool of hair oil into one cupped palm, and with both hands work it into his scalp so that his hair became slippery and soft; she would continue to do this until he shouted, 'Stop! Stop!', for fear of his hair and brain getting poisoned by oil. Then she would dress his hair, first making a parting to one side and then combing, combing, combing it with such heaving tugs on both sides of the parting that he would again shout, 'Stop! Stop!,' for fear of losing his hair by the roots.

Now he was older, and he bathed with much less grace than in his mother's hands, and combed his hair in much greater comfort than in Ayah's.

Over at school, before the classes began, in the Assembly, the Prayer that the boys said every morning – led by Father Armand, who carefully decelerated it to ensure that the boys would utter each word – this Prayer too, which on normal days was an oppression in the strengthening sun, became now vital and transporting. This, together with the effect of his mother's predawn bhajans, made it seem that the best time to establish a communion with God, as with teachers, was early morning, when alertness ruled perhaps in heaven as on earth. So it was with uncommon sincerity that at the start of each Morning School day Vipul recited, his voice lost in the electric hum of hundreds of others, a prayer composed by Father Armand himself:

> Almighty God
> Creator of all
> Life and sorrow and happiness;
> I ask of Thee
> To admit me to Thy
> Hallowed presence.
> Bless today
> My trials and endeavours
> That I may receive
> A little of Thy
> Divine Enlightenment;
> And pardon me my faults,
> My shortcomings, and failures,
> And make me worthy
> In whatsoever I undertake

Of Thy Grace and Thy Compassion
And Thy boundless Love,
Amen.

But the very last day of school before the summer holidays, and the one before any other, was marked by a curious violence and excessiveness. The boys were replete with goodwill; so much so, perhaps, that some of it could not be prevented from slipping over into warfare. They ruined one another's clothes. Vipul carried on him three fountain pens; he wrote the last examination with one; the other two were for use as inkjets, to splash others' shirts with. Everyone brought extra pens along, and, minutes after the examination was over, had emptied them upon others. Of course the boys came prepared; they wore discarded old school shirts. It was an imitation, blue-toned Holi.

There were also the fights that never took place: the pre-planned, predetermined fights, between entire sections of classes. Each class had three sections. In the coalfields of Bihar, Bengalis were numerous, and for Bengali boys there was section B; C was mostly Christian; A got the rest: sprinklings of boys from other states and other faiths. Sections A and B caused each other particularly deep chagrin. Section A held that the Bengalis of B were despicable swots, and, like all swots, were vainglorious and ignorant of their deficiencies, mainly physical, which A meant to lay bare; section B in its turn held that A was a pack of uncultured louts, who, like all louts, thought themselves stronger than they were, and needed to be taught, in their own language, some hard physical lessons. Immediately the ink-splashing ended, the two sections gathered in the football field, some distance apart. They began by hurling couplets of pithy ridicule, diligently rehearsed, at each other. This over, spontaneous abuse commenced; and after this, the unsheathing of arms. Boys in both sections had come equipped with leather whips (and those who had not, took off their belts), catapults, retired hockey sticks, knuckledusters. These they brandished, to the accompaniment of gestures of challenge and of might, and allegations of cowardice, and threats of annihilation. But the distance between the sections remained; no one really wished to risk either receiving an injury or inflicting one, no one really regarded his piece of armament a usable weapon. Thus they rattled on, building up to a fight that was never to take place. To see them at this hour one would be reminded of well-matched packs of dogs who, a safe distance apart, will interminably emit the reddest, most bloodcurdling snarls at each other, with neither of a mind to attack, and neither to retreat, and both happy, on being sapped by their own demonstrations, to lower their tails and repair limply back to their camps. So did the boys, after an hour or so, each section feeling it had cowed the other, threats still ringing feebly in the air.

The boys were also rich today, for their parents, for once, had given them both the money as well as the leave to feast on all the dirt they wanted, outside the school's gates. Puffed-rice mixtures, nameless sour powders, salted and chillied cucumbers, ices: each article certifiably pathogenic, and each certifiably, exquisitely, tasty. Vipul and Sameer were forbidden to have these on ordinary schooldays, and throughout the term they dreamed of this the last day, the day of academic and gustatory dissipation.

TWO

Outside school hours, and through the day on holidays, Vipul had taken to listening to the BBC at the times and the frequencies Father Rocqueforte had typed out for him. (Sheer joy it was, too, to Vipul, that father had typed out the list: Vipul had never received a typed note in his life, only dull handwritten ones; the piece of paper glittered with modernity before his eyes.) His hunt for the broadcast led him across the entire spectrum of short-wave radio, and this in turn became for him a subject of enchanted inquiry, a species of research enterprise.

He would scour the face of the dial for new sounds, new voices, new stations. Going across the short-wave bands was like passing through a series of crowded bazaars. At each metre band there would be an explosion of motley sounds. If you moved the needle quickly across, the speaker would erupt with squirts and spits and bursting bubbles of sound, gibberish, like a stormy squabble spoken backwards. And if you moved slowly, very slowly, the sound of one radio station would melt into that of its neighbour's, so that at the indistinct edge sometimes one nation spoke and sometimes the other, alternating nonsensically, bilingually, conversationally.

Just as Vipul characterized different nations by their postage stamps, so he characterized them by their presentations on short wave. The Russians were an earnest nation, disseminating formulae of statecraft and political ethic. The Chinese were excitable and soprano; the British punctilious. The Americans and Australians, imitation Englishmen, were desultory, forever short of things of substance to say, somehow filling up the time; other Europeans frivolous, transmitting for an hour or two every day in badly learnt English just for the diversion of it. But most wonderful of all was Radio Seychelles – remote, oceanic, sun-lapped Radio Seychelles, available serendipitously at just the one faint spot on the dial, yet so very thoughtful, giving such news and at such times as no other station would deign to. Such as the score, fresh off the field at twelve-thirty in the afternoon, at the end of a day's play in a test match between New Zealand and the West Indies at Christchurch, South Island; just the station for a connoisseur of irrelevancies.

Medium-wave radio, on the other hand, was a journey through a lonely district. Here and there during the traverse, and interspersed by long silent tracts, you came across a few relaxed, uncongested broadcasts; a scratchy record of Hindustani classical music superimposed on the scratchy air; the News at Slow Speed being read out, a peculiar and ataraxic activity, a timeless pastime, an apt complement to a sleepy afternoon.

With the BBC, however, Vipul became intimately acquainted. On holidays he would home in upon the signature tune before the broadcast began, and chaperone the World Service through its programmes. As the mains-powered Murphy at home was unportable, the size of a small suitcase, he inveigled his parents into buying for him, saying that Father Rocqueforte had recommended it, a battery-operated transistor radio which he took to carrying hoisted on a strained shoulder, close to his ear, wherever he walked. He memorized, through an osmosis born of listening to it day in and day out, the preamble to the broadcast:

'This ... is the World Service of the BBC, broadcasting to South Asia on 15.31, 15.15, 12.75, 9.74, and 6.195 megahertz, in the sixteen, nineteen, twenty-five, thirty-one, and forty-nine metre bands.'

A pause.

Then:

'This ... is London.'

And then the news began, and it was an example of the punctiliousness of the BBC: to usher it on there was its very own clarion fanfare; then at the start, after the headlines, the body of the news came quite without announcement, with just a weighty silent moment inserted there to give notice to the alert. And in the middle they said that the news came to you *in*, and not from, the World Service of the BBC; and the *main points*, not headlines, were repeated at the end. And the news lasted *nine* minutes, not a wholesome ten; and why any of it should have been done in the way it was remained for Vipul a source of bafflement and charmed wonderment.

Over the ensuing months he became conversant with the names of all the announcers. He thought that he should one day make a trip to England and meet them and exchange courtesies and news. He started listening to pop music programmes, and thought that he should cultivate the kind of laconic wit that their presenters possessed (how irreverently they mocked and slandered the Director General of the BBC!). He tuned in to the Sports Round-Up twice daily, growing staunch loyalties for football and rugby clubs going about their muddy business thousands of miles away. And in the summer the mullings, infallibly civil and pithy, of John Arlott and Christopher Martin-Jenkins, of Gerald Williams and Dan Maskell, took him through warm breezy evenings imagining, visiting, savouring to repletion, Lords and Trent Bridge, Wimbledon and its Centre Court, places that seemed not to be rooted in earth but to float green and lilting somewhere up in the sky, unsullied by worldliness.

But the BBC World Service commenced its broadcast only in the afternoon; and often there were programmes that, regardless of Vipul's best efforts at acclimatizing himself to them, eluded him, programmes on Western classical music and opera and British theatre. So there was time left during the summer holidays for other pursuits. It had been a standing ambition of Vipul's to write a ghost story; one as good as some of those he had read, the kind in which the ghost became so corporeal that it leapt out from the page and shimmered before his eyes. He wanted to write an unsparing ghost story, not a soft-pedalling one: the ghost would be malignant, and insidious, and extraordinarily callous. It would first manifest as an aura of evil that the characters in the story would only sense – in the way of a suffocating presence, a heavy weight on the chest perhaps, or a sinking heart. It would next work into their blood, making them behave eerily and ominously, and finally, one by one drive them to unnatural deaths. All the incidents in the story would take place late in the evening or in the deep of night, to the accompaniment of cloudswept skies, gales that howled, and the baying of wolves.

He wrote:

In the grounds of the manor, the dark evening was like a shroud upon the trees, which swayed in the angry storm. A giant bat, the symbol of evil, flitted between the trees, waiting to turn into a vampire at night. From the forest, the bloodthirsty baying of wolves could be heard. Mischief was afoot.

That was all right. Ghost stories had to unfold in castles or manors or in a Transylvanian wilderness, else they wouldn't be credible.

Next Vipul pondered on who should emerge from the manor to witness this chilling scene, and wrote:

Frederick and Susan, after their evening tea, came out of the manor into the garden.
Frederick felt a heavy weight on his chest.

Vipul liked the name Frederick. He liked its tough consonantal feel; and he relished the air of adventure and dash that it possessed by virtue of being the name of the West Indian opening batsman, Roy Fredericks, who was supposed to play his shots while entirely airborne, pouncing, mongoose-like, on the ball with his scything cavalier bat all awhistle. He wished he had been named Frederick; his parents had been quite unimaginative in naming him. And Susan was so soft and delicate a name, just the name for just such a ghost-afflicted girl.

For a moment he thought he should write a ghost story set in Khajoori, in one of its bungalows, perhaps their own, with ber trees and banana fronds in its grounds, with names like Mohan and Preeti for the haunted victims.

Absurd.

And the trees – what would they be in Scotland? (He had inspirationally chosen Scotland as the setting for his story, for the country seemed from many accounts to be adequately craggy, forsaken and prone to visitation.) Oaks and weeping willows, perhaps. Or poplars and chestnuts?

He considered. What did these trees look like? Were they menacing at twilight? Of all the English trees he had heard of he had seen only a picture of an oak in blue-skied sunshine, looking unequivocally benign.

For help he went to Sameer, who was busy pricking holes, with nails and a hammer, into the club of a hockey stick in order to oil it, and said, 'Bittu, what does a weeping willow look like?'

'Who asked you?'

'Nobody *asked* me. I just want to *know*,' Vipul said.

'Why?'

'How does it matter? Just tell me what it looks like.'

'First tell me why.'

It was clear that Sameer did not know. So Vipul said, 'What would English children have for snacks in the evening?'

'Tarts, crumbles and pies,' Sameer said.

'What do they look like?'

'White, with blonde hair, blue eyes, and red...'

'Uff, the *snacks*, not the children. I know about blue eyes and all that.'

Sameer gave pause to his hammering for a moment, thought it over and said, 'Who knows. But that's what they eat, and for breakfast they have ham, bacon, and fried eggs.'

'What's bacon?'

'Must be a kind of toast.'

Vipul decided not to return that day to his story, and squatted there to help Sameer muscle up the hockey sticks.

Any season could be enjoyed in two ways: in its indulgence, and in its exclusion. Vipul enjoyed the heat of the direct summer sun, but he enjoyed better, at times, the shelter of a room that excluded it entirely. He enjoyed getting drenched in a downpour, but enjoyed better, at times, remaining dry in a veranda, watching the play of rain upon foliage without; enjoyed the exuberance that cold air brought, yet enjoyed better the swaddling warmth of a quilt. He was thankful to climate for its severities, for without them there wouldn't exist the pleasures that attended their exclusion. The capacity to enjoy contrary conditions equally being intrinsic to his nature, Vipul could in good measure enjoy companionship and yet enjoy better, at times, the absence of it, the space afforded by solitude, and the circumstances that gave rise to it.

Vipul celebrated summer in both ways. He enjoyed being in the sun; he liked the way it made his hair hot to the touch, so that it seemed to be no longer black but bleached, perhaps cream-coloured. He liked the stillness it enforced daily around noon, sending the multitudes, perspiring, indoors, creating for him a welcome solitude. He liked the loo, too: the desert-blown loo that, even though by nature a gusty wind, rather than cool the skin dealt it slaps of heat, making Vipul think of the sandscapes whence it had sprung: of corrugated dunes, caravanning camels, earthen houses and a faded sky; of the moustaches and the nosegays and the hot-coloured turbans of the people of the deserts of Rajasthan.

And Vipul enjoyed equally denying the sun a sense of almightiness. Outside the house, he did so by bathing with bucketfuls of water drawn from the deepening, diminishing well. The well's water was cool at all times, unlike the water in the taps that, warmed in the tanks on the roof, issued scalding hot during the day. The well's water carried, too, the netherworld flavour of the algae and the ferns and the frogs, insects and occasional snake that lived there; and considering its copious abetment of life, it was surprisingly clean, transparent, not like the Damodar's water that came in particulate, earthy streams in the taps, making you anxious that your teeth might turn brown through brushing with it.

Inside the house, Vipul and Sameer often spent afternoons in their parents' room. Here, when there wasn't a power cut, an air conditioner, a mysterious machine that never inhaled, yet constantly blew a breeze of cool air from its kind icy heart, chilled the air to cosy wintriness. Or when they were in their own room, they heatproofed it. First they heatproofed the house, letting down the chicks in the veranda. Then they shuttered all the room's windows and drew all its curtains to make it as dark as possible. (And yet, even after the best arrangements had been made, there remained a gleam of light in the room, enough to see mistily by; was the sun so mighty that it seeped in through the very walls?) They sprinkled water everywhere, on the floor, on the bedsheet, on the pillows, sanctifyingly, and switched to full speed the ceiling fan, which revolved bodily even as its blades rotated, and issued plaintive noises, seeming apt to come crashing down, panicked arms flailing, any moment. Finally they lay down on their beds, lit their bedside lamps, and read or talked till they fell, for two interned hours in the afternoon, asleep.

THE PICTURE TOOTH

ONE

Some days before Veena masi, Vipul's mother's younger sister, and her six-year-old daughter Neha were to leave after their month-long stay at Khajoori, Vipul's mother made an unwelcome discovery. She found that Veena masi's gold bracelets, which had been entrusted to her care and which she had kept hidden and locked in her stainless steel almirah, had gone missing.

The bracelets were made of twenty-four-carat gold, and were heavy; on their weight alone, they'd have fetched two thousand rupees in Delhi's jewellery markets. What was more, their surfaces had been worked into sinuous, fragile curlicues and ringlets, and had been set flashing with opals and garnets in the workshop of one of Delhi's better respected goldsmiths. Their actual worth was therefore close to four thousand rupees. And four thousand in those days could have bought you a second-hand car in self-starting condition. To crown it all there was, as Veena masi called it, the sentimental value of the bracelets (which, of course, was inestimable): they had been gifted her by her late father-in-law, whom she had greatly feared and adored.

Vipul was not much affected by the monetary degree of the loss – the sum of four thousand was but an abstraction to him, and he could not reckon its magnitude in terms of things, such as marbles or tops or comic books, that mattered. But he was worried by the effect that the incident had on Neha: Neha, on seeing her mother suddenly urgent and anxious, had herself withdrawn into a shroud of sympathetic gloom, and brushed Vipul away when he tried to kiss her.

This pained Vipul, for over the month of summer that Veena masi and Neha had stayed at Khajoori, Vipul had grown to love Neha and, by the measure of his senses, every one of which was touched by Neha in ways they had never been touched before, had also fallen in love with her. When she was at a distance, he stared at her, marvelling at her small movements; when she was close, he liked the smell of baby powder on her neck and of coconut hair oil in her hair; and he liked to kiss her, her cheeks warm and yielding to his lips. He loved her in a way only a child can love another, and then perhaps as only an Indian child can love a cousin of his: intimately, in the absence of the denial of physical closeness; with an intensely brotherly feeling, and again with an undefined, confounding, unbrotherly passion. When they played, he treated her as a doll, and as a child; as a sister, and as a wife; sometimes separately and sometimes, inexplicably, as all of these together. He had once, in a moment of dizzy intensity, even applied his mother's vermilion powder to the parting in her hair, like the heroes in the Hindi movies did to their heroines at the unfailingly happy and cathartic finales; and he did so in just as grave and mournful a manner as theirs. That made them both embarrassed for the next hour or two: the play-acting had become too adult, too fraught with meaning; but they were back soon to their precocious ways. It became, then, a delicious and an infernal condition for Vipul, the condition of being a cousin to Neha: she was not his sister, and so he was not familiar enough with her to be indifferent to her; yet she was his designated sister – his 'cousin sister' – and so he could demonstrate his fondness for her as lavishly as he chose to. He was all the time hung between guilt and ecstasy.

One of the things that Vipul regularly asked Neha to do was to dance for him. She would do so, after putting on her special dress – her mirror-worked ghagra and choli. She liked to dance to the songs from the film *Hare Rama Hare Krishna* which was, as the magazine *Picture Show* put it, a towering box-office hit that year, Zeenat Aman in it sensational. When Neha spun around, her ghagra swirled and the hundreds of tiny flickers of light that shot from its mirrors were like a jungle of restless fireflies. Vipul watched her steps in fascination. They were elemental and uninstructed, and lagged behind the music; it was as though she had turned into a marionette, and the puppeteer could only do so much – and not enough – to keep all her joints moving to time.

When Vipul's mother made her discovery, she told Veena masi about it in a whisper, as follows: 'Veena, did you pick up your bracelets from my almari?'

And Veena masi knew what had happened. But first she said, 'Didi you know I've never touched your almari without first asking you.' Then she said, 'But have you checked the whole almari?'

They went to the dressing room and ransacked the almirah. It was like a desecration: the interior of the almirah possessed, as ever, the cool aromatic undisturbed aura of a sanctum, rarely accessed: there was gold locked away there, and Vipul's father's twenty-one-jewel Rolex watch which in seven years had been worn perhaps twice, and cash – ever the cash, to save them from having to go to the bank too often.

After the almirah they emptied out both the chests of drawers, and there too they did not find the bracelets. By the time they were done with their search the dressing room was fused with the stern vital odour of the naphthalene balls and the dried neem leaves strewn amongst the stored clothes to keep the moths and silverfish away. The room was now like a musty warehouse, and no longer the minor perfumery of which it was usually redolent, with the pastel odours of Pond's Dreamflower talc and Old Spice aftershave coasting its air.

They mulled over the disappearance of the bangles. Vipul's mother said that she had kept the almirah locked every single breath that she was away from it; it was a queer thing to happen. Only, she said, she hadn't kept the bracelets in the locker – here her voice trailed and she smacked her forehead with her palm in remorse.

Veena masi said that that was not Vipul's mother's fault; they had returned very late after dinner with the Bhatias two nights ago, which was the last occasion on which Veena masi had worn her bracelets, and naturally Vipul's mother must have been too tired to remember or to bother to put them in the locker.

Vipul's mother said that she wished she had also put on some of her own jewellery that evening, so that she might have remembered about the locker – but then she was so informal always with the Bhatias…

All this time Neha clung to her mother's sari, by her side, in that peculiar manner which tells of both the lending as well as the receiving of solace. Vipul picked her up and patted and kissed her and said distracting things to her for a whole hour, but Neha remained distraught.

All the servants were under suspicion.

Thapa, the sweeper, was in any case always under suspicion because of his red rotten eyes and his red clever teeth and very dark glinting skin. So now he was held to be almost certainly guilty.

Aansu, the kitchen boy, was now established to have been thieving from the storeroom, and had put on five kilograms in weight since the time that he had joined not so long ago. But what did he know of gold? When he had arrived, he did not know properly even of currency.

The gardeners – of course they were out there most of the time fooling around with the earth and its fecundity and looking ignorant of anything unrelated to soil and hydrodynamics and botany, but – but they did come inside the house from time to time to put up the flower arrangements or to air the indoor ferns and cacti when the plants started to ail.

Ayah, who had a name that nobody seemed to know, knew everything about the house that there was to know, and indeed made a point of being smart about it: so wise she acted at times, Vipul's mother said. But then she was also clever enough to realize that her cleverness would itself make her a target of suspicion, and so would she be likely to do it?

Then there were the guards, who of course never entered the house but who could have gleaned information from any of the others and masterminded the operation.

Everybody was questioned. Had they done it; did they know who had; if they either confessed or informed on the thief they would be forgiven, even rewarded.

Thapa was only amused. He became charming; his face cracked into his drunken smile. He said, 'Of course, memsahib, everything bad that happens in this house is because of me. Why don't you just hang me? I'm standing here ready to hang. You can hang me memsahib.'

Vipul's mother said, 'Why do you have to repeat this stupid thing every time? Can't you think of anything new to say? *How* can I hang you, even if I want to?'

'You can hang me however you like, memsahib,' Thapa said, with his red grin.

'Atrocious man. Go away and carry on with your cleaning,' Vipul's mother said.

In this way Thapa always won, by condemning himself more outrageously than any detractor of his ever could.

Ayah was deeply hurt and offended, and said she would forgo lunch in protest; everybody else was a little shocked and, it seemed, also a little pleased, and, of course, unknowing. There was no clue.

Vipul's mother wrote several little identical notes in her open loud handwriting and sent one to each of her friends and to other members of the Ladies' Club. The notes carried information on the theft, and a request for vigilance on clues. She sent, along with each note, a selection of vegetables fresh from her kitchen garden, arranged on a cane tray and covered with a clean white napkin.

Most of her friends responded with notes that conveyed their gratitude as well as their regret at being unable to help, and each note came with a selection of garden vegetables that differed from that which Vipul's mother had sent.

But one of the notes, when she read it, made his mother say aloud, 'Veena! See what Monisha here says. "I do not have information on the thief, but I may be able to help in another way. I'll come over in about half an hour."'

Monisha, Auntie Banerjee to Vipul, knew of an astrologer who, in addition to making the usual sorts of forecasts, had gained the reputation of being able to identify fraudsters and thieves and other criminals by a method that only he knew of. For instance, Auntie Banerjee said, her sister had inherited a piece of land in their village, and the land had been encroached upon while it lay unattended. The pandit told her sister – correctly, as it turned out – that the encroachment had been orchestrated by a most trusted servant of hers, one who had served her loyally for more than twenty years and would not normally have been suspected of thieving even a button, leave alone ringleading all this subterfuge in real estate.

The pandit, she said, was something of an ascetic, living by a temple on a hillock in the middle of a small forest in the neighbouring district of Gumia. So it was decided that faith, business and a picnic could be combined in one outing by worshipping at the temple, consulting the pandit, and then having lunch in a forest clearing.

TWO

The drive along the road that led out of Jadugoda was raggedy but for a patch that ran for a few minutes where it seemed that the road had been smoothened with emery paper and varnished to make it shine. At the end of this road they came to its junction with the Grand Trunk Road. At the junction stood a tall signpost with several arms pointing east and west, like a totem of a bird standing erect with outstretched wings, each blade of wing telling of impossible distances that the Grand Trunk Road stretched to, to the east towards Calcutta and to the west towards Delhi and Amritsar, in hundreds and in thousands of kilometres.

They turned on to the Grand Trunk Road. The Grand Trunk Road is an inconstant one, a road that changes its size and its character as it goes along, so that it is always consonant with the stretch of countryside or the town that it passes through. Sometimes in the towns it becomes simply another market-lane, constricted by shops on either side, arrayed with carts and stalls, peopled by a numerous antlike traffic – rickshas, bicycles, mopeds, scooters, tempos, milling about each other like molecules of a gas in random thermal motion yet miraculously avoiding collisions – and treated as a mall by all manner of pedestrians: human, bovine, canine, feline. It assimilates into the town so completely that it seems as though the town has digested it. And then when it passes into solitary countryside it expands and, like the villages that never border on it but always stand respectfully off to the sides, a kilometre or so away, it becomes reclusive and mysterious.

They were going through a quiet patch. The Grand Trunk Road plunged into shady patches under the mango and jamun trees that lined it and emerged from them in quick succession. From high above it must have looked like a thin long chiaroscuro strip, the alternating patches of dark and light like the blobs of pigment on a viper's skin. Concurrent with the play of light was a dance of temperature; a pulsatile, rhythmic oscillation of hot under the sun and just a little less hot in the shadows of the trees. Had you carried a sensitive thermometer in the car its meniscus would have bobbed up and down, nodding in happy agreement with some inaudible point.

Vipul's father's car was an Italian Fiat sedan, made partly in India. It had a protruding radiator grill, which imparted it a sort of smile, benign and feminine. Inside the car, on the dashboard, there was an idiosyncratic speedometer of an uncommon design. It consisted in a fluid strip that ran alongside a series of numbers, indicating speed as mercury in the stem of a thermometer indicates temperature. To Vipul this was the proudest feature of the car, far outshining its smooth gearbox and its steering wheel, both of which moved, his father said, as silkily as milk fat. Vipul liked the speedometer ribbon better because it created illusions of speed. When the car was at rest, it stood at forty kilometres per hour and when the car went downhill without the brakes on, it broadcast breathtaking speeds.

Where the road was smooth, Nizam would let his foot bear down upon the accelerator, driving the ribbon to its limit, where it would tremble with fatigue. A stream of asphalt would flow past them, alive like a river, and on either side the countryside would begin to rotate like a gramophone record. And the Fiat was the needle on the record, plucking off it and pluming forth the music of the road and its surrounds: yodel of goatherd, roar of overladen truck, boom of langur, low of oxen.

But after every few minutes of speedy progress Nizam would have to decelerate, brake, and swerve: the road would turn rough, and would be reduced to a thin writhing trickle of tar amidst an irruption of potholes, as though it had developed an allergic rash at the point. All roads in and around Jadugoda were like this: ever treacherous, ever in a state of unapologetic disrepair, intolerant of sustained speed. Every winter they were dutifully padded up, and every subsequent monsoon they weathered – utterly. They were of course designed to do just that, in the interest of maximum profit for everybody concerned – contractor, labourer and corporator. And there was a biological cyclicality about this ritual of regeneration and degeneration. The roads after they were resurfaced in winter were like devotional sacrificial offerings laid before the rain gods, which during the monsoon the gods proceeded festively to destruct.

Nobody said much during the drive. Vipul felt uneasy. Although neither of them would admit it, Vipul felt that a silence had grown between his mother and Veena masi. They spoke to each other in the manner of two normal people responding normally to each other, and not in the manner, which had prevailed all through the past month, of two slightly hysterical girls relating something hysterical to each other. Indeed all through their stay at Khajoori, while Vipul and Neha had played at their adult games, their mothers, it seemed, had reverted to girlhood. They became giggly, they teased each other and the servants and Vipul's father about, it seemed, nothing at all, joked about the relatives in Delhi: a balding scalp, a morose temper, somebody's sense of dress. Vipul's mother never normally said such things of her own accord; it was as though Veena masi had taken the lid off a stewing pressure cooker, letting free a sudden, startling fragrance. Vipul was both astonished and pleased every time this happened to his mother; the novelty of it never wore off because of the entirely different person his mother became in the intervening periods, sober, prosaic.

And while they talked, each made it a point to get shocked by the things that the other did and said, expostulating, 'You're so naughty! So *bad*!' At which the other would dissolve into a fit of chortles infused with wickedness and embarrassment as though to say, 'See? I've grown up, I'm no longer the little girl you used to know.' But neither of them was in any way being wicked or bad or naughty; and neither of them really shocked the other; their revelry lay in fact in shocking themselves by saying unaccustomed things, things that were really as mild and neutral as the taste of fresh curd – but then curd, too, when tasted for the first time or after a long interval, can play keen on the tongue.

And they did some of the things that Vipul and Neha did together, but with much greater verve and relish than did the children, the transience of their regained childhood spurring them to heighten each moment of it. They sat with their sides glued to each other on the wooden swing in the garden, swung as high as they could while sitting, alternately stretching and flexing their bodies, and asked Vipul or Neha to push them higher still. While swinging they sang songs together, songs of the rainy season and of swings and of love and of heartache, and all through the songs they laughed and sighed. One evening they both washed their waist-long hair and, before oiling it, let it hang loose to dry. They draped themselves in white thin saris, and went on swinging and singing till it became dark. Then there was a power cut, and in the murmurous light of the infant moon that night they looked and sounded like twin banshees reminiscing a happy earthly past, their white saris a thick ghostly two-lobed mist ruffled by the breeze.

Vipul also remembered distinctly the morning on which Veena masi and Neha had arrived. He recalled how his mother and masi had filled one section of the railway platform with noise, shouting inquiries, laughing with delight at having met after many months; how he and Neha had been tentative, like strangers; how on the way home, in the car, on the boat, and then in the jeep his mother and Veena masi asked each other, 'So! How are you?' or 'And! What else is going on?', time after time. And in each instance the immediate response would be, 'O, absolutely fit', or 'See for yourself, what do you think?' or 'Nothing much, what about you?', which made it appear that the conversation would die there and then. But these were just bit-replies, partly sham, and after a while there would come the real answer, dotted with particulars, from which it would become clear that a great deal was in fact going on in the lives of both women, and that not quite everything was fine. But even the particulars were not, indeed could not be, divulged entirely in the hour-long journey home; quite enough leads, however, were issued over that spell to keep them busy each day through the ensuing month, when they would pick up on one of these leads after another and tease it out to exhaustion. That conversation, then, was like the preface to a textbook, giving inviting glimpses of what was to be elaborated more fully in each of the chapters to come.

When they reached home, and after they had all lunched and bathed and slept a while, Veena masi opened her suitcase and laid out the gifts that she had brought. There was a T-shirt each for Vipul and Sameer with Walt Disney comic-strip characters printed on them, and a book called *The Space-Age Man* which told of the exploits of man on the moon and of the spaceships that went past Mars and Venus; for their father she had brought a metre-and-a-half length of a new kind of cloth, called terecrepe, that, she said, had become all the rage among men in Delhi lately. It had a fine-grained surface, like that of coarse rubber, was meant not to crease, and was hailed as giving to trousers a very good fall. And for their mother, Veena masi had brought a sea-green organdie sari embellished with a sparse threadwork, known as chikan, of paisleys and tendrils and vines.

As the gifts were handed over, Vipul's mother said, severely, 'But Veena, what's the *need* for all this? Your coming here is the greatest gift I could ask for,' and 'You shouldn't spend so much on the children, Veena, they'll get spoilt,' and 'Why do you have to spend so much money? You know I already have enough saris.'

To which Veena masi replied, 'Do you have to first need something in order for me to give it to you?' and 'Aren't they my children as well, isn't Neha your daughter too?' and 'One can never have enough saris, didi, and I've heard you say so yourself.' She spoke in a robust scolding way, and anyone eavesdropping on the exchange might have concluded that the sisters were quarrelling. But to both women the scolding and the chiding were as pleasing to the senses as a caress or a compliment: for the vehemence of Vipul's mother's objections to Veena masi's gifts was in direct proportion to the pleasure they evoked in her; and Veena masi rebuffed Vipul's mother's objections in a way that made it clear that she knew how the latter actually felt; and they persisted with the make-believe. Scolding each other this way was in fact an expression of deep intimacy, since one could only scold somebody whom one was very close to. From experience Vipul knew that the same sequence would be enacted when the time came for Veena masi and Neha to leave, except that the parts would be reversed, for then Vipul's mother would be giving the gifts and Veena masi would be vocally protesting and Vipul's mother would be reproving her for her protests.

They turned off the Grand Trunk Road into a nameless, unboarded branch road that led off it. This tributary was narrow and sharp-edged, allowing just one car or truck to pass comfortably at a time. Whenever a truck approached them, Nizam would have to take the car off the tarmac and wait for it to pass, for the lumbering trucks, menacing rapacious monsters, would neither give way nor slow down. At the sides of the road, thorny scrub and sal and teak trees had replaced the mango and jamun trees bordering the Grand Trunk Road, and these became gradually more populous until they seemed suddenly to turn into a forest. Here the air was thick with shadows, as cool and dank as night-time. The undergrowth condensed, creepers and vines constricting the trees and bushes. Occasionally a dense chirping, resonant and shrill as a tinnitus, would approach them, heighten in pitch and intensity to a crescendo, and then fade away, telling of a colony of crickets or of cicadas among the bamboo clumps. Langurs, black-faced as though tarred in punishment for mischief, leapt between trees and pranced across the road, their long insolent tails held up like flagstaffs of defiance.

After a while, the road lost definition. The asphalt crumbled away, leaving progressively larger patches of earth exposed between puddles of tar; it was as though a giant macadam-eating bird had haphazardly torn away at the road. Further on the asphalt had been picked clean, giving way, in turn, to firm earth, then to gravel, then to dust as thick as pulverulent sand. Finally, round a bend, the road ended, without warning or explanation, in a wide dust-logged clearing, at the foot of a hillock. Nizam had to brake suddenly again.

From this point there were two routes to the temple. On the slope of the hillock there was a kind of trail: the shrub had been cleared half-heartedly here and there, or had perhaps been trampled under with use, and at intervals there were slabs and cubes of stones for foothold, placed such that they suggested neither accident nor design.

The other approach was a constructed one. They didn't see it until Nizam spotted it. The road had not really ended; after expanding into this varicosity, it now issued a dendritic process that skirted the side of the hill to the right.

'But it's not safe to drive that way,' Nizam said, pointing up.

An aerial cableway ran directly above the road, throwing on it the swaying shadows of the cables. The cableway spanned a succession of tall pylons staked into the hillsides, the pylons grey-black and towering unprettily over the green carapace of the treetops, gaunt unvigilant sentinels policing the wilderness. On two parallel cables ran cast-iron telpherage buckets, in one direction full of coal and in the other, empty. The buckets were the shape of cubes of ice, and were either badly dented or badly made. They passed unhurriedly to and fro, gently rocking, their procession monotonous and businesslike and disciplined, as that of lines of ants trafficking towards and back from a carcass.

When they got out of the car, Neha said, 'I want to sit in a bucket.'
'Black you'll become,' Vipul said, 'like coal, like Ayah.'
Neha considered this for a moment, then said, 'Arms.'

Vipul lifted her, and held her at his side with her legs straddling his waist, and kissed her cheek. She kept looking at the groggily purposeful buckets, her arms round Vipul's neck, her bangles clinking by his ear, her hair blown just a little by the breeze, gold-edged strands of it breaking away from the general mass, leaving faint lines of tingling itch where they brushed against Vipul's face, and in the air, tracings of the scent of coconut oil.

On the skeletal path on the hillside, two women, one old and unsure of foot and propped up at the armpits by a small man, the other wearing a vermilion sari and a vermilion bindi on her forehead and vermilion powder in her hair, looking like a wound on the hillside, descended tentatively. Their eyes, from being cast down in concentration, made them look contrite, confessional, as though unexpectedly chided and shamed by the gods upon whom they had just called. The young woman held a baby just as Vipul held Neha; the baby stared with great interest at Neha, perhaps judging whether an immediate acquaintance might be in order.

Atop the hillock, the temple's precincts included three huts, one for the temple priests, one that functioned as a tea-and-paan stall and grocery-and-trinket shop all in one, and the third, set apart in a corner, at one edge of the hillock, where the pandit lived. Facing the temple there was a low wide wall, and on the wall sat a sadhu, perched there like a bird. His legs were close together, his knees pressed against his chest; his arms went round his shins in an embrace; he looked like a cold huddled old foetus. Round his waist he wore a saffron loincloth, and round his chest, going over one shoulder, a sacred thread. He was very thin, thinner even than Thapa, Vipul thought. He had long grey hair. At the back of his head the hair was rolled into a bun; in front it covered his mouth and hung down in a conical beard that ended in a sharply tapered plait. He looked pensive, yet he also looked mischievous. The way he perched, like a myna, seemed mischievous. His posture seemed mischievous, like a squatting monkey's. And there seemed to be mischief in his face. Vipul could not see the sadhu's mouth for his overhanging moustache, but, he considered, the moustache would not have been curving up at the sides as it was had the sadhu not been smiling underneath, smiling enigmatically, smiling at nothing and at everything, at Vipul and Neha, and not at them, at the pye-dog that slunk about like a hoodlum by the paan stall, and not at it, at the hills of Gumia and the sounds of the telpherage cableway, and at the softly fluttering leaves of the peepul, yet not at any of these; perhaps just at himself and his own prehistoric thoughts.

Veena masi and Vipul's mother went inside the pandit's hut. Neha and Vipul stayed out, inspected the grounds around. They saw an outcrop of low boulders and rocks that winked with shifting spots of lights, as Neha's ghagra did when she danced. They went there. The boulders were strewn with broken glass bangles. They were cheap, basic bangles: brightly coloured, slim, and unornate but for haphazard golden specks which seemed to have been splashed on them by accident. Some pieces were as small as granules of sugar; some were nearly whole; some bangles had been crushed, others merely snapped. It was as though some small festival had just been celebrated in which the act of faith had been the destruction of bangles, the crushing of coloured glass.

Vipul said, 'Neha, look, so many bangles.'

'But all broken,' Neha said, and even in her child's voice there was sadness: she loved bangles, and felt this a tragic waste.

They looked meditatively at the debris, each fragment of which caught a ray of the sun and turned it into a miniature lamp embedded in its crystalline belly.

Vipul said, 'What will you do with so many bangles if you have them?'

'I will wear a new set every day. No, every morning and every evening. Or I will become a bangle-seller. I will give lots of bangles to my mummy.'

Vipul said, 'Next time we go to Jadugoda market I'll buy you as many bangles as you want.'

'No, I don't want them.'

'You just said you wanted them.'

'Not if you buy them.'

'I *will* buy them for you,' Vipul said, not knowing how.

'Vipul! Neha!' came Vipul's mother's call. She stood in front of the pandit's hut, one hand held horizontal, a visor over her eyes, which were already shielded by large round sunglasses, those impenetrable jade enemies of light. She wore a green georgette sari patterned with large round rings, and it seemed as though two of the rings had jumped out, sat on her nose, and become her sunglasses. 'Come here,' she said, 'panditji is calling you.'

Inside the hut, which was a single large room, the pandit sat on a straight wooden chair behind a trestle table on which rested a few books, some paper, and a tray on which lay betel leaves, areca nuts, a nutcracker and other ingredients of paan, and, like a jewel among all these, a small magnifying glass. The pandit's face was as neatly arranged as his desk, with well laid out compartments for oiled plastered hair, spectacled eyes, and a careful smile underneath a faint mid-lip moustache. He asked them to sit on the two visitors' chairs made of beaten aluminium. He said to Vipul, 'Son, tell me about the servants in your home.' So Vipul told him about Thapa, Ayah, Aansu, the gardeners, and the guards. The pandit said, 'I see, I see. Now tell me more about this guard called Ram Parvesh? What kind of eyes does he have, what kind of teeth and hair?' Vipul told him. The pandit said, 'Now come here,' motioning him to a stool by his own chair.

When Vipul sat on it, the pandit said, 'Show me your teeth.' Vipul bared his teeth. 'Remain like that,' the pandit said. He picked up the magnifying glass from the tray on the table, and held it to Vipul's teeth. 'Ahh...' said the pandit. 'Ahh ... Good. Now you both can go back out and play; but send your mothers in again.'

When Vipul's mother and Veena masi came out the second time, they wore looks of satisfaction of the kind that arises from having driven a hard bargain. Vipul's mother said, 'What did panditji tell you, Vipul?'

'Nothing,' Vipul said.

'Good,' his mother said.

THREE

Then the time came to pray in the temple. First they cleansed themselves by sprinkling a few drops of water on their hands and faces from a brass pot which held gangajal, water from the river Ganga. They bought offerings from a stall by the temple: garlands of marigold and jasmine, a coconut, sweet puffed rice. The temple's sanctum was fringed by a wide square portico that ran all around it, forming an encircling veranda. Between the veranda and the sanctum, at the entrance to the latter, was a low threshold. Vipul's mother and Veena masi, who had both covered their heads with hoods made out of the free ends of their saris (so that they looked a little as though about to do something clandestine and unlawful), bent down at this threshold, touched it with their fingertips, then touched their fingertips to their brows. Inside the sanctum, they knelt and touched their foreheads directly to the cold stone floor. Vipul and Neha repeated all their actions, feeling somehow blessed as they did so, holiness rising from the stone.

The sanctum was a hollow empty cavelike enclosure but for dense incense smoke that moved about in placid swirls and eddies. Two fans hung from a wooden beam suspended from the ceiling; the beam was warped and cracked, and the fans, which were of the old design, with very long heavy arms and very large conical housings for their obese motors, were covered in so much dust and cobweb that they seemed never previously to have moved and never in the future to be able to. A large brass bell hung low from the ceiling. The women sounded it, then held up Vipul and Neha to do so. Brassy peals filled the sanctum and died away within it, mingling with the swirls and eddies of the smoke without splintering their placidity, sound congealing peaceably with matter.

At the rear of the cave, in a lighted recess, there lay a slab of red rock, and on it there stood an image, wrought on another red slab, of Lord Hanuman. It was not an easily deciphered image. The rock was not hewn; it had but a few faint undulations upon its surface that suggested, dimly and without edge or angle to it, a large face, a torso and a leg, and a mace laid to one side of the face. In the region of the face there were two small crescents coloured a bright yellow, and these were the eyes of the Lord. With no other feature to set them off, they looked demoniacal, like the shiny eyes of a cat caught in the beam of a spotlight. The priest, a small thin man in white dhoti and kurta, said, with a guide-like demonstrativeness, that the rock, a natural formation, had been found here, at the spot where the temple stood, centuries ago, and had been looked upon as an instance of the revelation to His subjects of the Lord.

The women handed over the offerings and some money to the priest. He placed reverentially the garland and the sweet rice at the foot of the red slab of rock, dropped the currency notes in a box, and threw the coins into a shallow gutter that ran along the temple's floor where he stood. He cracked the coconut against another slab of rock, and splashed and sprinkled the coconut milk on the image and on the floor. Meanwhile other devotees had arrived with their coconuts, and the priest cracked the coconuts one after another, and the sanctum was now filled with hard explosive reports, as though firecrackers were being set off. The coconuts squirted milk; the milk splashed into the gutter and washed clean the coins. He handed to each of the devotees a lighted incense stick; with these they traced small hoops of smoke ahead of their faces before handing the sticks back to the priest; the priest applied vermilion paste to each worshipful forehead.

Vipul contemplated, intrigued, the diffuse, indistinct image of Lord Hanuman on the rock. Such a frail image of such a robust god – the god of strength and valour – just a small chip here or an extra hump there would destroy it, rob it of its mystery and its force. Vipul felt calm and soothed. The vagueness of the image conformed to his idea of God as being simply a presence, without discrete form. Then they all folded their hands, held them up by their faces or down by their bellies, and prayed their silent personal one-minute prayers. Vipul wondered at the content of his mother's and of Veena masi's prayer. Were they still asking for revelation, or were they already thanking the Lord?

And after the prayers, they walked backwards on their way out; you could not turn your backs upon a watching, listening God.

SWAMIJI

Vipul was getting on in years but was showing no signs of growing tall, and this made both Vipul and his parents anxious.

The matter of the height of a child, or for that matter anybody's height at all, was of the greatest import to the people of Jadugoda, as it was to the people of all of India's other towns and cities. Children and their parents, at all kinds of events and places – at parties, in school, or on social visits – were asked, 'So how tall have you grown?', or 'Has your son touched five yet?', as inevitably and as naturally as they might be asked their names. A good height mattered a great deal: tall people had personality: at five-six, you began to be noticed, a head of hair above the crowds; at five-nine you virtually towered above them; beyond six-zero – a giddy dream – you rose like a monument. The inches mattered most of all for marriage. The parents of tall boys received proposals from the parents of the best cultivated girls. Like the alphonso mango, the gene for tallness was in demand as acute as it was in supply short.

And so all parents, including Vipul's, remained in perennial suspense about the state of elongation of their children, and in particular of their boys. They measured their heights every few weeks, against walls where little horizontal nicks marked the often painfully slow vertical progress of their bodies. The boys were administered growth-promoting tonics and fed vitamin-rich preserves. Parents whose children seemed never to emerge from the darkness of the Midgets' category in the school's annual sports day wore humiliated, cheated looks. They and their children prayed for sudden providential spurts of growth. In contrast parents whose children advanced problemlessly into the Seniors looked becalmed, as though half the exhausting, life-long task of decently settling their offspring had been automatically and effortlessly accomplished – which it had.

For Vipul there was further cause for dismay. The Bull, living up to his name, was growing prodigiously, and looked a likely five-niner, no less; Koyala had recently enjoyed a providential spurt; and the Mosquito, though still only as high as Vipul, had taller parents, and therefore greater potential.

Vipul had tried no few techniques of accelerating his growth. He had suspended himself from the rusty rungs of the cast-iron stepladder that led to the roof till his arms felt hot and his muscles torn. He had given up carrom board and table tennis in favour of badminton and volleyball, which were supposed to stretch the body and provoke growth. He had jumped and jumped to try and touch with the tips of his fingers the leaves on increasingly higher branches of trees, hoping to recapitulate in this manner some of the evolutionary achievement of the giraffe. The springs in his legs grew commendably strong, but Vipul's spine remained inelastic.

There was a waking dream into which Vipul would often wilfully lead his mind. In it he would be stranded in a jungle, and hanging by his hands from a high branch of a tree. He would not have the strength to pull himself up, but only enough to keep hanging. He would not be able to let go and fall to the ground because on the ground, directly below him, there would be a cobra, fanning its hood and hissing. In this state Vipul would remain until rescued, which would perhaps be days later, and by this time he would have elongated by an extraordinary amount.

And finally there was the neck rack. Known as the 'Extender', this was a recently invented device, introduced by someone who had gauged cannily the magnitude of the anxiety of millions of height-deficient Indians. He had collaborated with a Japanese firm to start its production in India. And he had grown very rich very suddenly. The advertisements for the neck rack said: 'First Time in India! Inches in Months, or Your Money Back!' and 'Your Chance to Grow Tall the Same Way as Millions of Europeans and Americans! Limited Period Offer!' The exact matter of how many inches in how many months, was left unaddressed. But the advertisements carried several persuasive 'Before and After' pictures of initially nondescript people blooming into svelte, lanky frames.

Tayaji, Vipul's father's elder brother, had gifted an Extender to Vipul through sympathetic concern: Tayaji's children, too, were midgety. This is how the Extender worked: the back of the head was placed in a fitting saddle; ropes that led from the saddle passed over high pulleys fixed to the wall; then the ropes hung down, ending in clasps. You now heaved the clasps downward – this hauled up the saddle, and along with it your head and neck, brought you to your toes, and stretched your spine, meaning thus to elongate it. Vipul did this exercise for hours every evening, feeling like a prisoner condemned to a rare routine of torture. It was an especially boring exercise: standing against the wall, staring at the blankness ahead, being stared back at by geckoes with pensive cunning eyes, and simply pulling and stretching, no call in it for any sort of skill whatsoever.

But even this drastic measure did not work. Vipul's spine was firm. The little horizontal nick on the wall stood callously still, an indifferent spectator to Vipul's worries. Something needed to be done urgently, but everybody had run out of ideas.

*

Then, in the summer, fresh hope arrived. A group of yogis set up camp in Khajoori. They came from Jadugoda, where they had a small headquarters. They came as evangelists, to instruct the people of Khajoori in the fundamentals and the benefits of yoga. In the early mornings, the air still crystalline and coaldust-free before the onslaught of the sun and industry began, the saffron-swathed yogis, sitting in the lotus position on the floor of the veranda of the Khajoori Guest House, told Khajoori's people how yogic exercises would tone their muscles, supple their limbs; or augment their powers of concentration and strength of will; or purge their viscera; or subjugate their bodies to their minds; or, most importantly for Vipul, impart chimeric physical virtues like height. And so it became imperative that Vipul should learn yoga.

The swamis at the camp had divided themselves into two groups. One, comprised of the elder swamis, took charge of Khajoori's adults. The other consisted in the younger Swami Suryaparmananda, alone in charge of the children. Vipul was glad of this arrangement. The elder swamis were intimidating. The most frightening thing about them was their preternatural serenity. It was almost deliberate; and it seemed to have been honed and perfected to an art. Theirs was the serenity that associates with abstinence and austerity. But it seemed to arise not from the abstinence itself, but from the sense of achievement of it, like the satisfaction that arises from doing well a job that may not really be worth doing. And the swamis wielded their serenity like an instrument, if not of castigation, then at least of reproof. People would wilt under the glare of their censorial serenity. Under its transmuting influence utilities seemed to turn into comforts, comforts into luxuries, and luxuries into sin. The elder swamis inspired strong feelings of guilt and self-indulgence: in tailored clothes, mattressed cots, good food, and the lack of will to renounce these pleasures. Their glances, as they swept about, seemed to reprimand the furniture, the hangings on the walls, the ornate lampshades and carpets, for simply being there. Often they came to Vipul's home for a meal, and every time, without uttering a word of recrimination, succeeded by the time they left in leaving the family feeling inexplicably remorseful. And the collective remorse of Khajoori's families had the effect eventually of raising a handsome subscription for the camp.

Swami Suryaparmananda, in contrast to his elders, was milder. He was not more than a few years older than Vipul and his friends. His eyes spoke not of serenity but of a worldly restlessness which against his holy-looking shaven head and saffron robe made him appear an imposter, a fraud.

But he was most definitely a yogi, and he knew his yoga. Every morning, after he had instructed the children in the elementary asanas, he would stage demonstrations of the difficult ones. Then his body seemed to turn into rubber; it was as if his joints forgot that they existed, and his limbs turned into octopusine tentacles. His legs went over his head, and round his neck. His arms went under his legs and up his back. His back arched into a hairpin. His limbs were like infinitely adjustable flexible tubing: you could have knotted them. To some of his asanas he ascribed names which sounded as impossible as the postures themselves: Poorna mastyendrasana, Parivritti janushirshasana. Thus, at the end of each lesson, he showed off.

They called him Swamiji. He instructed them to bid him 'Hari Om Tatsat' instead of 'Namaste' in the mornings. He taught them a clip of the Gayatri Mantra and made them chant it time after time, slowly, in one breath each time, until the mantra seemed to become a reflexive part of the very act of breathing, so that with each exhalation the incantation 'Om' seemed to emanate naturally from the recesses of the lungs. And he taught them to sing over and over again:

> Hari Om,
> Have no home,
> Food nor money nor wishes have I none,

Still ... ll I will ... ll
Be Aa ... aa ... anandam,
Hari Om

This they all chanted, the children who came from and returned to comfortable homes, who harboured a hundred ambitions each, but who savoured, through the chant, a little of the arcane flavour of the swamis' asceticism. It was somewhat like the Bible History lessons Vipul had to take at school. They studied the parables of the Old and the New Testaments, they learnt how to judge the allegorical significance of the colourful happenings in the lives of the prophets; for forty minutes on each of three days every week they dived into all this, and for the remaining nine thousand nine hundred and sixty minutes of the week quite forgot about anything to do with the Bible, and turned heathen unedifiable minds to marbles or ants or comic books or Lord Krishna or Goddess Durga.

Swamiji taught them all the simple exercises, of strength, of endurance, of agility, of meditation. He seemed at the time of the lessons to be much older than they were, and much wiser. He knew mantras and shlokas, could recite them offhand in Sanskrit, and casually said primal-sounding things that seemed to render him an anachronism.

The days went by; many of the children, including Vipul, became plastic and strong to varying degrees, but ... Vipul was not gaining any height. Swamiji had not so far taught them any specific height-increasing asanas, and Vipul was not bold enough to make the demand. His father or his mother would ask after every lesson whether the all-important asana had been taught or not. Then they would say, 'Probably a right time for every asana; its time will also come.'

Eventually Vipul became impatient. After class one morning, and after Swamiji had shown off some more of his contortionist tricks, he went up to him and said, 'Swamiji, I want to learn a particular kind of asana.'

'What kind?' said Swamiji.

'One that can make me grow tall.'

Swamiji laughed. He said, 'I knew you would ask for this. Everyone asks to be taught such asanas. I always teach these right at the end because once they learn such asanas people forget about the others, leave the camp. All they want is to grow tall, as high as date palms. How high do you want to grow?'

'As tall as Tarzan,' Vipul said.

'Tarzan! How tall is he?'

'Must be six-six at least, judging by the pictures. Or even as tall as Tony Greig.'

'Which comic book is that?'

'No, no. English cricketer. South African-English mixture. He's six–seven and a half. He scored a century against Australia some days ago and also took nine wickets in the match. A great all-rounder, and very good-looking,' Vipul said.

'Cricket I cannot understand. But listen. Do you have any Tarzan comic books?'

'Tarzan comics? Of course. But why?'

'May I read them?'

'You?'

'I want to read them.'

'You must be reading only religious books, but.'

'Those I have to. But comics I like to.'

'Then you must read some of my comics.'

'Do you have any others? Richie Rich, Laurel and Hardy, the Phantom?'

'I have all these, and many others too. Swamiji, you know a lot about comics.'

'When should I come to your home?'

Swamiji came the same evening. He looked around at the appointments in Vipul's home in a way that was quite different from the way the elder swamis looked. There was neither displeasure in his eyes nor rebuke. He seemed captivated by everything he saw.

Vipul showed him the collection of comics that he and Sameer had built up. Their father had sanctioned each of them the purchase of two foreign and two Indian comic books every Saturday, when they went to the Jadugoda market. It was understood that this was their pocket money, in kind. Books were under a separate head, debited from their mother's account.

They bought comics sensibly. They collaborated with the Bull. They did not buy the comics he bought; and they exchanged comics with him. The Bull had different tastes. He preferred Superman and Wonder Woman and Flash Gordon and Zorro: 'Action Comics', he called them.

They cherished their comics. They handled them with a care that approximated reverence, turning their pages delicately as though they were archival material, sensitive to the touch. They preserved them in neat stacks in cupboards, and had them bound into volumes of twenty-five each. Each volume, with its flower-papered hard cover, became a treasure box that would periodically be reopened and its contents re-examined with as much fresh enchantment as when they were first read.

They went through the comics studyingly. They looked long and deep into the clean simple luxurious worlds that they contained, illustrated in sunny, fruity colours, particularly in the American comics: just-right houses; just-right lawns, skies, trees, avenues; everything pastel and easy on the eyes; placid dustless uncrowded manicured towns; and an all-pervading air of quaintness and of wealth. All so different from – so superior to – the coaldust-shrouded, glamourless, congested towns that Vipul knew. How spartan yet how voluptuous everything there seemed to be, and how lush yet how indigent everything here was.

Swamiji looked at the books greedily. He picked up all the loose comics one by one, and as he riffled his way through each, said, 'Can I take this?'

Then he leafed through the bound volumes. Continually he made noises of recognition and of pleasure. He seemed to want to borrow them all. Eventually he picked two, Woody Woodpecker and Dennis the Menace.

Vipul's mother had prepared toasted curry-potato sandwiches and a sweet lime drink for the evening snack. Swamiji had his share with gusto and at an astounding speed, and asked for more. He did not raise the issue of abnegation. As he ate he said to Vipul, 'You have a nice home,' and 'Your mother is very nice,' and 'Do you have snacks like this every day?', and 'What great comics! I shall really enjoy myself.'

Vipul asked Swamiji about life at the ashram. Swamiji said it was 'a little that way'. Which way, said Vipul, and Swamiji told him. The swamis got up at three-thirty every morning. They said their prayers and freshened up by four. Then for two and a half hours without a break, they practised yoga exercises. After this they washed, bathed, put on fresh saffron robes. Throughout the day there were several chores to be done. Being the youngest and still an apprentice, he had to shoulder the largest fraction of the chores while the other swamis meditated, disputed, studied, and held court for visitors and sponsors. In the mornings he swept and swabbed the floors of the ashram, cleaned the toilets and bathrooms, prepared lunch. In the afternoons, after an hour's nap – that much was granted – he swept the courtyard, tended to the ashram's vegetable garden, made tea. Then there was another hour of yoga, and another bath. Finally he helped prepare dinner. Dinner was at seven-thirty; by nine the ashram was asleep.

He said, 'Staying here at the camp is like a holiday. Everything is taken care of by the guest-house servants. I'll have plenty of time to read the comics.'

'But where will you read them?' Vipul said. 'Will the other swamis not object?'

'I have a padlocked trunk in which I keep a few things of my own. No one will see the comics. And sometimes these days I am on my own.'

As Swamiji was about to leave, Vipul said, remembering, 'Swamiji, those height-increasing exercises?'

'Of course, of course. In the next class I'll teach you one. Within weeks you will have learnt several of them. All the ones I know I'll teach you. You can be sure you'll grow tall. Yoga is like magic. Hari Om Tatsat.'

'Hari Om Tatsat,' said Vipul.

Swamiji turned to go, then turned around. 'In fact, we can have an arrangement,' he said. 'Among friends ... now we are friends.' He patted the bundle of comics that he was clutching under his armpit. 'You keep lending me comics, and I'll keep teaching you those asanas. Will that go?'

'It'll go fine,' Vipul said.

'Hari Om Tatsat,' Swamiji said, and walked away, and in the distance his vestment rippling about him was like an unquiet saffron vapour.

During the weeks that followed Swamiji taught Vipul a handful of height-increasing asanas. The most effective, he said, was the Tadasana, or the Heavenly Stretch Pose. For this Vipul had to stand on tiptoe, feet together; interlock his fingers, evert his palms; then raise his arms, stretch his neck and spine to the utmost and fling his head back so that he looked straight up.

To Vipul this felt suspiciously similar in both sensation and procedure to the neck-rack method of the Extender.

But Swamiji said, 'That is artificial. This is natural, it is yoga. The natural way is the best way to gain height or to change body function in any way. In fact most probably the maker of the Extender got his idea from the Tadasana only. But remember, in yoga you must *meditate* on what you are doing. Bring your thoughts down to your backbone as you do the Tadasana, then lock them there. Try to feel each segment of it. And with the power of your mind, extend it, force it to stretch. All the power is in the mind, none in the body itself. You must *feel* yourself grow.'

Swamiji subsequently taught Vipul the Chakrasana, or the Wheel Pose, and the Ushtrasana, or the Camel Pose, which were also purported to rouse his spine from its slumbers.

Vipul performed all these exercises with diligence. He did yoga for an hour every morning and for another hour every evening; of this he spent almost half the time on the Tadasana. Swamiji had also told him that the Tadasana could be performed informally – that is, by simply walking in the prescribed posture during the course of any routine activity. So Vipul started going about the house in this fashion, arms up, craning his neck, trying at the same time to cast his eyes downward to see the way.

While on tiptoe, Vipul projected his mind down on to his spine and dreamed of glorious imminent height. The nightmarish prospect of hanging from a high branch while a cobra fanned its hood below receded. Now, with the help of the Tadasana, instead of stretching downward from above he would rise from below…

Five … six … seven feet tall. Then he would show them all. He would show the Bull. Inch for inch, pound for pound, he was certain he was stronger than the Bull. But the Bull had so much more height and mass. Vipul determined first to grow tall, then to put on weight. He would exercise profusely. Every day he would eat half a dozen fried eggs, and drink three big tumblers of milk. He was sure that if he had a spurt of growth he would immediately begin to relish milk and eggs: surely a taste for these was contingent upon proper growth, and not the other way around, as people in general, and in particular his mother, deludedly believed. He would insist on being given some non-vegetarian food every day. Up he would go, up and up, and beyond the Bull. He would thrash the Bull with ease, as he had done before the Bull had discovered his self-respect. He would thrash many others, on the trivialmost counts. He would become a scourge. He would be particularly severe on Koyala.

'Good,' his mother said when she saw him going about in the Tadasana. 'If you keep it up you'll soon cross five feet.'

Swamiji came twice again to Vipul's home and borrowed more bound volumes of the comics. He seemed as voracious and attentive a reader as Vipul and Sameer themselves. He had a precise memory of the frames of illustration; he could relate the stories in vivid detail, quoting with admirable accuracy the bubbled dialogues.

He said that he enjoyed the Richie Rich comics especially.

'What a life it must be in America, no?' he said. 'Every second man is a millionaire.'

Vipul said, 'And even those who are not – even labourers – have cars and electric blankets and televisions.'

'Labourers even!'

'You don't see them in the comic books. But I know. I once read an article about coal miners in America. The pictures showed their cars, TVs and fridges. And just look at our Indian mineworkers.'

They reminded themselves briefly of Khajoori's mineworkers, housed in tight dark barracks, carless, TV-less, fridge-less, happy if they could afford themselves a new bicycle or a medium-wave transistor radio or a shiny frilly nylon dress for a child once a year, around Diwali. Vipul felt ashamed.

Swamiji said, 'And how free children are with the elders. They call them by their names, Mr Wilson, Mrs Grundy, Mr this, Mrs that. None of this "auntie-uncle" business that goes on here.'

Vipul reflected upon the Bull calling his mother 'Mrs Uberoi' not 'auntie', and felt almost enraged. However, he conceded that Swamiji had a point. He said, 'And children get pocket money, in dollars and cents. They can act like adults even when they are just our age.'

'Does your mother give you pocket money?' Swamiji asked.

'No, but she buys us books.'

'Not the same thing.'

'Not at all.'

'And boys and girls are able to meet each other freely-freely there.'

'Totally freely. And how forward the girls are. They wear small clothes, they go here and there with boys, unaccompanied by parents, imagine, unaccompanied, totally, for dinners and for picnics and for pictures.'

Swamiji said, 'But really, girls should be shy and should feel shame. Without shyness and shame what is a girl?'

'Yes, that's true,' Vipul said. In his heart he preferred shy girls to brash; Chetna, for instance, to Sushma didi; one could weave loftier romances around the former. But surely there could be a compromise – surely girls could shyly date.

'Still, it would be nice to be like Richie Rich.'

'That it would.'

The time came for the yoga camp to move on to Victoria Jubilee colliery, some distance away to the other side of Jadugoda. Swamiji came to Vipul's home to say goodbye.

He said, 'I'll be visiting Khajoori off and on, because I've made friends like you here. I'll return your comics by and by. At the moment I feel like rereading them. Now, since I won't be back for some time, can I take two more volumes?'

He took a volume of Classics Illustrated, saying that he would like to read *Moby Dick* and *Kim* and *Tom Brown's Schooldays* because he had heard the names of these books, and a volume of Laurel and Hardy.

After the camp had departed, Vipul practised the entire set of asanas that Swamiji had taught him, every day for months. There was no appreciable result. The nick on the wall remained resolutely immovable.

Swamiji called round on a visit some six months later; the swamis were reviewing the results of their camps. Vipul was alone at home. Swamiji had not brought any of the comics back with him. He said, 'Vipul, I just forgot. But next time I'll return them all together. In any case, whenever you want them, you can come across to the ashram in Jadugoda and take them. But can I take just a couple of others?'

Vipul thought quickly and said, 'You'll have to ask mummy.'

'But they are your comics, no?'

'I know. But mummy has forbidden me to lend them to anyone without her permission. Even the Bull can't borrow them without mummy's permission these days. Actually it's nothing to do with you, it's all the fault of that boy in my class...' here Vipul invented a name '... Dipen. He started denying that he had borrowed them and even started stealing them.'

'I see...' said Swamiji.

'Swamiji, those asanas you taught me...'

'Which?'

'Those ones for height.'

'Yes, yes, I remember.'

'Swamiji, there's no effect.'

'No effect?'

'My height – it's still the same.'

'Who says?'

'Papa measures it every month.'

'But Vipul you have grown. I'm sure. You *look* taller. I'm cent per cent sure. In fact the first thing I thought when I saw you today was, "Wah! Vipul has grown by inches!" But I wanted to say sorry first for the comics, so I didn't say it then.'

'But according to Sameer I haven't grown taller.'

'Where do you measure your height?'

Vipul led him to the spot and showed him the unmoving nick.

'Give me a book and a pencil,' Swamiji said. 'Now stand there. Straight. No, absolutely straight. Chest out. Head up. Neck straight. Up to your full height.'

Swamiji placed the book on Vipul's head and marked the wall. 'Of course you've grown! See? Look at this.'

Vipul came away from the wall. Swamiji's pencil mark was a clear inch above the mocking nick. 'I told you you had grown.'

'But, until a few days ago, there was nothing.'

'These things can happen suddenly. As a yogi I have seen incredible things happen. Do you know, we once had a swami in our ashram in Patna who came from Nepal and so he had very little chance of growing beyond five feet. One night he grew two and a half inches – overnight, while he slept! He woke up in the morning saying he was feeling thinner. We couldn't recognize him at first.'

'Could that have happened to me?'

'God can do anything. See this mark. You too must have had an overnight spurt. A couple more spurts like this one, and you'll soon be reaching where the Bull stands.'

Vipul felt warm and triumphant. He said, 'Swamiji, it's all due to your asanas.' He paused for a moment and said, 'Swamiji, I've thought of a way you can take the comics.'

'No, no, leave it if it's any trouble with your mummy.'

'No, listen. Mummy and Sameer are not here. You take them now – I'll explain to them later.'

That evening Vipul kept going to the wall and looking at the new mark. When Sameer came back, Vipul said to him, 'Do you know, I've grown taller.'

'Where?' Sameer said.

Vipul showed him the new mark.

'Stand there,' Sameer said.

Vipul stood there and drew himself up to his fullest height.

'You're still at the old mark,' Sameer declared.

'But this pencil mark?'

'Who made this?'

'Swamiji.'

'He was here?'

'He left a few minutes back.'

'Took more comics?'

Vipul was silent. Sameer smacked Vipul's head.

'Idiot!' Sameer said. 'Why did you let him?'

'He taught me those asanas. That's how I've grown.'

'But where have you grown!'

'Put a book on my head and see, properly.'

'Why put a book on your head, when I can see anyway?'

'I'm up to the new pencil mark.'

'You are as far away from the new pencil mark as ever. Idiot!'

'How can you keep calling me idiot!'

'Why not?'

'It's an abuse.'

'It isn't. Even if it is, you are an idiot, so you are.'

'You can't call me an idiot.'

'Who says? I'm calling you one now.'

They started grappling, and there was a fight; Vipul got beaten, and he cried.

*

It was some months before they could visit the ashram in Jadugoda. Vipul's parents thought that it was time they should pay their respects once again to the swamis. They also needed to get professional advice on niggling matters such as how to combat the stiffening of joints or the ever-escalating rate of hair fall.

They sat on a thin cotton sheet on the mud floor of a room that was bare but for a few framed pictures of gods and goddesses and of renowned swamis, and a squat earthen water-pitcher in a corner.

Vipul's parents told the swamis how beneficial yoga had turned out to be for them, how enlivening and how becalming, and invited the swamis to drop in at any time for a meal or even to stay. The swamis listened serenely – even the way they listened was reassuring, as though their very audience solved all problems. They then recommended specific asanas for each complaint that Vipul's parents had broached.

Vipul waited, keeping a discreet lookout for Swami Suryaparmananda, but he was nowhere to be seen. Vipul wondered how he might raise the question of the comic books. He had assumed that he would find the swami sweeping the courtyard or chopping vegetables, and had thought he would act as though something or the other reminded him of something in the comics, and so bring up the question. He was too overawed by the elder swamis to ask them directly.

Then, as they were leaving, his mother said, 'But Swamiji, I don't see the younger swami today? The one who was very popular with the children?'

Vipul said, quickly and audibly, 'Swami Suryaparmananda.'

'The little boy has a sharp memory,' the elder swami said, considering Vipul beatifically. 'Our young swami has left.'

'Why?' Vipul asked.

The elder swami said to Vipul's parents, 'Everybody dreams and even thinks that they can live this life of hardship and penance, but in practice very few can.'

Vipul gathered up his courage. 'Swamiji,' he said, 'did Swamiji leave behind any comics for us?'

'Comics?'

'Comics.'

'What comics, son?'

'Like Tarzan, Swamiji, or Mandrake or Donald Duck, Swamiji, or ... or...'

'My son, we devote ourselves to other kinds of studies,' the swami said, through a laugh. 'We have given up comics along with a lot of other things.'

'No, Swamiji, not his own comics. They were ours. What had happened was...'

'Vipul, it doesn't matter, son,' his mother said. Her voice was coaxing but her eyes were censorious.

Vipul kept quiet.

Then his mother said, 'Swamiji, there was another small problem.'

'Speak, my daughter, speak,' the swami said.

'You see how our Vipul is short for his age.'

'Is he? Which class are you in, son?' The swami chucked him on his neck.

'Seventh,' Vipul said.

'Yes, a little short in that case,' the swami said, sizing him with his eyes.

'Yes, just a little,' his mother said. 'But last summer the younger swamiji had taught him some asanas for gaining height. But they don't seem to have had much effect.' Then she added, apologetically, 'Perhaps he is not doing the asanas properly?'

'Quite possible, quite possible,' Swamiji said. 'Just what I would have guessed. If instructions are not followed to the letter, yoga exercises cannot be expected to have their desired effects. Like mathematics. They may even harm. Are you following the instructions correctly, my son?'

'Just like Swamiji had taught me,' Vipul said. 'Exactly like that.'

Swamiji said, 'Good, very good. Then you're on the right track. There's no need to worry. Keep it up, continue with it, even increase the amount of exercise you do. You will certainly grow tall. One day you will find you have grown up overnight. Hari Om Tatsat.'

'Hari Om Tatsat,' they all said.

THE FLOOD IN THE RIVER

ONE

'It's good it's the rainy season,' Vipul said softly to himself, as he lay in bed unable to sleep. 'At least it's likely to rain if I pray hard enough for it.'

He glanced yet again at the pocket watch that stood against his schoolbag on the table beside the bed. Its radium-embedded hands formed an acute 'V' of firefly-green luminescence, encircled by a witch's halo of dots, the mechanism of the emission of light by the dots and hands as mystifying and as ancient as the firefly's.

It was eleven, and already two hours past normal bedtime. Keeping awake late made Vipul feel not only restless but also, unaccountably, guilty, as though he had brought upon himself some manner of retribution for some inadvertent sinful act. On the occasions when there seemed to be no discernible reason for this retribution – such as twisting the arm of a weaker boy, or salting earthworms, or abusing someone – he simply prayed a routine prayer to God for the speedy administration of sleep. But tonight a particular anxiety kept his mind awhirr. He had not done the craftwork for the class test tomorrow. He would fail. And he could not repeat the insolence that had somehow rescued him in the previous test. Twisted Spine would not suffer such audacity again.

He needed to pray for rather thoroughgoing intervention. He had decided that it would not do to say a casual and perfunctory prayer, repeating reflexly the daily requests and admissions. Tonight's contingency demanded of earnest prayer, and for that he had to engage his mind into a special mode. He closed his eyes again, shutting out the embryonic light of the cloudy night outside that came in like a weak mist through the window. As he did so, the sounds of night grew louder, and nearer. Grasshoppers and crickets, frogs and geckoes, the wind upon the trees, were all engaged in a gentle symphony that played upon the air. Inside Vipul's head it seemed as though a fleet of minute instruments had started playing: some stridulating, others crackling, or trilling, or rustling, or swishing. Although the sensation was pleasant, he strained within to shut it out, to wipe out all interference, so that he might project his mind away from the here and the now.

Once the impinging sensations had been repulsed, he imagined himself floating up into the high air, and launching into space. He became a spaceship without physical substance, a travelling consciousness. Escaping earthly limits, he felt himself coasting past the planets, entering stellar space. There he continued his flash-fast journey, past the stars that streaked by him in currents of sepulchral blue against a background of nothingness. Most of them were in busy familial clusters, gossiping, and the rest solitary, like distinct and lonely bachelors.

After a short while his mind felt at peace. He sensed an astral presence. It was God. For Vipul this was God's only true manifestation: as an intangible Presence, nebulous as the image of Lord Hanuman in the temple at Gumia. To sense it one had to travel to where it resided: among the stars, in empty space. Perhaps starlight was God. Vipul never had an idea of God's shape. He did not look for it. The moment he sensed the astral presence, he started praying.

'O God, you must know already what I'm going to pray for. You know my mind, and everybody else's. But first I must pray for mummy and papa and Sameer and all the relatives in Delhi. Please bless them and grant them their wishes. Please grant papa an early promotion and mummy a win on her lottery ticket, if possible.' Here a twinge of guilt surfaced, so Vipul hurried on. 'And for me, God, please make it rain tonight. That is all I ask for myself. No money, no fame. You know why, you know everything. Please make it rain up in Gumia, so much that the Bhorighat dam overflows. Please cause a flood to happen in Damodar, so that we can't go across tomorrow. Please don't let me be humiliated. You know how Twisted Spine – Sir George, Sir George – is. He won't let me off this time. You alone can do it. Everything is in your hands, rain, sunshine, or famine. Thank you, God. And one more thing. Please give me sleep soon. Please. How long can I lie awake like this? Please give my mind peace and sleep. I just want to sleep...'

The stars dimmed and melted away; everywhere was nothingness.

It had been imperative for Vipul to pray hard. His ineptitude in Arts and Crafts had become a red blotch of embarrassment on his marksheet. His fiascos owed partly to what he considered to be Twisted Spine's blinkered thinking. The man was entirely in favour of the Crafts, and utterly cold-shouldered the Arts.

'I'll teach you sons of managers and businessmen how to use your hands to *make* things,' he would say.

Vipul, however, was all right in Arts and hopeless in Crafts. He could draw passable likenesses of mountains and rivers and foxes and English-looking girls, but when it came to building anything, his mind blanked out. He hadn't the first idea: he couldn't picture designs in his mind, much less execute them; he couldn't tie a knot, couldn't see how things were hinged to each other, hadn't ever been able to pick up the rudiments of nailing and sawing. So he had been continually dismayed as, throughout the year, Twisted Spine persisted in assigning Crafts exercises, week after week; and the boys were compelled to make models of the obscurest artifacts: igloos, steamrollers, Red Indian wigwams, hydroelectric dams. It was miserable but just about manageable for the normal classes; some help was always to be had from the Bull or Koyala or the Mosquito. But for tests, where it was a matter of marks, his friends turned suddenly, vaguely, helpless, making ingenious excuses for not being able to come to his aid.

Tomorrow was the third test, and much depended on it. In the first two Vipul had been plain lucky. For the first they had been asked to make a house. Vipul had gone with the problem to his mother. 'A house! What does he think, am I a carpenter or something? How can I build a house, ma? I don't even know how the roof stays up.'

'Tell Jamuna to do it for you,' his mother said, recognizing the futility of such assignments.

Old Jamuna, the tobacco-drunk gardener, his lower lip forever ballooning with a quid tucked behind it, proved to be a considerable craftsman. With cotton thread and firm straw from the cow pen he knotted up, in front of Vipul and almost conjuringly, a four-walled enclosure with openings for doors and windows and ventilators. There next appeared within the enclosed space two floors and various rooms in each, and on top a gabled roof; and finally doors and windows, properly hinged and latched, like real ones. Although Vipul watched the fabrication with rapt fascination over two entire afternoons, he had not at the end of it learnt to knot together two pieces of straw in the way that Jamuna did.

On the day of the test, no one had a house that could rival Vipul's. Some houses were made of cardboard, some of thin wood, some of humble laughable mud. Each was in some way third-class or ungainly compared to his.

'How did you make it?' the Bull asked. In his eyes there was zero envy or admiration, only suspicion.

'Do you have eyes or buttons?' Vipul said. 'Does it look made out of iron?'

'Where did you get the idea to make it this way?'

'Idea? What idea do you need? A house is a house. Haven't you seen your own?'

'But this one is very nice. Twisted Spine will like it. You made the doors and windows and everything?'

'Who else do you think? Was your father missing from your home on Saturday and Sunday, that he could help me with it?'

'Don't bring my father into it.'

'Don't bring my father into it!' Vipul sang parrot-like, exasperated by the Bull's cross-questioning.

The gong was sounded for two forty-five, a needlessly protracted series of resounding peals that seemed after a while to issue from the very walls of the school.

A few minutes later the slight frame of Twisted Spine entered, his torso pivoting dangerously on his hips. Each step he took seemed to transmit a vicious torque to his pelvis, which shook and swung in a way that would have been immodest even in a woman. He was like a puppet sprung at the waist. 'Twisted Spine' was the least sexual and most respectful of the several monikers the boys had endowed him with. He sat down, compulsively smoothed his hair with long bony fingers, and forthwith called out, 'Roll number one, Amit Ahluwalia, yes, up here with your house!'

One by one, alphabetically, they went up to him with their efforts, and returned to their desks scowling or swelling with pleasure or entirely unaffected, as their marks dictated. Twisted Spine set no store by the notion of privacy. He announced vocally the marks he awarded to each boy. This was another thoughtless trait of his. Marks were meant to be like sisters, untalked about and protected until the time appropriate for their release into the world: marriage for sisters, the end of the year for marks.

'Fifty-six, seventy, sixty-five and a half, thirty-two,' Twisted Spine shouted. His voice was profoundly soughing and hollow, touching first the gut of the listener and then travelling upward to the ear. It was as though his mouth, with its bulging cheeks, was a reverberation chamber where whatever he spoke gathered its own deep echoes before it left for the unenclosed air.

No house had been given more than seventy marks by the time Vipul's roll number was announced. Vipul went up looking pleased about something invisible inside him, like a newly pregnant woman. He put the straw house on the teacher's desk preciously, as though it were a gift. Twisted Spine drew back, looked at it as if from a remote distance, smoothed his hair, and then looked at Vipul. He examined the house with a peer, turning it around slowly. He pulled and pushed at the doors and windows. They swung perfectly.

'Very nice! Doors, windows, two floors. Very nice! How much time it took you to make this?'

'Two full days, sir,' Vipul said.

'Very good! Did anyone help you?'

'Who could help me, sir?' Vipul said, in a way that indicated that, with due respect and humility, he thought the question absurd.

'You have suddenly improved in Crafts, Vipul. Well done.' Smiling, he started writing on the list, and called out, 'Forty-seven marks! Next! Roll number forty-one, Sudhir Verma.'

'But, sir…'

'No discussion.'

'Sir, don't you like it?'

'Back to your seat.'

'Sir…'

'Back. Roll number forty-one!'

In the corner of the classroom, the Bull and Koyala were swaying and smirking.

*

For the next test, Twisted Spine asked them to build ships – a task even more obtuse than building a house. Vipul had never seen a ship. The object that in his experience came closest to a ship was the pontoon, decrepit and grand, square and shapeless, that stood on the river like both a waterlord and a rueful relic of the iron casting industry. Its vocation was unknown. Never did it move anchor. But it had its own energetic slave, a dredge that scampered up and down a rail on the valley's slope, hurtling down now to dive splashing into the water, now holding its breath till the tenuous last, till you thought it had gone under, only to part the river's surface and rush up again with its scoopful of sand ferreted from the riverbed, depositing it finally on a conveyer belt that carried it over to the mines to douse their fires with; then it hurtled down again.

And this time Vipul would not ask for Jamuna's help. After the previous test Vipul had entered the house with a dark villainous face, flung the straw house on the floor, and blamed his mother and Jamuna for the debacle. Forty-seven was a disgrace – a third division – and in the next test he must get at least seventy to win back some respectability. But Twisted Spine had dashed all hopes of that. Vipul gave up.

The evening before the test found him not having done anything about the ship. At eight-thirty, after dinner was over and only half an hour remained for bedtime, and he still hadn't drawn any inspiration, Vipul went for a walk in the compound to balm his nerves. Rover came with him, tail joyously upcurled, sniffing out the path ahead, serving as his antenna. Vipul wandered about the lawns, went along the gravelled driveway, then turned into the vegetable garden. While Rover was a master at detecting rats, snakes, scorpions and the like, he did not give warning of inanimate obstacles; Vipul's foot crashed into something hard. His toes stung with pain. Cursing, he raised the stubbed foot and massaged it.

Looking down, he saw the offending object. It was a block of wood the shape of a fat spindle, about two inches high. Vipul picked it up and, forgetting the pain in his foot, ran back inside, Rover rearing and prancing beside him like a horse, expecting the block of wood to be thrown for him.

In the light of the fluorescent tube in the veranda, the block revealed its full potential. It was very nearly the shape of a ship; almost no fashioning was required. At one end the spindle was sharply pointed: the ship's cutting fore-edge. The only enhancements required were a hollowed-out deck and a mast or some other superstructure. Vipul had neither the time nor the knowhow to scoop out a deck without ruining the block. But a mast ... he rushed into the drawing room. On the mantelpiece above the unused hearth was a brass galleon that his parents had brought back as a memento from Tamil Nadu, its shine dulling with age. Vipul tested the mast. It felt detachable. He wrenched it out. He went to the storeroom, brought out the Brasso and polished the mast till it glinted like tinsel. He fished out a screwdriver from the toolbox and scraped and screwed a hole in the centre of the block. Into this he jammed the stem of the mast. It stood, if a little angularly and precariously. His ship was ready.

The following morning the Bull, looking pleasantly at Vipul's ship, said in a heavy guttural, 'No one to help you this time, crab?'

'In fact this time your father did come to help and this is what he produced,' Vipul said.

'Keep my father out of it, do you understand?'

'Keep my father out, keep my father out,' sang Vipul.

Now Vipul put his handicraft on Twisted Spine's desk the way someone might hand in a letter of resignation, dully and with only the least curiosity about the reaction it would elicit. Even passing with forty-five would be enough, he thought.

Twisted Spine, looking it over and turning it about, was smiling ominously again. In the cold light of day it was quite apparent that the piece of wood was accidental and not contrived. 'Very good, very good,' he said. 'Made this yourself?'

'Yes, sir,' Vipul said.

Twisted Spine fingered the mast, pulled it out, and regarded it. 'Made this yourself too?'

'No, sir, just the ship,' Vipul said.

'Good,' said Twisted Spine, running a finger along the rim of the cavity Vipul had scraped. 'It's a good ship.' He handed the block back to Vipul. He sat back. He smoothed his hair. Then, writing, he announced, 'Seventy! Next! Roll number forty-one, Sudhir Verma…'

Vipul did not stay to express his surprise. Speedily he carried the ship back to his desk. He felt warm; Twisted Spine spiralled in his esteem. Perhaps he was one of his favourite teachers, Vipul felt.

This time there was absolutely no hope. Jamuna was on leave, getting his son, who was a year younger than Vipul, married. And there had been no windfall discovery of an artifact that might resemble the prescribed task. Such discovery was in any case quite improbable: Twisted Spine, dipping deeper into his reserves of perversity, had this time asked them to build a model of a coal mine, complete with pithead, underground shafts and tunnels, and coal wagons and mineworkers. His eyes had glinted cleverly and his voice was hollower than ever with glee when he announced the assignment.

TWO

In the morning, the first thing that Vipul heard on waking was a dense decrepitation, as of the sound of eggs frying in hot oil. He jumped up and looked out; sheets of fast fat raindrops occupied all visible space, seemingly having displaced the very air. He heard and saw more: the digestive licks and gurgles of water disgorging from the overflow pipes leading down from the roof; leaves huddled together in collective misery, meekly receiving the lashing from the clouds, no breeze about to raise their spirits; on the ground, a network of instant little streams and pools, pimpled by a dancing myriad of thin glassy ampules of watersplash made by the raindrops that struck their surfaces.

Vipul became hopeful. But he started to get dressed as usual: he had learnt that to guard against hope was the wisest thing to do.

Just as Vipul and Sameer were sitting down to breakfast the news came: a phone call from his office informed their father that the gates of Bhorighat dam were going to be raised.

Vipul's mother said, 'So that's decided. There's no need for the children to go to school. They'll get stranded on the other side in the evening.'

Vipul's father said, 'They simply said the level of the water will rise. They didn't mention anything about any flood. They can still go.'

'No, baba, no,' his mother said. 'It's happened before. Whenever they lift the gates of the dam, the river always gets flooded within a day. They can miss a day. Far better than getting stranded on the other side.'

In his mind, Vipul recited a short standard prayer of thanks to his God.

'When the rain lessens, let's go and see the flood,' Sameer said.

The shower thinned after about two hours. By this time the grounds of the bungalow had been converted into a full-blown waterworks. Rippling ochre rills of muddy water ran here and there and carried on their backs swarms of bubbles, like baby scorpions nesting on their mother's back; the bubbles were spontaneous and ephemeral, ballooning into existence at the touch of a drop of rain and bursting dead at the slightest toss. The earth where it rose above the rills and pools was a glistening russet, like moist caramel. In the distance, beyond the compound wall, past the sloping bush, a flowing patch of beige now became visible for the first time this year: the Damodar's first floodwater had arrived; Bihar's annual Sorrow had begun.

They went down to the riverbank after collecting the Bull from his home. Clutching firm sticks in their hands, they waded through and stamped about in the watery ground, and troubled the earthworms that, shocked survivors of a cataclysm, crept in blind confusion all about, alternately shrinking and lengthening like living elastic. 'Snake!' the boys shouted at the slightest movement in the undergrowth, probing the bushes with their sticks.

Everywhere about them, as they walked, there was notice of that communion salient to the monsoon, the exchange of gifts between the air and the earth: the air granting its wealth of moisture to the soil, the soil opening up its pores to clothe the air in its long-withheld humus fragrance, a smell of millipedes and last year's leaves and sprouting mould.

And the phenomenon of rain apparently so spontaneous, was in reality so woven into the loop that entrained it – sucked up from the oceans by the sun in cloudfuls; compelled shoreward by the great winds; settling, as rain, on land; swept back down to the sea on the backs of rivers; sucked up again by the sun – the circulation of water rivalling in cyclicity that of the coaldust, fuelled daily by Thapa, in and out of Vipul's home, or that of the yearly sacking and regeneration of the roads of the coalfields.

They went down the slope of the valley. On the way, nearer the upper end, was a milestone that said

HIGH WATER LEVEL
5 SEPTEMBER 1951

They halted by it, and tried to picture what the river might look like when it had risen this far. It was a forbidding thought. Compared with the day before, the Damodar had already put on a radically different appearance, even though it was only just starting to flood. In colour it had gone from greyish-blue to beige. Instead of unfussily rippling along it was now affluent with water, coursing in visible important currents, and turbid and opaque with suspended mud. In width it had markedly prospered; the bank opposite seemed twice as far away, remote. And on the surface of the river there floated and bobbed a variety of objects that did not belong to water, objects it had ravaged from its banks: leaves, twigs, branches, and occasionally entire uprooted plants, which told of the maiming that the monsoon and the rain had perpetrated the night before.

Now the river was not merely a vision, but also a sound and a smell: hissing like a snake, reminiscent of the exudations of a freshly killed rainy-season insect. Downstream the pontoon had been lifted closer to the sky, held aloft by the swollen currents, a fluvial offering to the riverine gods. It looked grander still and even possessed of a debonair intent, liable any instant to elope with the urgent river, away to the infinity of the seas. Its moleish dredge, though, had called off for rest and recuperation, and crouched now at the top of its rail at the valley's rim, watching its master's tussle with temptation.

And on its banks the river showed the appetite and wiles it had developed overnight. Its margins were no longer polite linear borders with the sand; all along, thin twisting fingers of water abruptly branched out from the mainstream, boring their way into the bank. After a few inches of incursion they turned to course parallel to the mainstream for another few inches; then they curled inward again and rejoined the parent waters. Small islands of sand were thus cordoned off; the river's margins became picoted with loops of water. Presently these islands were engulfed by the fusion of the loops of water with the mainstream. Repeating this manoeuvre, the river rose perceptibly as the boys watched, nibbling at and finally devouring the bank little by little, insidiously as a snail feeding on a leaf. Along with its tendency for annexation there were also signs in the river of an inner disquiet. Its waters turned back upon themselves, forming small angry whirlpools and eddies; water got sucked into and drowned by water; water reared up into knife-edges and, whipping down, gashed its own skin. The drizzle that still fell covered the Damodar's surface with a close array of pinpricks.

'Ey! A scorpion's nest!' the Bull shouted. He was pointing to a spongy foamy mass, dirty cream in colour, the size of a hockey ball, which came floating along.

Vipul had seen these objects before, but had never known their origin or their function.

'A scorpion's nest?' Vipul said. 'How do you know?'

'I've broken some of them before,' the Bull said. 'Huge coal-black scorpions live in them, much bigger than you ever see on land. They breed within these nests.'

'Can't be. Scorpions live under the ground, how can they survive on the surface of water? It's exactly the opposite condition.'

'These scorpions are another kind, that's why. And much more poisonous than the land scorpions, as poisonous as cobras.'

'But the oars of the boat often squash these things, and I've never seen a scorpion come out.'

'Those nests may be empty. The scorpions leave them after they have multiplied.'

The nest was now within poking distance. Vipul said, 'Shall I break it now? I bet there is no scorpion inside. Bet five marbles?'

'Not five marbles. I bet two rupees there will be a scorpion inside.'

'Okay, two rupees,' Vipul said, rashly, for he hadn't recourse to so much as four annas, and stabbed the nest with his stick. Although it looked foamy and soft, the nest did not yield easily. Vipul thrashed feverishly at it, running alongside it as it floated downstream. It spattered. A small black mass dived instantly into the water.

'There it was,' the Bull said.
'Don't shoot gas. Wasn't a scorpion.'
'Oh yes? Then what was it?'
'Something else.'
'You'll have to give me two rupees.'
'What two rupees?'
'That two rupees, what else.'
'Measure your way home.'
'I won the bet.'
'Prove it was a scorpion then.'
'It's gone. But you saw it.'
'All gas! I saw nothing.'
'Prove it was *not* a scorpion?'
'I didn't see one.'
'Cheat, bastard.'
'Ho! Be careful how you talk.'
'Cheat, liar, thief, ass! Give me my two rupees.'

'You want two?' Vipul said. 'Here, take two,' and struck the Bull twice with his stick.

While over the next half hour they thwacked and scratched and chased each other about on the sand, Sameer assisted the river in its imperial design by drawing with his stick runnels in the sand along which the water hungrily and gratefully slithered.

It was Sameer who first noticed the arrival of the mammoth cloud in the west, upstream of the river. It had crept up from the horizon stealthily, like a prowling big cat. Now it occupied a good mass of the western sky. Its underbelly was eloquently dark. It was so bulky and ponderous that there could be no doubt that it would shed some of its load presently. It was attestably one of those clouds that to the boys were known as King Clouds, which occasionally, and memorably, visited Khajoori in the monsoon. Subordinate cloudlets, unthreateningly ashy grey, scuttled attentively about the King like minions while it made its stately untroubled way forward. The western horizon had already sunk into a gunmetal gloom, which now advanced towards them. The cloud was fronted by a sheer veil, a membrane of rain. The King suddenly shot a thin blinding squiggle of light at a smaller cloud, as though impaling it with a kinked electric spear. The thunder that followed was as bold and sharp as the discharge. It hurt the ears.

Presently a damp skin-cooling breeze built up, which in turn progressed into a turbulent gale that the cloud seemed to sweep before itself with violent flourishes of an invisible giant feather duster. On the slopes of the valley, the branches of trees tugged this way and that, straining to break free of their trunks, mutinying. Leaves fluttered uncontrollably, as if possessed by some botanic ague. Many detached themselves from their stems, and the air became dotted with leafy agitation. The boys' hair was thrown up and back, and their faces looked years older with their foreheads, normally veiled by the hair, now fully exposed, hairlines visible. Their shirts were pressed into their chests by the gale, and at the back billowed and ruffled like weather vanes. Up at the brow of the valley, lamps had begun to be switched on in homes. These feeble yellow globules of light in the rapidly darkening morning seemed somehow to issue a challenge to the elements, and Vipul imagined that each family in each of the homes was at this moment scurrying about to prepare to battle the storm: gathering tarpaulin sheets for leaky roofs, shuttering windows, and in the kitchen, stoking fires over which they would make spicy fried snacks that would be an apposite culinary accompaniment to the rain.

Although not a little unnerved, the boys were impelled by fascination to stay and watch the oncoming spectacle here by the river, in its natural theatre. Just as it had crept up unnoticed, the cloud had imperceptibly gained speed, and was now bearing down on them with dour intent; it was like a languid bull that had suddenly turned frisky and bellicose. It was at war. It flung frequent shots of lightning at other clouds; and although the others retaliated, their bolts, slight and undazzling, were as the nips and yelps of curs beside the pantherish swipes and roars of the King. There was now a cacophony of bangs and rumbles, the rumbles not getting a chance to die down before the bangs erupted again. And the veil loomed ever larger and heavier; it became now a thick curtain of rain that blanked out all vision beyond. On the river its advance could be clearly seen. Nearer the boys, the water was still dotted by the pinpoints of light rain; in the region of the curtain, now less than a hundred yards away, they could see the surface of the water dimpling. Headlong this leading edge of dimples careered along the river, beating its current for speed.

'Here it is! Here it is!' the boys shouted. Standing on the narrow sandy bank, they spread their arms out and turned their faces upward, as though to receive a skyly benefaction, to catch and gather the rain as it fell.

Within the first few seconds underneath the cloudburst they were drenched; after that it was just a matter of how long they wished to shower. Swiftly the sensation of wetness saturated; but the mechanical effects of the rain, its pounding and its slithering, could still be enjoyed; and it felt to Vipul as though his skin itself were melting and turning into drops of water.

But they could stay no longer, for the battle overhead had grown bitter, and there was now a chance of falling victim to the crossfire. And the glowering King had started shooting bolts of lightning down at the earth too. They saw a couple of flashes snake down to somewhere near Vipul's house. A deafeningly high-pitched skiddy squeak filled the valley, the sound as of glass rubbed hard against steel, clawing at the senses. It foretold devastation. As if in response, the lights went off in all the homes. It was the usual outcome: all preparations against such storms were futile: the monsoon always won on such days.

They decided that they were frightened, but they said it was getting late and their parents would be worried, and so they started back. They repaired homeward through the watery windy gloom, each wishing with the fervency of a prayer that none of the now proliferative flashes should squiggle down on to his head. They were almost at a run. As they ascended the margin of the valley, Vipul recalled the anxiety of the previous night, and felt at once both relieved and concerned afresh.

FOUR-ANNA HERO

ONE

Across the road from the spot where the children boarded the school bus stood a row of four shops, only one of which opened with some regularity. The shops were fronted by a cool veranda whose pillars advertised Coca-Cola, and a locally made health soap, and a Family Planning message with its few-happy, many-sad puppet heads. In the shop that opened, Banwari, its owner, could be seen sitting cross-legged on a divan, his back against the wall, unbusy and seemingly indifferent to custom, musing on nothing. His teeth, visible only at their very tips when he smiled, were the colour of tarnished bronze, and interrupted by large gaps. In his inactivity he resembled a torpid cat, drowsy, gruff, unimpressed by events around him.

'Banwari seth!' A thin boy dressed in a tight flowery shirt and expansively flared bell-bottoms had swaggered up to him and now stood before him, his legs apart and arms combatively akimbo.

The shopkeeper's eyes opened infinitesimally, the way a window shutter might be raised peepingly in wartime.

'How about a cup of tea, Banwari seth?' The boy's voice was misleading: an old man's voice: two-toned, grainy in its ground, sharp-edged on the surface.

Banwari's eyes moved in a slow and stiff arc, as though cramped by exertion, towards Kishenlal, his shop-servant. Kishenlal got up wearily, and wearily melted into a recess at the back of the shop, to make the tea.

'Went to see a picture last night, seth! *Deewar*, first day first show. Wah! What a picture, seth! If you see it you'll also start liking pictures. What fights! There is one thing you have to say: No one can fight like Amitabh Bachchan. And Parveen Babi? What stuff, what a treasure. Seth, is there a Parveen Babi written in the lines of our hands or not?'

Rajna spoke at volume. It was not really Banwari he was addressing, but the schoolgoers across the road. He spoke with great aplomb, as of a sizeable achievement; which, to see a hit picture in Jadugoda, first day first show, it admittedly was.

'Did you hear that?' Sameer said.

'Must have got the tickets in black,' Vipul said.

'Does he have that much money?' the Bull said.

'He might know the owner of Shiva Talkies.'

'He? Know a picture hall owner? Drop it.'

'But he knows people. He knows all kinds of people. Don't you hear him talk?'

'All bluff and lies.'

Sameer said, 'But he has seen *Deewar* first day first show and I know Shiva Talkies is giving no advance reservation for it, and I know that three-rupee tickets were going for not less than twenty rupees.'

The boys looked at Rajna and wondered at his wealth and connections. Rajna looked neither wealthy nor connected. He had a skullish face. His hairpin jaws produced an unintended long-toothed grin when he talked, and a rictus when he smiled. Conscious of this, and feeling a grin to be at odds with his standing as a rogue, he would downcurl his lips when he spoke, so that he looked torn between amusement and melancholy.

He went about in style. Bell-bottoms, and heels, and bared chests were in fashion; and it was Rajna's bell-bottoms that flared the most bounteously; his heels were platform and gave him four inches of extra, much needed, height; he wore his shirt unbuttoned down to the navel in spite of his unbefittingly glabrous chest. On his brow he affixed goggles, the blackest ones to be found; round his neck hung a golden pendanted chain and round his wrist, a thick steel bracelet.

Rajna elaborated on his experiences of the first day first show, and the boys across the road kept listening, pretending the while to be memorizing Lessons to Learn in the Moral Science book or the names of the major African rivers for the Geography class.

They learnt in this manner of all of Rajna's exploits. If he wasn't holding forth on his high living, it would be on his tremendous escapades – bloody fights he had cavalierly got into, or how ruthless he had been in 'cleaning up' his enemies. He would recount the incidents surrounding the knifings he had received or inflicted. Doing so, he pinched out from his bell-bottoms' rear pocket a flick-knife, and unsprung it, and slowly rotated it, so that its blade glinted intermittently in the sunlight like a lighthouse beacon. And he said – just as an aside, of course – that he also had a pistol hidden away for grave contingencies. Banwari, his surrogate audience, absorbed all this in his unseeing, unlistening, unflappable way, proof to being swayed by even the most extraordinary tales.

Rajna studied at Macaulay College, having groomed himself in the necessary ways at the Dudhiya school. The St Francis boys had several names for him – Roadside Romeo, Street King, Don – but the best favoured was Chuvvania Hero, or Chuvvania for short: four annas', a quarter of a rupee's, worth of hero.

*

Presently the school bus came into view, a small motionless patch of grey which occupied the width of the road in the distance and with time swelled gradually into shape, bearing disjointedly towards them, rocking to this side and that, as though a giant Sushma were gyrating inside it. Karim, the driver who should have retired years ago, but never did because – as in all such cases – no one could prove his age, could now be seen, his head swinging to the left and to the right and sometimes to the back, alert as a general leading soldiers to battle. It was said that Karim had not once looked directly at the road for some years now. The bus went on unbusy routes, and forty years of experience had taught Karim the exact location of each pothole, each bump, each twist and bone-jangling rut on the way. He could let his practised rhythms take care of the driving, while he looked for changes in the unchanging scenery about him, the pitheads and mounds of coal and quarries and quarters, or twirled about to shout at the schoolboys if their noise rose above that of the shivering engine under the bonnet at his side.

That morning, just as the bus started from the stop, a piece of paper, folded into the shape of an aeroplane, flew in through the window by which Chetna, the elder of the Marwari sisters, was sitting, and landed stiff in her lap.

When the contents of the unfolded aeroplane came to light, nobody was sure what action should be taken. Had another schoolboy done what Rajna had, he could have been shown easily. But Rajna was an unknown, a forbidding quantity: flick-knives, Macaulay College, hoodlum streets. He was menacing enough without being provoked; what he might do when confronted was imponderable. But when Sameer heard about it he said, 'A love chit to an ICC bus girl! Tomorrow what will he do? He'll start singing songs at them. We must keep our honour.'

'But how can we straighten such a rogue?' the Bull said.

'He has a knife,' Koyala said.

The Bull said, 'And he must have greater rogues for friends in Macaulay College. We can thrash him today, he can retaliate tomorrow.'

Koyala said, 'And anyway, Chuvvania looks weak but he is probably very strong. Most of these gundas may look weak but are really very strong, from all the fighting they do with one another.'

But Vipul said, 'Look, strong or whatever, should he be beaten or not? Are we to show him or not? Are we girls?'

And this convinced the others that something ought to be done.

It was imperative for Vipul to have thus provoked the others. The reason was Chetna. Over the intervening months, he had grown to develop a palpable affection for her. He had had time and occasion to observe her closely; and now he felt that his initial judgement on both the sisters, that they looked like men in the process of turning into girls, had been unwarranted, even harsh. Chetna had begun to look more and more a girl to him; had even begun to strike him as pretty. His continual fugitive examination of her features led him steadily to fancy the depth at which her eyes lay – it gave her that canny, enigmatic air – and the tufts of hooked hair at her temples, which arabesqued her profile. And he felt her hair had now begun to recede from her forehead, and her eyebrows to thin; she was, truly, very much a girl-like girl.

Above all else, there was her silence, and her shyness. She was still thrown into shock and alarm when addressed by a boy. Vipul had been picking up courage, some here some there, learning from Sameer's ways, to speak to her. Of course doing so in public – in the bus or the boat or the jeep – was still out of the question; but he could chance his arm when, infrequently, their families exchanged visits. Then too the usual clumsiness reappeared. They would be, for instance, in the girls' room at their home, Vipul and Sameer and Ratna and Chetna, settled cross-legged on the bed to play cards, drenched (but for the gallant

Sameer) in discomfiture, and Vipul, having nerved himself against all conceivable consequences, would at last ask Chetna, 'So have you seen any picture?'

And Chetna would turn in consternation to Ratna, as before; they would exchange twitching glances, their lips would flutter; finally, the question being resolved as not too lascivious, Chetna would murmur an abject 'Yes', as to a private wickedness.

'Which picture,' Vipul would ask.

And Chetna would again turn in collapsing distress to Ratna, and again...

Uff this girl was just too shy.

Which was why Vipul felt arrested by her. So shy, so quiet; certainly, then, a girl of excellent character; yes, of splendid virtue, timid and helpless, just the kind that Swamiji would have applauded – and not a bit like Sushma didi.

The fondness in which Vipul held Chetna was different, appositional, to that in which he had held Neha. For in Neha's case the object of his fondness was Neha the girl, Neha the being, Neha the strands of hair itching his face and warm cheek yielding to his kiss; whereas in Chetna's it was Chetna the impression, Chetna the vision; Chetna no more than the slipstream of air which her swirling skirt caused to brush across his face when she walked past him in the bus. And he knew that Neha would remain corporeal, there for him to see and sense years from now, but Chetna might prove to be as insubstantial as her cloak of fenugreeked air, and remain unknown; she belonged, firmly, elsewhere, to the Marwari world and its financial flavours.

So, because Vipul could not talk to her most of the time, and because she was unable to respond for the rest, he had to content himself with imaginings; with long bejewelled dreams that unravelled themselves before open vaporous eyes...

Such as. He would get to know her by and by. He would; she simply needed to be handled with care, with delicacy. He would draw her out of her shell. She would no longer be shy; she would share his laughter, reverberate to his moods. Her parents would be relieved (they must be so worried about her too-excessive shyness); her father would shake hands with him and say, in his particular English, 'Thank you, Vipul. You have hugely helped us. We were, I mean, worried about her so much.'

Or. He would get to know that she was bad at Maths (girls were meant to be bad at Maths), and he would bail her out. Now he himself was not so good at Maths, but he would surely be able to help her (girls were meant to be *hopeless* at Maths). He would help her pass (she must be flunking her Maths). Mr Aggarwal would call him over to their home – him alone – and shake his hand and say, 'Vipul, how I can thank you. We had given up hope for her in Maths.'

Or yet. Her mother would be perilously ill, in urgent need of being removed to the hospital at Dudhiya. Late at night. Vipul would drive her in the jeep (of course he would know by then how to drive, even though Sameer and Nizam were still being bloody-minded about teaching him the jeep – all the skills would come upon him quite naturally, obligingly, in an exigency). He would brush everybody else aside, and himself row the boat across the river, and himself pedal the ricksha to Dudhiya – at the speed of a car, amazing the already marvelling Chetna sitting at the back, her mother's head in her lap – and reach them to the hospital in the nick of time. They would all be so grateful to him. 'Thank you, Vipul, thank you, thank you, thank you.'

Vipul the teacher, Vipul the saviour, Vipul the hero.

And at the conclusion of each of these heroics, after the thank yous, there would be the ineluctable, delicious upshot: everybody would be agreed that he and Chetna should, when the time came, marry. And meanwhile they should be given both the freedom and the arrangement of circumstance to go about together, as family-approved friends. Even – bless the thought! – as boyfriend and girlfriend, like in America, like in the comic books which Swamiji had borrowed!

Vipul felt giddy; he ached with delight at the prospect, and felt concomitantly a chill moroseness at the memory of the lost comics.

And so it was Vipul who was the most perturbed of all about Rajna's transgression, which is why he asked whether they were to show him or not and whether they were girls. But other than this he feigned no more than average concern, for he wished not to give away any sign of his designs on Chetna.

It was decided then that Chuvvania should be beaten up, and that the four strongest boys in the bus, Sameer, the Bull and two others, Partha and Gurjit, should do it. A plan was drawn up. When the bus stopped at Sameer and Vipul's stop, Gurjit and Partha would alight. The four would go across the road. Karim would keep the bus idling. Sameer would confront Chuvvania about the chit. Chuvvania would deny all knowledge. An argument would churn up. Chuvvania would become, doubtless, rude and insulting. At the first abusive word from him Sameer would fist him on the chin. Chuvvania's head would turn; Partha would punch his belly. Then Gurjit, broad and stout, would use his wrestler's vice and trip him to the ground. The Bull would hold his arms down, and the others would thrash him nice and well. Then they would board the bus and drive away.

The sequence would have to be executed with despatch. They would require to rehearse. So they took to assembling after school and, while waiting for the bus, rehearsed, asking Vipul to be the dummy, practising their fisticuffs and nelsons and feints on him in the football field. Vipul swivelled his head, and doubled up, and flung himself to the ground, and had his arms pinned with such verve and flair that he astonished himself. Once or twice the mock blows overshot, and he was hit; after this there was a brief, earnest tussle for revenge, then the shadow fights took off again.

At the end of a week, the fighters were finely drilled.

'But,' said the Bull, 'Rajna is not going to be a soft pillow to beat like Vipul.'

'Soft pillow, ha?' Vipul said. 'You've forgotten the early days, ha? When I was walking over you like you were an earthworm?'

Then they had a few mocks with Vipul offering real resistance, and they were all set.

On the fateful day, though, events did not quite unfold according to plan.

It was all too incredibly simple.

When confronted, Chuvvania readily admitted to having written the chit; but his rictus made him inscrutable – his admission itself might be an untruth. This unbalanced Sameer, who had expected a prelude, and, having nothing to say, and failing to improvise, he delivered the blow.

Chuvvania fell at once to the ground. No further skill or force was necessary. The others carried out an almost perfunctory, mild beating. They could not hit hard: Chuvvania had gone limp. He looked bewildered and hurt. He did not look enraged. His bewilderment was like the Bull's, when he used to be set upon by Vipul and Koyala.

They could afford to stroll back into the bus at their ease, and Karim did not need to drive away any faster than usual.

Chuvvania did not appear at Banwari's shop the next day; he did not appear the day after that; wasn't to be seen for over a week.

'Must be gathering his Macaulay College friends around,' Partha said.

'And all the other street heroes he knows,' said Gurjit.

Sameer said, 'May be collecting knives and chains.'

'May be too embarrassed to show his face,' the Bull said.

Gurjit said, 'Unlikely. He's planning something. He's pukka planning something.'

The unease spread. It infected everyone in the bus, and particularly the fighters, mildly at first, then with virulence. They had walked away after the beating as after a conquest, but now it appeared that in spite of Chuvvania's subordination, that foray might have been just an invasion, and now they might be trapped within the fortified walls of Chuvvania's kingdom; by resorting to violence, they had admitted themselves to his realm. And the invaded was regrouping; he had become a guerilla; he would ambush them just when they least expected him to. They started carrying weapons, prying them out again from their hideaways where they had lain since the last day of summer term – chains, compasses, leather knobs – and everyone wore a belt at all times.

After a week Chuvvania reappeared. He stationed himself, as before, at Banwari's shop, had tea there, but did not talk much. He spoke so softly that what little he said did not carry across the road. He only threw occasional inquisitive glances at them, as at newcomers on the scene.

He remained thus, mutated, for another week.

The boys' unease grew into a frazzled anxiety.

But Chuvvania just kept appearing at Banwari's shop, and continued to do exactly nothing; and, remarkably, betrayed no sign of anger or of vengefulness.

Then one day, once the schoolgoers had boarded the bus, he ran across the road and boarded the bus before Karim could rev it up again. 'Don't move it,' he said to Karim. 'Not one inch.' A hush fell upon the bus. Boys felt about inside their boxes and bags for their weapons. Some started loosening their belts. Chuvvania came down the gangway, towards the back, where the bigger boys sat. They all got up.

But Chuvvania was alone. The battle-ready companions that everyone had expected to troop along in his wake did not appear.

He came up to Sameer, and extended his arm.

'Shake hands,' he said.

Sameer, still red and stiff, every muscle taut and on the blocks, looked at him warily. He shook hands. Nothing happened; no sudden pull or twist from Chuvvania. On the contrary, Chuvvania's hand, soft and limp, yielded to Sameer's like a piece of foam.

'You,' Chuvvania said, using 'aap', the respectful inflection of 'you', 'have taught me the right way, bhaiya. From now on I am reformed.'

Then Chuvvania shook hands with all those who had roughed him up. He addressed them all as 'aap' and 'bhaiya'. Then he got off the bus; and even after the bus had rolled off, the boys kept expecting an attack, an ambush.

As with his absence for a week and his silent presence for another, nobody knew what to make of his declaration of apology and fraternalism. It was a ruse, a hoax, a trap; it was to lull them into complacency; he was modelling himself on a Hindi-film villain, ironically sweet before the villainy.

But Chuvvania proved himself consistent. He would daily come over from Banwari's shop across the road, start talking to Sameer and Vipul and the Bull. He kept repeating that he had been taught a good lesson, that he had reformed; kept shaking hands. He started calling everyone 'bhaiya' or 'didi', even those younger to him. And to Chetna he apologized as feelingly as he had done to the boys.

With each passing day, there was less and less room for doubt. It seemed he had been straightened.

Vipul felt a rush of possibilities arise. Chetna might get to know in course of time of his role in Chuvvania's straightening, and see how jealous he was of her honour. And the inescapable consequences would, dreamlike, follow. He hoped, though, fearfully every time it occurred to him, that she wouldn't incline to one of the beaters instead – even the Bull perhaps – thinking them to be the real heroes ... She should be made aware soon of how it was he, Vipul, who had talked those cowards into doing the honourable thing ... but there was just no way to tell her of this.

TWO

Vipul was ambling to and fro on the chabutra one evening with the BBC held to his ear, listening to a comedy that he could not catch the funny words of, but smiling, even chuckling, in considerate sympathy with the peals of laughter that issued from the evidently deeply appreciative audience in England. This required the sternest attention to be paid, for the accents, too, of many of the players were elusive: cryptic with elision, and so very bouncy and discomposed and adolescent compared with the measured evenness of the BBC's newscasters and commentators. Through his frowning absorption Vipul sensed in the periphery of his vision the gate to the bungalow being drawn and a figure make its way along the drive. He supposed it must be Thapa or Jamuna or Aansu, but at the flick of a glance he saw that it was Rajna who was advancing. Rajna, smiling his fleshless smile, his rictus disconcerting.

Vipul was troubled and dismayed, wary of his visitor – and loth, as ever, to be distracted from the goings-on on short wave.

Rajna explained first how he had asked his way to Vipul's home, how it had taken him so many hours to get there from Dudhiya. Presently he said he wanted to talk about something serious. Vipul turned off the soup of the BBC's words and laughter, the rest of the world's crackle and squeals.

'It's a matter of my honour,' Rajna said. He gave Vipul the sort of look that signals that enough has now been said for the sensible to understand.

'A matter of honour?' Vipul said.

'You know.' Rajna's look turned stern.

'I don't. What happened?'

'You *know*, bhaiya. What do you call me? All you people?'

'What?' Vipul's guard went up.

'Chuvvania, is it not?' Rajna's face had become darker and more gaunt still. 'Chuvvania?'

'We all call each other names,' said Vipul. 'It happens to everyone.'

'But it should not. You are officers' children. You go to a good school. And yet you say such things. And…'

'I said, no, we all give each other such names.'

'… I give you people so much respect. I did make a mistake, but now, I told you, I have changed. I treat you like my brothers. But you call me Chuvvania, Road Romeo, Street King. I've heard all of these names. I don't like it. Talk to the others about it. Tell them I don't like it.'

'I'll tell them,' Vipul said.

Chuvvania, pacified, said, 'Vipul bhaiya, I'm going for the first day first show of *Kala Heera* on Saturday. My father has given me this.' He brought out a plastic wallet from his trouser pocket and from the wallet, a currency note; and when he held it up, Vipul saw that it was a hundred-rupee note. He looked at it as at something contraband, fearsome; Rajna considered it with fond pride.

'Your father gave you one hundred rupees?' Vipul said. He had never been trusted with more than ten rupees at a time; and in any case his parents were not, so far as he could tell, wealthy enough to dole out to him a note on as grand a scale as this.

Rajna said, 'My father is like that. He is proud of me. Sometimes he just showers me with money. Sometimes he lashes me with a horsewhip. You'll come with me for the picture?'

Vipul, still under the spell of the note, said that he would.

*

Kala Heera was showing at Sri Hanuman Talkies, near Jadugoda. They went there in a share-taxi, an Ambassador. Fourteen people were stuffed into the car, including two, at concessional fare, in the dicky, where they sat demurely holding up the roof like a sari's pallu over their heads. The taxi driver squeezed himself into a glyph of space, narrow as a blade of grass, between the seat and his door, and from there broke out into paroxysms of ballistic lunges and furious workings of his arms and legs without which the stiffness and friction of the gears and pedals could not be overcome; the passenger next to him, in order to avoid being clouted by the unannounced flails of his limbs, swayed and dodged with a boxer's watchfulness.

At the picture hall there seemed to be no hope of getting tickets. The box office was closed, a board over it said 'House Full' in phonetic Hindi alphabet, and dozens of young men stood about, seeming to refuse to give up hope, waiting for a miracle to happen. Rajna left Vipul, went to one of these men, led him aside, out of earshot for a doubtless solemn conference, and returned flourishing two tickets in his hand.

'Twenty rupees each,' he said, the bones in his face shining in triumph through his skin. 'He was asking for thirty.'

'How did you manage?'

'I told him you were an officer's son. I told him you were the son of the Superintendent of Police.'

'Wait! Wait!'

'What wait-wait. I got the tickets.'

'But police may find out.'

'No chance. All officers' children look the same.'

Sri Hanuman Talkies was a semi-cylindrical grain godown converted with haste and parsimony into a picture hall. Rows of tin chairs had been placed on its slopeless floor; a white cotton sheet, probably a reimagined shamiana awning, had been put up at one end; a projector whirred and droned at the other. The roof was a lowering semicircle of heat-emitting corrugated iron; fans, adventitious outgrowths on the walls, added to the heat with their paralysed promise of breath.

The hall was patronized by locals, and no effort had been made to see to it that they watched the film in comfort. But the audience was vigorously participatory, and barely thought of comfort; what really mattered was the threat, from challenging and numerous sources, to the clement existence of the hero and the heroine, and the heroics necessary to scotch the threat. And participation today was fevered. For the film was set in the coalfields, and when it took time off from its main point – the love story – it dwelt on the exploitation by mineowners of mineworkers, on flash floods in underground mines, and purchasable trade unions, and death and grief. At one stage, when the villain, the mineowner, was being uncommonly fiendish and the hero, a rebel miner, uncommonly heroic, men in the audience started to rise to their feet and to bellow exhortations at the latter: 'Kill the bastard!', 'Why do you sit so quiet!'; but the hero would not listen, and kept lapsing into noble rhetoric, which, whilst not a wholly satisfactory response, was rousing enough to earn cheers and claps, which in turn drowned out the villain's vile retorts.

And Vipul, accustomed so far to the flattened involvement of the balconies and the dress circles of the amphitheatre picture halls, soon found himself getting won over to the froth and fizz of Sri Hanuman Talkies, and himself started cheering and clapping and baying with all his might, and exchanging fraught glances with Rajna during scenes of high moment.

Ah, cinema! The hero challenging the audience to confront him if they had drunk their mothers' milk. The heroine smiling unbeguilingly, as though known to them, sociably, for years. The parents of the heroine obsessive about some illogical archaic point. The villain chewing cigars, hypnotically weird and unethical and charming. The moll forever festive, forever partying, brandishing overspilling goblets. The children so mature, so tragedy-stricken, so cute and hateable. The comedians absurd-faced, absurd-mannered, absurd to the absurdest degree. The songs mere excuses for music; the music all-excusing; and life an excuse for cinema. Vipul saw that cinema was truly Rajna's world; here it was that he was fashioned and sustained.

Rajna became a regular visitor to Vipul and Sameer. He would arrive in the evening, ensconce himself in one of the deckchairs in the veranda and, reverting to type, go on about his exploits. Often their mother received and welcomed him, for Vipul and Sameer would be getting changed after school. After a few visits, Rajna started calling her 'auntieji'. And he started calling Sameer and Vipul 'Bittu bhaiya' and 'Bitty bhaiya', having overheard their mother addressing them. This unwished-for slide into familiarity caused them a gnawing unease. Vipul resented Rajna calling his mother 'auntieji', just as much as he would have resented the Bull calling her 'Mrs Uberoi', like an American. This term of address, and the more so their own nicknames, were zones of regulated access, to which only those with the correct credentials were given admittance. Parallel to this there existed an exact physical demarcation of access: only friends on nickname terms were admitted inside the house, and furthermore into the boys' room; others were not invited in any further than the veranda. The names by which you were allowed to address each other, and the space in the house that you were invited to grace, determined precisely the coordinates of your affiliation.

Taking things a step further, Rajna had started making unsubtle hints that he should like to be taken inside, into Vipul and Sameer's room; he would bring up subjects that would reference their room, and he would immediately say, 'Come, let's go to your room, and I can have a look at it' – a carrom board, or a table-tennis racquet, or some such thing. But the boys would offer instead to bring the object in question into the veranda to show it to him, making it out that they were doing so purely from kindness, so that he did not have to rise from his seat.

A new and bewildering friendship was being offered them, and Vipul and Sameer did not know how, or whether, to arrest it there and then or boldly to let it run its imponderable course.

THE NEW ONE

ONE

The Puja vacation, in honour of the goddess Durga, and in deference to those who would worship Her for days together, had begun. Vipul never looked forward to this break. It was just the wrong duration: immediately you started to feel you were on a long leash, you were dragged back to school. And the holidays fell in an indeterminate part of the year: late September or early October, a seasonless time. Summer had been left firmly behind, the rainy season was blowing away its last clouds, and winter was yet to arrive. And in his part of India, as in most other parts, there seemed to be no such thing as the autumn that Vipul read of in books; no distinct interval of transition between summer and winter; instead, there was an imperceptible progression of the air from moist and cool to cold and dry. Leaves did not fall from trees, nor did the colour of rust come upon them.

It was like an illegitimate holiday, with no sound underpinning to it, for Vipul only associated holidays with the distinct and severe seasons, when school closed up its gates in order principally to shy away from the extreme weather; even in the rainy season they had their rainy-day holidays. During the Puja holidays all that happened was that the days grew discernibly shorter and the evenings heavier with smoke, a dreary transition. But the Puja season did presage Diwali, and in that act of heraldry lay its partial redemption.

During these holidays, then, Vipul found himself listless, bereft of an agenda; and he tended to spend most of his time with the men who worked in the bungalow.

Two gardeners, Mali and Jamuna, trained the garden. Their work had the merit of being slushy and soily and even suspenseful. They created elaborate irrigation networks for the vegetable garden, comprising canals, bandhs and weirs, which directed sluices of water to a set of plots; the sluices could be magically switched, by the release of one bandh or the creation of another, to instantly feed an entirely different set of plots, like the activation or silencing of electrical circuits at the touch of a button. And they often happened upon scorpions that scurried away upon the turning of a stone, or snakes that skimmed the surface of the low-lying vines of gourd. Vipul often joined them in their work, even though they urged him not to, for he was prone to sabotage it with good intent.

Jamuna had sharp, long, intelligent features but was really quite unintelligent – according to Mali. But Mali himself looked a mixture of an ignoramus and a saint, with his clean-shaven head and the long wispy tuft that helixed down its back. He was too old and too knowledgeable about the grounds of the house – he had worked there more than forty years already, and his age of retirement, like Karim the bus driver's, and like Govardhan the boatman's, was never reached – too old and knowledgeable to be called by his name by anyone, so he was called Mali. Indeed he possessed a calm daring which only those approaching sainthood may. He would pick up live, recently unearthed scorpions and bring them across on the palm of his hand to show them to the boys. He said no scorpion ever stung him. And the scorpion, black, diabolically lowering, its beaded sting curving stiffly up like Rover's happy tail, would somehow get immobilized on his palm, perplexed and strangely cowed. Then Jamuna would ask for a pair of scissors, and with the care of a tailor shaping a piece of cloth, snip off the sting, and ease the scorpion down back upon the ground. It would scurry away, toylike, unbalanced and humbled without its venomous ensign. And Vipul saw himself in some of his heroic dreams to be possessed of Jamuna's taming force, imagining that he could turn snakes into friendly and obedient creatures, executing his commands, as Rover did, to sit or stand or beg or drink milk.

Thapa's wife, Champa, kept the floors of the house clean. Had she not taken the rash step of marriage so early on in her life, and had she been fairer, Vipul was sure he would have fallen in love with her. She was small and bony all over except for her face, whose roundness, fleshy cheeks, and scared eyes made Vipul wish that he could make lifelike drawings of it. Champa's job was to swab the floors that Thapa had swept, and to clean the bathrooms. Owing to the calls of her job, she was ever to be seen shifting backwards, swivelling on her haunches, as she swabbed the floor before her first on this side and then on that with a dilute solution of Essence of Phenyl, which for a few minutes after her ministrations left the house smelling clinical.

Vipul found Jamuna and Mali companionable and Champa arousing, but for entertainment he turned to the untrustworthy Thapa. Thapa had a boyish gaunt body which should have stood under some other face – a younger, more ingenuous face – not his leathery, pleated, incorrigible mask. Thapa had so many faults. He was a latecomer. He broke precious curios. He never arrived sober. When he arrived he was either less drunk than always or more drunk than always or hopelessly drunk. In this last state he would be stumbling and reaching out to the walls to break his fall at every singing step, and Vipul's mother would have to send him back and report to the foreman to note his absence for the day. Thapa could be violent too. Champa would now and again come to work with her cheeks looking even fleshier than usual, and shining with colour, like ripening fruit. This was the only thing that Vipul held against Thapa, that he should have married such a sweet round-faced girl only to beat her. But Vipul did not really feel sorry for Champa; with her weak nervous voice, receiving body and the way she sat on her haunches, sloping forward, she seemed ill-fated to invite a certain amount of violence.

One late September morning, Thapa came to the house more drunk than always, and very late. Vipul's mother denied him entry into the house and threatened to have him chargesheeted.

Thapa protested. There was a reason why he was late, he said, a reason of faith. The Ramlila had come to Khajoori. Last night's had been the first show. How could he miss it? Was it a sin to celebrate the staging of the life of Lord Ram? He wanted to know.

Vipul's mother told him to get out and not waste her time.

Thapa said, 'It was only to worship Sri Ramchandraji. Otherwise, do I ever drink? Last night was a different matter. Still, forgive me. Have me lashed, rain shoes on me, I'll lick mud, but let me not be chargesheeted.'

Vipul's mother told him to get out and not waste her time.

'I promise,' went Thapa, 'in the name of Sri Ram, in whose name I drank – by mistake – I promise to get sober by the other side of noon. Then see me, see how I work – the whole house will be shining like a mirror by evening. Have faith in your Thapa.'

Vipul's mother told him to get out and get back at three.

Thapa returned sobered, but not sober. A leavening smirk still troubled his lips, and his eyes were watery-red on yellow. He did more or less as he had promised. With great speed and in high humour, he dusted, wiped, swept and polished; he broke nothing; then at five he announced he would stay on to do overtime – gratis overtime, no, no, he would not think of extra wages.

He said to Vipul, 'Baba, let's talk a little while I press.'

Now and then, Thapa would talk to the boys in the pantry where, of an afternoon, he would steam out the creases from cottons or softly persuade synthetic fabrics back into shape – or forget about the iron and singe a prized shirt. He told them stories of the people who had lived in the bungalow in the ruled past. He told them of times when all was grand, pompous, and shipshape, when the kitchen outhouse, kennels and incubators were used strictly in accordance with their deemed functions (not like now, when the outhouse was a godown for hay, the kennel a refuge for reptiles, and the poultry incubators derelict). When they kept horses that they rode. When twelve gardeners, five sweepers, two cooks and three bearers kept the bungalow in condition, when two dozen fresh flower arrangements were brought into the house every day. When he himself had only to polish shoes, nothing else, but polish thirty – oh, even forty – pairs of shoes daily, polish them so that they were like wet slate, so that they mirrored the whiteness of the sahibs' faces – and what generous baksheesh that would earn him, not just on Holi or on Diwali as nowadays, not just as a surrogate offering to the gods, but from time to time throughout the year, in gracious token of a job well done. And now, although he had been promoted from shoeblack to sweeper, he felt insulted: a general dogsbody, dusting, sweeping, swabbing, ironing, everything – no longer a specialist, downgraded.

Today he said, 'Vipul baba, memsahib is harsh on me.'

Steam from a damp, hissing handkerchief that lay over a sari rose, dissolving the edges of the iron. 'Too harsh. But you'll understand. The Ramlila – how can one not see it? You also went to see it on a couple of nights last year. I remember, sahib and memsahib did too, and memsahib was looking very nice, just like a manager's wife. After all, every Hindu must go to the Ramlila. And baba, this year the Ramlila is something else. There's an addition to the company. Of the name of Naiki. She has set Khajoori on fire. She kept a crowd of many hundreds up all night last night. Till five-thirty in the morning. She is the best thing to come to Khajoori since the time of the English.'

'Naiki?' Vipul said. 'It's a strange name.'

'The new one. It's what she is called. Her real name could be anything.'

'I'll come.'

'Then ask memsahib, and because you will be going that side, you can have dinner at our home. I'll come to take you at seven.'

Thapa was not late this time; at seven he was there, dressed in a nylon shirt and polyester trousers, shining and well creased, and his hair oiled and shining and combed, and his feet covered in shiny shoes. He looked unnervingly genteel; and fake, copper clad in gold. Vipul too wore his shiniest shorts, his newest shirt; it was an occasion.

They walked to Thapa's house, in the workers' colony. The colony was an array of low-roofed concrete hemicylinders stacked atop with chimneys, each chimney signifying a 'quarter'. Inside, there were two rooms to each quarter, and a courtyard for general use. Wood- and coal-smoke arose from the courtyards, for it was time for them to be used as kitchens. Vipul's eyes stung. But the smells that the smoke carried, of the locals' cooking, were enticing, abounding in tomato and turmeric. On entering Thapa's home the flavours grew full-bodied, heady; Champa was stirring them up, squatting, forward-sloping, as always, by a fire-pot.

Vipul was happy to eat the food at Thapa's home; he liked the overuse of tomatoes and turmeric in the vegetables, and he liked the chapatis made in the local way: thick as a book, and no bigger than the palm of his hand; liked their chewiness and roastedness. He would often ask his mother to have chapatis like these made at home, but she, pointlessly sensitive to inelegance in foods, a stubborn champion of thin-as-paper and soft-as-muslin chapatis, would never agree.

He was not so comfortable to be in Thapa and Champa's home. The signs of their poverty, always there, but recessed until the food lasted, emerged again to trouble him after dinner. The bare paintless walls breathing arrack; the low-power electric bulb, sapped further by the weak voltage, its ochre filament clearly, unhurtingly visible, shedding an ailing light that amplified the gloom; the low sooty ceiling; the neatness born of lack; the absence of windows along the barracks, just a small opening at one end, looking out on to other solitary openings; above all, amidst all this, Thapa's in-spite-of-all-this high humour, Champa's continued, suffering silence, and Thapa's and Champa's rich, make-believe clothes for today.

At the Ramlila grounds, where they went after collecting the Bull from his home, Vipul was in unaccustomed terrain. The crowd was composed entirely of mineworkers, market-people and villagers. He was inundated by sensations he never encountered at home: women smelling appetizingly of tamarind and turmeric, and babies of kohl and mustard oil; bright, iridescent saris and nylon ribbons and nose rings everywhere; the blunt native tones of village-speak and the incessant clinks of bangles. It only disquieted Vipul if his thoughts wandered to the homes they came from, homes like Thapa's. In the background there was the grumble, resembling that of a distant tractor, of a diesel-powered generator, the Ramlila's electric bulwark against load-shedding.

The stage was empty, although the curtains had been drawn aside. Vipul could already hear the word Naiki being uttered hither and thither among the audience, in tones of hushed, parched anticipation. Then a man came onstage from the wings, tapped the microphone, and said 'Checking hello one-two-three-four, four-three-two-one hello' a number of times, and, on hearing his nonsense amplified and booming over the ground, went back pleased. The chatter in the audience subsided. With quick rustles of saris and clicks of joints and clinks of bangles, they settled down to watch. Presently six monkeys danced on to the stage, complete with masks and arced tails and dazzlingly sequinned loincloths, shouldering a gleaming bronze mace each. They arrayed themselves three on either side and burst into energetic mace-fights. The air was now full of battle cries and clangs of bronze on bronze, produced by a man in the wings clashing cymbals, and the stage was aglitter with leaping monkeys, flailing arms and metallic flashes.

For a while the audience was spellbound by this display of simian agility and strength. But the monkeys capered on and on, seeming greatly to enjoy themselves, forgetful of the real agenda at hand.

So someone from the audience shouted, 'Naiki!'

And another shouted, 'Stop all this and get Naiki!'

The monkeys stopped. Sequinned not just in their loincloths but also, now, all over, in droplets of sweat, they, maces formidable on shoulders, glared through their masks at the audience. One of them came up to the microphone. 'As you wish,' he said. 'We'll stop. But you could give us some baksheesh before we go. Each mace weighs ten kilos.'

'Go, go, fool someone else,' some shouted.

'All baksheesh for Naiki today,' said the man who had shouted first.

'Monkeys can live on nuts. Why do the devotees of Lord Ram want money?' the second said.

There were approving, derisive noises from the audience, but a few sympathizers passed some coins along on to the stage, and then the monkeys left, as lackadaisical in their departure as they had been vivid in their entrance.

At the curtain's next draw expectations went up again. But there was no Naiki. After another cameo by the 'Checking hello one-two-three-four' man, there began the enactment of a scene from the Ramayan. On came Lord Ram and Sita, accompanied by Laxman, and set about the task of establishing a picture of domestic sufficiency in the forest clearing of their exile, prior to Sita's imminent abduction. It was an undramatic scene, replete with inaction and contemplation; Lord Ram was instructing Laxman in good ways. The audience became restive again.

Thapa said, 'They'll bore us tonight. They are deliberately holding Naiki back to sharpen our appetites. Even if Naiki isn't there, there should be something exciting on the stage, a fight or a chase or a spat. The monkeys were better than this.'

Shouts for Naiki recommenced. The actors, their philosophical trance broken, paused in front of the microphone and gazed regretfully at the degenerates before them, then continued. The shouts, too, continued. At length Lord Ram, unable to bear the rupture of one of his choice passages, squared himself to the audience and said, 'What kind of people are you? Are you not ashamed being disrespectful to your gods?' He continued in the same sonorous tone that he had been using with Laxman, and hooting laughter broke out. Lord Ram gesticulated grandly to the others, and they all marched off the stage with great unconvincing dignity.

Thapa said, 'How he came, hoping to make a speech about respect.'

For some more time nothing happened. The audience saw only the huge backdrop on the stage, a tapestry on cloth depicting, in its middle, Sita's engulfment into a bottomless fissure in the earth, and around it anecdotal scenes of war and bow-breaking and arrow-shooting. Again the restlessness grew, and became almost a tumult. The crowd's tenor had travelled from request to demand to threat; they were clamouring now not for Naiki, but for the manager of the show. Meanwhile hawkers did good business in the crowd. They carried slung about their necks trays containing plastic trinkets for children, flowers and bindis for the women, betelnut and beedis for everyone. Thapa bought a packet of beedis, and offered them to Vipul and the Bull.

Vipul took a beedi, flung it aside and said, 'Don't teach me wrong things.'

Thapa laughed. 'Baba, if not today, tomorrow you will start. Today's a good occasion.' He advanced another beedi towards Vipul.

Vipul said, 'If you try once more, I'll tell mummy you tried to spoil me.'

Thapa desisted, and Vipul looked at the beedi on the ground with some regret, some curiosity, and some righteousness.

The loudspeaker twanged. 'Checking one-two-three-four. Brothers and sisters! We know what you're waiting for. Give me just a few more minutes. She is getting ready. She is oiling her hair, reddening her lips, blackening her eyes! She is doing all she can to make this an unforgettable night for you!'

Just then a woman rushed up to the microphone from the wings and gave the compère a rough push.

'Useless man! Stop blabbering and let me come on.'

Thapa turned to Vipul and the Bull and said, 'Baba! Her!'

She stood on the stage arms akimbo, rocking her waist. There was much fair waist to be seen. The blouse was worn high, the sari wrapped low, its pallu wrung thin between her breasts. She had none of the roundness and pulpiness that was the hallmark of all the other women of the Ramlilas. She was angular, her crimson lips thin, going on cruel.

The compere said, 'Naiki, it's come to my ears that you've prepared today an especially intoxicating song for the menfolk of Khajoori – the virile menfolk of Khajoori.'

Naiki rocked her hips. 'Virile menfolk! Ha! It took six of them last night just to keep me awake. But before I sing the song, I would like to know who is here tonight to appreciate my charms. Is the foreman here?'

A pocket of voices indicated where he was. Naiki said, 'Foreman sahib! May God grant me my dishonour at your hands tonight.'

The foreman's head sank into his chest, and he looked at nothing but his feet.

'But what about an advance, Foreman sahib?' Naiki said.

The foreman, a shy man, shook his head in anguished disbelief, dug into his trouser pocket, and took out a note. This he handed to a man in front, who passed it along, until it reached Naiki.

'Two rupees! Wah, Foreman sahib, is that your standing in Khajoori? But even the loaders who work under you advance me five or ten. Foreman sahib, is everything all right at home?'

The foreman, still weak with thrill and pleasure and agony, passed on another note through the ranks of crowds.

'Ten more straightaway! Now that is an honourable act from an honourable man. Foreman sahib, you are a man after my heart.' So saying, Naiki, with deliberate prolonged care, eased the note under her blouse. 'And you live here in it.' And she patted her breasts.

A hot tremor of joy and embarrassment passed through the crowd, and Vipul and the Bull exchanged a furtive glance, even though they knew that Naiki was really a man.

And Naiki continued in her tangy, slighting way, ragging a few more people for money; but after a while she did not require to rag them, for the baksheesh had begun to flow spontaneously and copiously. She spoke in Bhojpuri; and that made her the more popular. The rest of the Ramlila was conducted in formal Hindi. To this the audience took no exception, even if they did not entirely follow the language; it gave them a sense of classicism, of being claimed by a possessive ancientness; but they soon tired of it, and liked it better when Naiki broke out in Bhojpuri, which they did not require to strain to follow.

Naiki sang, too, the song that had been promised. It was her pièce de résistance; she sang it at two in the morning, with three similarly fraudulent women chorusing after her. And this was her ditty, specially prepared for Khajoori's redoubtables:

Karwa le wa, karwa le wa;
Saya uttha ke
Marwa le wa
Marwa le wa

which meant:

Get it done, get it done;
Raise up your hem and
Get it rammed,
Get it rammed

And on it went in the same vein, for several verses, each rivalling the next for imagery and unmelodiousness.

Vipul and the Bull were delighted, and hoped that nobody could see them now.

Thapa was more than delighted. Whenever Vipul glanced at him, he had on his face the stunned look – mouth half open, half asmile, eyes fixated – of someone witnessing a miracle, pleasure and awe and incredulity alloyed.

Vipul went the next evening, too, to the Ramlila; and the next; he started going every day (but his mother absolutely forbade him to have dinner with Thapa after the second). He too was getting addicted to Naiki, and became impatient for the preliminary, necessary, scenes from the Ramayan to end. He was also developing, he realized with dismay and wonderment, an undeniable fascination for her. He tried very hard to dispel the images of the red mouth and the exposed skin and the swaying hips that kept pulsing at the back of his eyes, certain that they were incorrect and defiling, but they always caught him unawares. Then when there was no escape he would let the visions hold sway, and evolve as they would, reined in by no conscious restraint. And afterwards he would wait hungrily, guiltily, for his next visit to the Ramlila.

Most unsettling was the finding that his visions of Naiki were now vying with those that he entertained of Chetna, even displacing them by virtue of their greater vigour and – could it be confessed? – affinity. He understood deep down, too, that the mesmerism Naiki exercised on him was meretricious and facile, and that Chetna it really was who embodied his ideal. But Naiki's hold grew irresistibly stronger, and soon Vipul found himself easily submitting to, then gladly sailing on, those languorous outsize fancies whose centre stage Naiki, rather than Chetna, now occupied.

Vipul found consolation in the fact that others, too, had fallen to Naiki. The Bull himself, so impassive towards girls, once asked him, 'How do you think Naiki looks when she's not doing the Ramlila?'

'Oho!' Vipul asked. 'Why do *you* want to know?'

'No need to oho, understand?' the Bull said. 'Just like that. Don't you feel like knowing what Jeetendra looks like outside the films?'

'Is it the same thing? Hanh? Where's Jeetendra, and where's Naiki?' Vipul said, and thought he detected a flush sweep over the Bull's face.

And at the Ramlila it was becoming plain that more than a few others had been reduced to prostration by Naiki's magic. Of these of Naiki's well-wishers, whose baksheesh surged with every charming lyric she rendered, the one who fetched himself greatest notice, by merit of a brawny pair of lungs and a matchingly brawny sense of crudity, was one Gopi, a trader who made himself quite a substantial living by the artful adulteration of essential commodities. On his occasional visits to the local market Vipul had been struck by the hoarding on his shop, each letter on it painted in multiple colours to say: NOVELTY GRANE STORS FAIR PRICE SHOPE (dwarfed by a transliteration in Hindi, also spelt subversively), with each nook of remaining space given over to a miniature golden goddess or god. From inside the shop, you could always hear Gopi's opinion on this and that and the other. He chewed, with indefatigable perpetualness, paan loaded with supari and gulkand and lime, and emerged every few minutes to spit out its instigations, adding to the scarlet that already, in swirling layers, carpeted his shopfront. His words, for having to pass through the succulent thicket of fibre and saliva in his mouth, seemed to Vipul to come to his ears squelching and squashing in mud.

One evening at their conference at the ironing table Thapa said to Vipul, 'Baba, Gopi seth is a drowned man.'

Vipul, sensing confirmation of suspicion, pretended unawareness and asked why he said so.

'Don't you see how he riles her up?'

'So what? She does the same to everybody there.'

'Ah, but these stage people don't like being the target. This they cannot stomach. And they have a dangerous sense of revenge.'

Vipul had seen why things should have come to such a pass. There was now a nightly exchange of pleasantries between Gopi and Naiki. The trader would pass on a tip and when it reached Naiki he would shout, 'That's for you to meet me tonight, my collyrium-eyed packet of magic,' or some such invitation. To which Naiki would say, slightingly, as was her custom with Khajoori's locals, 'Meet your homemaker tonight, seth. I don't want you to remain up all night and ruin your morning's business tomorrow, and yet not satisfy me.'

Or Gopi would flatter her: 'In the annals of beauty / There's no mention of faith / You say you'll love? / But love's not your trade … What is your trade, Naiki, tell us all a little about it, what is it?'

And Naiki would say, 'Whatever it is, my friend, at least it's pure. I don't adulterate my charms to rob people, as you do your stocks. I give my very best.'

At first it seemed just another of those instances of persiflage that Naiki traded with her victims in the audience, such as the foreman. But to this banter that she carried on with Gopi there had gradually attached a new, and portentous, dimension: that of earnestness. For Gopi would take exception to remarks such as these and, helping himself to a bracing swig from his quarter bottle, would abruptly switch modes to roar succulent vilification at her, saying that he well knew what she was, and she was not worth the cheap sari that she wore, and that he could *buy* her with only a sand's grain's worth of the wealth he possessed, what was she talking about satisfaction ... he would *buy* her, and then they would see who was satisfied and who not.

Which would incense Naiki, and she would ask him – attacking the microphone with such venom that the loudspeakers around soared into a reverberatory ear-clawing squealing wail – ask him to tell her why, if he had all this wealth, did he not own anything better than that rathole shop of his, where not even a eunuch would think of stopping off to demand his extraction, and why, if he was the satisfying kind, was it that he had a homemaker who daily looked hungry for something fresh and sharp, even at midday?

And the continued reference to his property and family would drive Gopi to red wrath, and he would resort then to the purity of uncouched abuse and calumny; and Naiki would respond to brick with stone; and thus things would proceed, both tongues loosened free; and so it came about that mere badinage grew to taunt, and taunt to scurrility, and all decorum wholly collapsed.

And now the Ramlila, which to Naiki had already lost much of its telling, became yet more quagmired as the show's ambit further contracted, taken over by this squabble between artiste and audience. Not that Vipul and the Bull minded this unduly, for it was but another brand of entertainment. It was instructive too, in the homegrown techniques and traditions of retort and repartee, revilement and debasement. Added to which, it afforded them a spot of sport on the side; they wagered between themselves what might finally befall the vanquished. It was clear who this should be: Naiki was too adept and knowledgeable for the lala; a thoroughbred, with several seasons and extensive journeying through the roughest districts behind her, and he a mere local merchant with a good juicy voice. There was much room for speculation, though, as to what precise shape his drubbing at Naiki's hands would take.

In all of this it was apparent what the wellspring was of the sincerity in Gopi's demeanour: it was born of a livid, mounting ardour. He for his part had commenced each exchange with an invitation or a compliment, but Naiki there and then, through habit and professional persuasion, had disgraced him, whereupon he had been drawn progressively into a row. It was strange, certainly, to hanker after Naiki thus, but amongst the audience there wasn't an absence of sympathy for him; and Vipul himself, given the new flights of imagination that besieged him, felt he could understand something of Gopi's predicament, as well as his dismay at being spurned.

And Thapa, too, said, 'He's thinking too much, that is his problem. He must stop thinking about her. We all think about her, but by the grace of God we cut our thoughts at the right place. A man must know how far to let his thoughts run, baba, and how far not. Still. It has made the Ramlila even better than at the start. It's the best Ramlila I've seen. May it go on like this.'

But then Gopi suddenly spoiled it all, in the middle of a show, at two-thirty in the morning, with Naiki in full flow, by shooting her. No one got to know whether he intended to kill her. The bullet struck her hip, and she fainted on stage, and was taken away, and of course there was immense commotion and a small stampede, and the Ramlila was stopped for that day. It continued the day after, without Naiki.

Vipul was forbidden by his mother to go. 'What a place we live in,' she said. 'Whoever wishes to, carries a gun or a knife or something. I don't want to lose a son to a crossfire between thugs and nautankiwalas.' (So Vipul heard the rest from Thapa. In Naiki's absence, the telling of the Ramayan made up a great deal of the ground it had lost to her, though its audience was decimated.)

In the end, the motive of the offence was established to be jealousy; Gopi, Thapa told Vipul some days later, had confessed to having fallen passionately in love with Naiki, and could not brook her whoring around with everyone (he said) on stage.

'But I don't understand why he had to shoot her, though I can understand why he would have wanted to shoot her,' Thapa said.

And Vipul thought he agreed.

TWO

Sometimes a house guest other than a relative came to stay. He would usually be an apprentice mining engineer, a nephew or a son of a friend of Vipul's father, deputed for a month's training to Khajoori.

One such, Manohar, arrived towards the end of the Puja vacation. He was a very neat man. He kept a small comb in his trousers' seat pocket, and set and reset his hair with the same fastidious, needless care with which Pinki didi rearranged the pleats of her skirt. Cultured, too: he spoke in English only, and his diction was reprievelessly idiomatic, and velvet.

He said he was not cut out for a career as a mining engineer; not his cup of tea. In college, he would much rather have flirted with the Arts, perhaps Geography or English or Music. But his father was an engineer, and wanted him to follow suit. There had been difficult times, times when he was up in arms against his father and was looked upon as the black sheep of the family. Eventually he had been forced to toe the line; and what a thorny garden the School of Mines had been!

Now he was between the devil and the deep sea: he couldn't run the gauntlet of unemployment, nor could he bear the thought of day in and day out running a colliery; after all, he admitted, he knew sweet Fanny Adams about mining, so little had he burnt the midnight oil in college, and he did cut rather a sorry figure in those underground tunnels, being quite a square peg in a round hole; and the way he was now going he was riding for a fall, and knew that soon he would have to look for greener pastures.

And even in the recounting of his troubles he seemed not so much agitated as emotionally moved by them, so that they had the same uplifting effect on him as on his audience.

He impressed his hosts in many other ways. He was the first person Vipul had come across who was inclined to Hindustani classical music. He set aside an hour after lunch every day to tune into medium-wave radio, on which, broadcast by Ranchi Station, the recitals came. He rolled and nodded and swayed his head joyously at points and passages which to Vipul sounded like lamentations. At the peak of his intoxication he let out a 'wah', not loud and congratulatory, but shallow and wondering, as one might murmur 'hmm' at a question well posed.

He ate with great delicacy and calculation. He eschewed the use of fingers, but if compelled to use them, he made sure only their very tips got soiled. The way he ate rice was exquisite: with a fork and a spoon, piling up the rice in the spoon with strokes of the fork, guiding the spoon measuredly into his mouth.

And every morning he took a walk in the garden, sometimes with Vipul's mother, and asked after her flowers and ferns and cacti. And he addressed her as 'ma'am', and not 'bhabhiji', as all the other juniors did. And so on.

Vipul's mother decided that Manohar was a very cultivated young man, and told the boys that they should learn some etiquette from him.

*

One day Manohar asked Vipul's mother if he couldn't possibly use her bathroom and dressing room to get ready, instead of the guest room, if she wouldn't terribly mind. He said he liked to get ready properly, ma'am, and needed the comfort and equipment to do so, which were to be found on ma'am's dressing table, and not on the one in the guest room, which was a little less well appointed. Vipul's mother was taken too much aback at this profession in a stranger, and a man, of love of grooming, and immediately said yes, of course he could, most welcome.

Manohar began to use Vipul's mother's bathroom and dressing room; gradually he began to occupy them. He locked himself there much of the morning, leaving his hosts little time or space to get ready themselves. One could hear him humming inside. He clearly relished being a member of that most privileged, unberatable class of people – a guest, his hosts unable to demur.

And when he emerged from ma'am's dressing room he was a cadenza of powder and perfume and puff. And his skin, though fresh from a shave, was smooth, undotted, shiny, as though the shave had had on it the effect of unction rather than abrasion.

The upshot of his use of the dressing room was in the nature of a depredation; simultaneously, many bottles of perfume became clear-topped and glassy, until pathetically low levels of the amber or ochre liquids remained, clamouring for preservation.

No, no, Vipul's mother said, he was such a cultured, sensitive young man, you couldn't really say anything to him; he might get so very hurt.

By stages Vipul was to discover that in his emptier hours his gentleness took leave of Manohar and was replaced by an unsentimental tendency to a mixture of love and mild torture. In the afternoons, Vipul and Sameer would lie down with Manohar for the sake of his conversation in English. On the radio, Manohar would receive the music broadcast.

As he listened, he spoke, and as he spoke, he started taking a desultory physical interest in Vipul. He would pinch Vipul's cheek, twist his ear, squeeze his hand. He would rub Vipul's leg with his own, kiss him on the forehead and temple. Vipul was not unaccustomed to physical attention; in his family, among his relatives, embraces and kisses were the bare minimum tokens of kinship; and to demonstrate affection was to lie down together, exchanging candid fondles and strokes, such as those to which he had grown accustomed with Neha.

But Manohar's attentions grew from being affectionate to being exploratory, involved. Sometimes he would pinch Vipul's cheek so close that his eyes would start to burn and then, as though to atone for the pain, he would kiss him, throwing his arms around him so ardently that Vipul would feel short of air and spoilt.

And all the time Manohar would be going on most idiomatically, so that Vipul could not push away. It was as if the physical probings were central to the rendition of what Manohar said, gestures of elaboration, and to Vipul's appreciation of it. As he spoke, and alongside pinched or rubbed or kissed Vipul, he had a benign smile fixed on his lips; and Vipul, with the child's fascination of a genial tormentor, was disarmed.

So Vipul was relieved when the Puja holidays were over, when he could be away at school all day, particularly around lunchtime. When Manohar left – when finally (although only a month after his arrival) Manohar the dandy, the loving tormenter, the ace aesthete, left – he took with him, without informing anybody, exercising the prerogative, no doubt, of a guest, several of the new bottles of perfume that he had charmed Vipul's mother into bringing out from her almirah.

TO THE CITY

ONE

Vipul's journey to Delhi began with a walk in the grounds of the house just before the jeep came to take them. He did this every time he was to go to Delhi, for even a month's separation deserved a farewell, if a silent wandering one.

In the garden, the winter flowers had bloomed, making it briefly, resoundingly colourful. There were slim rectangular beds of flowers skirting the lawns, and circular beds inside them; there were large iron flowerpots with sawtooth rims, islands of soil in which the flowers grew as in exile from the earth.

His mother, and under her supervision the gardeners, had worked hard through the nondescript months of October and November to rein the garden in from its unruly green abandon that the monsoon had incited, and marshal it to the less lush, but disciplined, spectral display of today. First the overgrown grass and bush had been cleared – a haircut for the grounds – and then the seeds had been planted in the makeshift nursery by the unused, perhaps haunted, kennel (Rover, spoilt and wilful, slept only in the veranda at the back, and gave the nightguards company). During this time his mother had 'stood on the gardeners' heads', she said, 'twenty-four hours a day', to make sure that the manures – a different manure for each flower – were correctly prepared, the saplings carefully nurtured, and the transplantation – that most critical and delicate process – done at just the right time. During the transplantation the gardeners needed to be on their best form, exercising all the finesse at their command when they uprooted the saplings from the nursery with plugs of dripping soil still attached to the roots, and when they hoed and tamped them into their beds, the latter operation reminding Vipul of the way his father tucked the quilt around and under him, when he was put to bed like the flowers.

Nearest the terrace, on one side, were the heavyweights of the show, the dahlias. Vipul's mother prided herself on the diameter they attained – thirteen inches at times – and she had a few new colours this year: lavender, maroon, purple and carrot, called respectively 'Henry Pinkerton', 'Brazilian Velvet', 'Wild Passion', and 'Mrs P.C. Chatterjee'.

The names sank into Vipul's memory; they could not but, once his mother had mentioned them; names as colourful as the petals of the flowers, and as supremely imaginative as Bitty and Tipsy for boys or Betelgeuse and Spica for stars.

On the carroty Mrs P.C. Chatterjee, who was a handsome nine inches across, a tiger wasp alighted and began its probing search for nectar; Mrs Chatterjee's colour did not change.

In the centre of the main lawn there stood the poinsettia. In season, just after the rains, it had whorls of scarlet leaves at the tips of its branches, and they looked like flowers, while the flowers themselves, pitcher-shaped, green and gargoyle-like, hid shy among the leaves. A month later the plant shed its leaves and flowers, and now it had the appearance of an outlandish sculpture, made from thongs of bare, ribbed leather.

Vipul's favourite flowers were the cosmos and the sweet pea, and to their beds he went last. He liked the cosmos for their name and for their fragility: the petals so membranous, always shivering, delighted with what the breeze whispered to them; the colours pastel; everything about them, their name and their form and their colours, redolent of a celestial grace, a lightness of spirit. And he liked the hedge of sweet pea, wrapped in its own cocoon of densely scented, cool air, the frail tendril stems clinging on to the training sticks, the flowers' colours inspired by those of sea fish, salmon and purple and pink and cerise. Vipul did not much care for the calendula, a word that sounded like medicine and a head of flower that was overcrowded with blunt, small, wormish rays.

The jeep had to make two trips to the riverbank; and there, the boat had to be rowed twice across. Vipul's mother had packed lavishly for the trip. Across the river, their car was equipped today with its occasional headgear, a luggage carrier, clamped on to its roof. At first the carrier looked like a crown on the head of the car, or like its own television antenna, and lent it some grandeur, but, soon after, when the luggage had been put on it and tied up with coarse rope, the car looked commercial and needy, like one of Jadugoda's taxis, whose luggage carriers were permanently, beggingly, fixed on their roofs.

The Fiat sank nearly to the ground under the weight of the luggage that lay on its roof and in its dickey and within its cabin; and it came nearly to a stop, even though in top gear and roaringly declutched, while ascending the steep slope that also left Rekhai's ricksha-propelling muscles sore and disarrayed; and its axle nearly broke when it grazed one of the abrupt bumps in the road; and it went very, very slowly, like a man rejected in love.

Vipul's mother had done all their packing herself. She did not trust the boys and their father to pack sensibly; she knew they would pack the wrong things, and much less than they required to, and that would create work for her in Delhi, spoiling her holiday. She packed many sets of clothes for each of them, and in particular she packed many sweaters, for she had herself knitted them, and wanted the relatives in Delhi to admire her creations. For herself she packed large numbers of saris; for saris, even though remarkably adept at keeping grime and dust at bay, needed nevertheless to be changed twice a day and – and she couldn't *repeat* a sari in Delhi. Even as she packed she kept updating a list, which at the end went:

Trunk – 1, Suitcases – 3, Holdalls – 2
Shoulder bags – 3, Water jug – 1, Vanity case – 1
Food bag (Air France bag) – 1 (journey food)
Vegetable and fruit basket – 1 (to give)
Food bag (Lufthansa bag) – 1 (to give)
Handbag (self) – 1

The vegetable and fruit basket and the Lufthansa bag contained, respectively, the produce of her garden and the results of the various metamorphoses she had wrought upon the produce; she had spent the previous three-odd weeks salting, pickling, baking, frying, and syruping. These creations she took along because her family in Delhi (poor, helpless family) could never taste garden-grown vegetables or home-made preserves: they had to buy them from the market: and she was convinced that market vegetables grew not in soil but in some other, spoiling, medium, and tasted, remarkably, of nothing.

They were travelling in a cabin – a curtained enclosure designed, thoughtfully, to accommodate precisely a family of four – in the air-conditioned coach of the Howrah–New Delhi Deluxe Express, for which they had reserved their berths more than a month in advance. Into this cabin they had now, somehow or other, crammed all the luggage, giving it the air of a minor godown. Two hours from Jadugoda Junction, they entered the forests of the Hazaribagh National Park. On the way, Vipul's attention had been held by the landscape of the coalfields giving way by and by to that of the forest. Coalfine-slurried streams gave way to nullahs whose water grew progressively clearer, sandbanks creamier. Pitheads and mounds of coal and the grey haze in the air receded; in the forest there were hills covered in browning and green, and ravines whose bouldery depths were invisibly dark. On the outskirts of the forest, near the town of Koderma, another kind of mining went on. This district was rich in mica, and just as coal lay all about, profligately unnoticed, in Jadugoda, so did specks and lumps and sheets of mica lie about here, scintillating at the train, the earth bedecked in silver spangles, partially sterling, partially pinchbeck.

The forest, like any forest worthy of its name, held promise of a glimpse of a tiger or a panther – or at least a wild boar or a python. So for the two hours that the train steamed through it, Vipul detached himself from the game of cards that the others played and sat by the window, looking out, screwing his eyes up so he shouldn't miss any of the scenery, and trying to judge whether every shadowy wriggle in the underbrush that sped by was not really a camouflaged panther. He had been through this patch of forest several times, on the way to and from Delhi, and was in the future to do so several times again, but he never once spotted anything that mattered; only indolent sunny groups of cattle being grazed and scrubbed by indolent sunny herdboys.

But there was one landmark in the middle of the forest with which Vipul kept a tryst on every journey, renewing his wonder every time he saw it. Here it came now, beyond one of the tunnels where space seemed to shrink and light to be impounded by the belly of the hill. A building – a small brick building, with two or three rooms, house-like – a ruin. The roof had fallen in in parts. But for a few straggly patches the paint had been washed away, laying open the plaster; and at many places the plaster too had peeled off, showing wounded red brick. From the fissures in its walls, trees had started to grow: peepul, guava, sal, ber. Creepers and liana clambered over the walls. In the crepuscular light around it bats and nightjars, whose home it was, flitted and swooped. There was a door to one side of the building; it was padlocked. And on the front wall, a rectangle had been cleared of the creepers and in bold yellow letters whose paint was fresh and screamed through the dusk, it said:

ABANDONED

Such a needless, desolate, fulminant announcement of the plainly evident; and whoever had had the word painted there might have felt a little like a judge making the pronouncement: Condemned to be hanged.

Vipul thought of how good it would be were the house still intact and he to live in it, in the heart of this grand green-bound solitude. Momentarily he worried about where the electric power would come from, and where the water supply, and where the books to read; but immediately he dismissed these thoughts as unedifying quibbles, and allowed himself a dream of an encounter-ridden day in the life of a jungle, partaking in some of the heroics of Kenneth Anderson's son Donald.

Near the town of Dehri-on-Sone, late in the night, came the bridge over the river Sone. Vipul could not see the bridge: they went over it; and he could not see its scaffolding, for it was dark. But he immersed himself in the sounds of the passage, the train and the bridge together producing an interweaving, rhythmical drumming and clanging and castanetting, a phantasmagoric percussive mosaic. It was not only the quality of the sound, but also its duration, that thrilled him: for it went on and on, for minutes on end, telling of the immense span of the Sone, and of the sweep of the river when inflamed, a hundred times mightier than the flooded Damodar at Khajoori.

Of the railway stations that came on the way, the Express superciliously refused to acknowledge most – it did not so much as slow down to give a passing nod – while at some, classily called Junctions, it came to rest for a spot of breath. Railway stations are paradoxes.

It is here that a town's name is most energetically proclaimed, from the fat black letters on the mustard hoardings at each end of the platform. And yet railway stations are completely anonymous, for each is very much like every other: the A.H. Wheeler book-and-magazine shops selling railway-station books and magazines, the very sweet very dilute tea hawked in earthen cones; the same crowded waiting rooms and unattended offices; the same beggars; the same hopeless stranded passengers waiting for hopelessly late trains.

As Vipul never got any idea of the large towns of Uttar Pradesh beyond the facades of their railway stations, to him it seemed that they all must be very much alike, like Benaras perhaps, which he had once visited – seething with cycle-rickshas, cattle, mendicants and silk shops. But he did associate certain towns with certain things of which specimens were available on their railway platforms: Allahabad was good for big pulpy guavas, the pulp pink as one's tongue; Mughalsarai had the airiest cane hand-fans; at Kanpur the tea was a must – it was, surprisingly, almost like home tea; and Etawah was good for nothing, but did have a lilting name.

The train was late. At twelve the next morning, they should have been at Delhi, had time and the signals been on the side of the Deluxe Express. Instead they were near Kanpur, halfway across. Although the train went fast when it did, it spent just as much time at rest as on the run, and got ever more delayed. It would stop for hours at spots that seemed even more removed from the touch of man than those that Vipul knew around Khajoori. On the Indian railways a train running late is as regular an occurrence, as naturally inexplicable, as anxiogenic, as a delayed childbirth; it obeys the same extenuating axioms of probability; no significance or moral can be read into the phenomenon. And time itself with folded hands waits for trains to arrive.

*

When they neared New Delhi station, it was close to midnight. Vipul's mother had grown anxious. Perhaps Balram mamaji, her younger brother, unable to ascertain their time of arrival (railway inquiry numbers never, but never, worked), wouldn't be there at the station to receive them. There were considerable dangers that they might have to face if this happened. The coolies were crooks. When they saw their luggage they would rejoice, for without them the family would be stranded, and then they would certainly overcharge, particularly at this vulnerable hour. They might even run off with the luggage; some were known to do so; they usually walked so very fast. Then the taxis would demand exorbitant surcharges on top of the already doctored meter readings – late-night surcharge, heavy-luggage surcharge. And then the taxi driver would take a wrong turn here and a wrong turn there (as if by mistake), and inflate the bill. The worst of it was that the driver might take them into an out-of-the-way, deserted alleyway, tell them to get out, loot them there. And then ... oh, God help at this hour, Vipul's mother said.

But nothing sensational happened, because Balram mamaji was there on the platform, with mamiji and their two-year-old son Pankaj, who was in a very sleepy state. He was soon awakened, however, by the noise of the exchanged greetings, and started to gurgle and say half-intelligible things.

They came to the house, in the old quarter of Delhi, at an eerie hour, and the silence all about, ruptured only by the few dim fluorescent lamps here and there, made it seem to Vipul that he was entering a house of recent passage, of mourning.

The foreboding was dispelled, however, as soon as they'd ascended the high-stepped staircase to the first floor, where Arjun mamaji, Vipul's mother's elder brother, was up waiting, and in whose room the lights were all on. Here though the exchanges were hushed so as not to wake up Vipul's grandparents in the room across, and everybody else downstairs. Vipul looked about the room and confirmed that it still held true to the way it existed in his memory: the walls had withdrawn at several places from the paint, leaving it hanging stiffly loose; the ceiling had the same irregular patchwork of fresh plaster slapped on to stem its leaks. Vipul felt excited to be here again, and looked forward to re-exploring the many crannies and corners of his ancestral home, as he did yearly. But that would have to wait till tomorrow, for everybody was crushed with tiredness now, the travellers and the awaiters. They immediately changed and repaired to the sitting room which, at night, doubled as a bedroom, its floor arrayed with bedsheeted mattresses, coversheets, pillows, quilts, and bolsters.

TWO

In the morning, Vipul was woken by the sound of a Paath, the recitation of the Guru Granth Sahib, the holy text of the Sikhs. There was a gurdwara close by, and the Paath was broadcast on a loudspeaker. It was loud enough to seep into Vipul's sleep, at first making him dream of having become a finely robed priest with a flowing white beard and kind eyes, and then stirring him slowly and piously from it.

It was a pleasant wakening. The Granth Sahib is recited in rather a solemn and doleful way, shot through with minor keys; it is very different from the Hindu kirtans, whose recitation is meant to, and often does, drive the reciters into a sacred fever, when the singing becomes explosive and ecstatic. The Sikh recitation, however, fills you with a quieter joy, a joy rooted in tranquillity rather than exultation.

Vipul did not open his eyes directly he awoke. He wanted first to assimilate all the other sounds that, one by one, came to his notice. Sameer was awake, and was talking excitedly to mamiji about the beating of Chuvvania. His mother was talking to Balram mamaji, and, as is mandatory for an elder sister, was heaping censure on him, telling him off for not having had his tooth extracted when he should, for having let his hair grow too long, for not having got the jangla strengthened, for being too scrupulous in his business dealings. His father and Arjun mamaji were taking stock of more substantial and ponderous things: the price of property in various quarters of Delhi, the gathering powers of Sanjay Gandhi and his philosophy of political control. Little Pankaj, called Pinky, was playing with papaji, Vipul's grandfather, who spoke to him of things and in words that Pankaj was meant to but did not understand. Vipul could sense that everyone except Arjun mamaji and his father (both of whom sat on chairs) was on the floor: sitting or lying or reclining against the sofa. He couldn't hear his grandmother, who must be in the kitchen, unobtrusive and private and preparative, as ever.

When he opened his eyes Balram mamaji said, 'He's got up, he's got up,' in a celebratory way, as though there had been some fear amidst them that he might never arise. 'Come here,' he said, extending one leg and tickling Vipul's his waist with his toes. 'You haven't come to Delhi just to sleep.'

Vipul got up, and went straight to where Balram mamaji lay, his head propped up by a satin-wrapped bolster. Balram mamaji said, 'A kiss.' He gave one to Vipul on his forehead, and received one from him on his cheek. Arjun mamaji said, 'What about me?' 'Later,' Vipul said. 'Pig,' Arjun mamaji said. Vipul crept into Balram mamaji's quilt, by his side, and, lying there, put his head on his uncle's chest. Mamaji moved a hand over his face. His hand felt like cardboard. It was a large, reassuring hand, protective like his mother's arm over him.

Later, when Balram mamaji was about to have a bath, the hair at the back of his head crushed and mangled where it had pressed against the bolster, Vipul, touching him on his arms, said, 'Mamaji, show me your muscles.'

Balram mamaji rolled up his sweater's sleeve over his left arm, and flexed it. His biceps rolled up into an unquiet ball of flesh that caught the light and bounced and wobbled it about.

'Look,' mamaji said. Vipul looked at it from below. His lips curved downward in awe. Mamaji looked at it himself, down his nose. He smiled. It was the sort of smile that might come to the face of a writer who is considering a book of his that has been successful; the smile retrospective and slight, but immeasurably proud, telling of the smileless days and years spent in gestating, grooming, fostering the finished work. The flesh is at least as difficult to work into any kind of excellence of shape as is a product of the mind, and Balram mamaji had accomplished a tremendous working of the flesh.

Vipul felt it would be a great entertainment to set up a fight between Hari the boatman and Balram mamaji. He said, 'But maybe you can't beat Hari.'

It worked. 'Who's this Hari?' mamaji said, his chest expanding.

So Vipul told him about Hari's muscles from all the rowing.

Mamaji's chest expanded further. 'Bitty,' he said, 'bring me all the Haris in the world together, and just see how one, just one blow from this hand' – here he clenched his fist – 'will knock their thirty-twos back into their throats.' And he gave the air a sharp uppercut.

'Show your muscle here,' Vipul said, wanting to feel the shining ball on his arm.

Balram mamaji sat on his haunches. Vipul poked the muscle. His finger buckled; the muscle did not dent. Stone, simply stone.

'Hit it,' mamaji said.

Vipul boxed it. His knuckles hurt; the muscle yielded not a jot; it gave back better than it received.

'Harder,' mamaji said.

Harder.

'Harder, come on. Aren't you a tiger?'

Vipul took a step back, clasped his hands in a double fist, and brought the fist down on the muscle from behind his back, like a hammer. No effect.

He was beginning to feel frustrated and cheated by this muscle, this ball of stone parading as flesh. He said, 'Wait a few years, mamaji, and then I'll ask you to box *my* muscles.'

Balram mamaji said, 'That's my tiger!' and, standing up, lifted him up in his arms. Then he threw Vipul in the air, and caught him.

'Higher,' Vipul said, the same charges of thrill trickling through his groin as when Lakhan massaged him.

While mamaji bathed, Vipul took a walk around the house to see if anything had changed – inspectingly, like Pinki didi's siblings on their holidays in Khajoori. The house was like a stack of doughnuts, each floor a ring. Only the annulus of each doughnut was roofed, and had rooms; in the centre, the large hollow area formed a courtyard on the ground floor and was empty sun-letting space above. On the roof of the house, the central hollow was ringed by a parapet of brickwork, but on the first floor, where the family stayed, there was only the jangla, a two-foot-high latticeworked fence wrought from thin iron, very flimsy, frailly embedded, so that if you prodded it it swayed, and if you were to lean on it you, and it, would crash down into the courtyard on the ground floor, becoming dear to the gods. Vipul prodded it; it swayed; Vipul was satisfied that things in the house were still in order.

A few days after Vipul and Sameer arrived, their cousins from Bombay turned up, in a train that arrived on time.

These cousins, Karan, a boy, and Nikita, a girl, were about the same age as Vipul and Sameer, and intimidating. They were intimidating because they were from Bombay; and because they knew so well what it meant to be from there.

They played their parts. They were smart, and said crisp things, using the smart language of the streets of Bombay, a kind of Hindi that had been made laconic and bold, so that it always sounded as though some hurried business transaction were taking place, even if all you were engaging in was light chitchat. All superfluities had been whittled away, and only the core of any expression had been retained, often cryptic. Thus if they meant to say 'How are you?', they said, 'What!'; or if they wanted to say, 'I am fine', they said, 'Enough!'; and if they wanted to make a speech, they could not, because there were never enough words to make it with.

And the things they talked about, and the things they were asked! Vipul and Sameer were asked only about school, and what subjects they liked best, and what hobbies they had; for no one was interested in accounts of their games at the riverside or their desultory, timeless pursuits during power cuts or about the lives of Khajoori's people.

But Karan and Nikita could hold everybody spellbound with accounts of, merely, the things that kept happening to them, never needing to recount what they themselves did.

They talked, for instance, of the film stars whom they had happened upon, right out of the void. 'I almost *touched* Rekha, you know, she was standing there just beside me in the shop – just like that, shopping, like any other, any *ordinary* person,' Nikita said. And everybody considered Nikita in great envy and in some disbelief and with much respect, as if she were one of God's Chosen – for to whom else could epiphanies so theatrical as this present themselves, just like that, on a perfectly ordinary day?

Or they retailed the latest news on the smuggling dons of Bombay (how they operated, where they lived, what they were *really* like, as persons, in private, with their families – yes, just like you and I), or of the film shootings they had been to, or of the latest, tallest building to come up at Nariman Point. Up to the point of their arrival Vipul had thought Delhi to be an impressive place, but these cousins made the city seem derisory, saying that it was – *compared* to Bombay, of course –

a village; following which Vipul was again forced to consider where, in that case, Jadugoda ranked, compared to Bombay – a mud hut? – and what about Khajoori? – ah, Khajoori, unmapped, unacknowledged Khajoori was as distant and immaterial and expendable to the world as the passing flicker of a shooting star, just a speck of coal dust. But for the fact that Vipul lived there, there seemed to be no compelling reason for Khajoori to exist. And he sensed that here in Delhi he was perhaps the 'local', the one whose prerogative, and decreed limit, it was to listen in wonder and puzzlement; to only receive, for he really had nothing of note to offer. And to try and think of the consequence to the universe of the land beyond Khajoori, and of its inhabitants – antemodern, ante-industrial, antedated – was, surely, useless.

In the evening Balram mamaji said to the children, arrayed around a carrom board that produced miniature pistol-shot noises from its walls, 'Who wants to have meat tonight?'

'I,' they all said, except Karan, who said, 'Fish! Fish!'

Balram mamaji said, 'Fish for Kuku some other day. Come on. We'll get the meat.'

'Two minutes. After this game,' Sameer said.

'Let me play, then,' Balram mamaji said, and then to Vipul, for he was the youngest, 'Come on, Bitty, be my vice captain.'

Vipul was glad to do this, and leaned on Balram mamaji's back, arms around his neck, looking over his shoulder, as he played.

Balram mamaji was a fair player of carrom, and he supplemented his skill at the sport with a virtuoso sleight. While everybody looked earnestly at the board, at the course of the striker on its way to cannoning a smaller disc, stared at it as at a map difficult to read, Balram mamaji slid one small disc, which lay close to him and close to a pocket, into the pocket with a deft, incidental, silken wave of his hand, as if he were merely invoking upon the board a gentle blessing. Vipul saw this, and nudged mamaji's neck with his arm and laughed aloud within.

But the next time mamaji did this Nikita caught sight of it, and with eyes as wide as the others' became when she told them about having almost touched the very popular film star, she said, '*So! Cheating! Mamaji!*'

Balram mamaji put his large hand on the carrom board and swept all the discs to one side. 'Game's over,' he said. They protested and boxed him on his muscles, and he led them down to the car.

They drove to a road that curved through an old section of the city and had exclusively two kinds of shops at its margins: rubber-tyre shops on one, butchers' on the other.

Balram mamaji sang as he drove. To sing as you drive in old Delhi – that is, to sing in tune and to drive fluidly – is to perform a feat of the most stellar control and equipoise. Every faculty of yours must be trained and busy: your hands on the steering wheel and gear shift; your feet on the pedals, your eyes and ears on the road, your mind juggling with all these simultaneously, maintaining that all-important poise, so that nothing ruffles you into either braking or accelerating too hard or swerving too much, either in your driving or in your singing. Balram mamaji drove with as much lilt as he sang, the inflexions and changes of key in his voice animating the sways and the runs of the car.

Indeed to drive fluidly in Old Delhi traffic, even when you are not singing, is in itself a commendable feat, for nobody else seems to be of a mind to allow you to do so. Moving things of any description – vehicles, people, animals: two-legged and four-legged, two-wheeled and three-wheeled and four-wheeled – will stall in front of you; they will creep up from behind and cut sharply across; they will emerge at great speed from non-existent bylanes; they will do all kinds of unforeseeable things calculated to fray your nerves to a hash.

Through all this Balram mamaji sang:

Naache man mora,
Magan tikk-da-dheegi-dheegi;
Badara ghir aaye,
Rut hai bheegi-bheegi...

That is (quite unfittingly for the month of deep winter he was singing it in):

My soul dances,
Ecstatic, tikk-da-dheegi-dheegi;
Clouds amass over,
The air's moist, oh so moist...

And through the chemistry of some subliminal, vivid association that the song touched off in his brain, Vipul imagined a peacock, its fan spread aloft, dancing in rapid stationary steps to the rhythm of the song – perhaps also singing the song – its beak directed upward, scenting the heady moistness in the air, plunging into ecstasy.

They were on the side of the rubber-tyre shops. To get to the other side, the side of the meat shops, the car had to be slinked through a small gap in the road's divider. There was a rush of oncoming traffic on the opposite side; but although Balram mamaji slowed the car down, he did not pause while he turned. Inch by inch he infiltrated into the other side: the traffic there had to take care of itself. It glided in a smooth arc, first around the car's front when it had just nosed into the road, and then, when it stood across the road in the middle, around it on both sides, in neat streamlines that diverged and then converged, like currents of air over an aerofoil.

At the butcher's, entire skinned headless goats hung by their ankles from a wooden beam at the front of the shop, their arms dangling straight down in inverted surrender, vanquished, it would seem, by the armies of houseflies that, between bouts of hovering, lovemaking and preening, feasted on them. And at the places where the goats had been fattest when alive, they were now slimmest, their bellies gutted. Their paws had been dehooved; thus abbreviated, they looked like the hands and feet of lepers.

Balram mamaji said to the butcher, 'No useless pieces today, miyan. I have to buy two whole kilos. Each and every piece must be good.'

The butcher said, 'Have I ever given you bad meat?'

'No, but don't today, either.'

'So you have guests?'

'Don't you see these children?' mamaji said.

'I see, I see. Who are they?'

'These are my nephews and my niece. My sisters have come home,' he said, and Vipul was flattered to discern a note of something like pride in Balram mamaji's voice when he said this.

'I see. Where have they come from?'

'These two, Kuku and Nini,' Balram mamaji said, patting Karan and Nikita on the head, 'are from Bombay.' ('Wah, wah,' the impressed butcher said.) 'And these two, Bittu and Bitty' – here he patted Sameer and Vipul – 'are from Khajoori.'

'From Bombay and from?'

'What do you cook your food on?'

'Why?'

'What is it, tell me?'

'Fire.'

'No, no. Think further.'

'Flames.'

'Arey, miyan, you're off your game today! Okay, what sends up the fire and flames?'

'Coal.'

'Coal!'

'Coal.'

'Yes! And your coal comes from Khajoori!' mamaji said, triumphantly, as though he had clinched an involved argument.

'I see, I see,' the butcher said, and laughed weakly, as though *he* had just forfeited the involved argument; and Balram mamaji seemed, finally, very pleased to have offered this piece of information to the butcher, and the butcher seemed very pleased to have received it, the name of the place where his coal came from, and so he started carving the meat caringly and attentively, giving the best of it to Balram mamaji.

Papaji washed the meat, running tap water over it and repeatedly squeezing and rubbing the pieces with his fingers with a sensuality that, in many other contexts, would have been construed as wanton. He wasn't partial to cooking in the kitchen; he preferred the courtyard, where he stoked a small iron fire-pot the size of a stool. He had primed the fire-pot earlier with wood fire, and now only thin wisps of woodsmoke rose from it. On its surface there was a patchwork of deep black and dancing orange, made by the coal and its trickles of flame. He sat on a cot beside the furnace, and stoked it. Then he set on it the kadhai, into which he poured groundnut oil. When the oil was hot, which he tested by sacrificing a shred of onion in it, which shrank and crisped into a dark writhing squiggle, he dropped into it a mixture of whole spices: black pepper pods, fat black as well as thin green cardamoms, cinnamon sticks, cloves, bay leaves. In a minute the spices, turgid with oil, turned dark, and swelled, and some of them popped, and let loose their entrapped flavours. Then he added a fistful of pounded ginger and garlic and green chilli, and a little later, when these had tanned, onion and tomato and salt and curd; and then an ineffable compound aroma arose, of the kind which only an eater of mutton curry will know, and will, like me, be unable adequately to describe, except to say that it reminds him of goats, of their ribs and of the marrow in their bones, and of the fragrant Gobindobhog or the Basmati rice, which make to the curry the perfect foils. All this time papaji stirred the masala, unbrokenly and tenderly, and finally slid the meat in along with some powdered turmeric and coriander. The next half hour he spent in roasting the meat, coaxing it to drink of the juice of the spices.

Between his fingers papaji held a cigarette, of which he never let go. His fingers were as habituated to pressing a cigarette between them as his lungs were to soaking up its smoke. Every now and then, when he drew a determined puff, the smoke, which between puffs was forever escaping in sinuous fugitive trails from the red tip of the cigarette, would be sucked back in, drawn through the tobacco, and poured down papaji's airways. And the cigarette smoke seemed to contain the vaporous buds of papaji's thoughts. Every time he inhaled it, he assimilated these buds; which then effloresced in his mind, giving birth to utterances ruminative and apt and wise:

'A cardamom must turn the colour of rust, and no darker.'

'Balram has bought good meat. A young, tender goat.'

'To prevent sticking, water. Not too much, not too dry.'

'Stir and stir and stir. Don't stir for a moment, and give the meat to the dogs.'

'Bad cinnamon. Crumbling to dust. The strongest sticks the idiots export.'

After the meat had been cooked, everyone gathered in the drawing room for drinks.

Balram mamaji went to the dressing-and-almirah room where, rather than in the drawing room, he kept his stock of spirits. From there he brought out a bottle each of rum, whisky, and gin, and also one of Coca-Cola, to mix the rum with, for the ladies. The whisky was called Aristocrat, the rum, Old Monk Very Old Vatted XXX, and the gin, Napoleon Dry. Like good luck charms, the English names of these Indian spirits had never been discarded by their distillers. And had they ever done so, and replaced them with equivalent Indian names, perhaps Chitragupta Gin or Nawabzada Whisky or Pandit Rum, one was certain that the spirits' fermentation would somewhere get perverted, and they would start then to taste of mustard oil and turmeric and tamarind.

Balram mamaji measured out the drinks into fine glasses whose surfaces were etched into patterns of leaves and grapes. A finger's breadth each for the ladies, two fingers' breadths for the men. He didn't use his fingers; his measures were spot-on from vast experience.

From the fridge Balram mamaji took out bottles of soda water, unimaginatively called Mister Fiz, with Mr Fiz's jolly clownish head imprinted on the bottles' ribs.

Then he poured the soda, from a small height, the way Vipul poured milk that was too hot to cool it down. This brought a happy froth to the surface of the drink, and mamaji said, 'Good soda.' He liked soda; without soda whisky was not whisky, he said; and with good soda Aristocrat emulated, almost, Johnnie Walker Scotch. A soda's merit was measured by how fulminantly it caused the whisky to froth. And as the smaller or the larger heads of froth formed with each falling taper of soda he declared, 'Bad soda,' or 'Good soda,' rather as one would laud or admonish a performing pet: 'Bad dog, Rover'; 'Good dog, Rover.'

Vipul helped Balram mamaji carry the drinks to the drawing room; and from the glass of each person to whom he handed it he received the inaugural sip.

If thought were contained in the smoke of papaji's cigarettes, then smiles lurked unseen, waiting to spring, in the amber, golden, and black drinks. By the time two or three sips had worked their way into their skins, everybody's faces loosened, and the lines and dents left by the day's business thinned away. Then the liquid worked on their eyes, which became vague, and at the corners of their lips, giving rise to smiles, smiles that were born not of satisfaction, nor of contentment, nor yet of pleasure, but just of grace, of a moment easily lived.

But in the smiles of Vipul's mother and his mamiji there trembled also the extra curve of thrill: thrill at the camouflaged drink – the drink camouflaged from no one but themselves, but thrilling still, as though in fact the world were watching, and were each moment being fooled.

They talked of things that a reassembled family must: common memories: the glue that kept them coherent, that kept them from losing affection. Vipul and Sameer reminisced the gurgly sounds that little Pankaj used to make a year ago. Karan and Nikita reminded Sameer that he had been dumb up to the age of two and a half, and Vipul that he could never repeat 'road rolling roller' without lapsing into a skein of lo's. Balram mamaji said that Kuku and Nini had better remember that they had been told to their faces by their music teacher that it would be easier for him to teach a stone to sing.

Vipul's mother said that Balram mamaji had needlessly wasted his childhood scaring and trapping pigeons on the roof, only to let them go later.

Arjun mamaji said that Vipul's mother had once been so frightened when he leapt at her from behind a door that she had fainted.

And so they reminisced, in an age-wise chain of arrows, each person remembered by somebody just elder; but the chain could not be looped: there was no one that little Pankaj could reminisce about, and no one could reminisce about papaji. They were the lonely ones, one with nothing to offer, the other with nothing to receive.

The talk moved on to other relatives, and varied in temper from gossip to evaluation to analysis to condemnation, as each merited. Then, towards the time for dinner, it came, inevitably, to a sadness in the family, a worrisome canker. It was an uncle of Vipul's mother's; one who had become very close to them once upon a time when he had lived with them for three years in the middle of a difficult phase when neither degrees nor jobs seemed to attract themselves to him. He was like another brother. They did not call him 'chacha', as they should have lineally, but 'praji', or elder brother. He was now host to a condition. It had already destroyed his sense of physical balance, and was now gnawing into that of his mind. He had become toddling and fall-prone, and insistent and fussy; unmanageable. His wife, Savita bhabhiji, had turned against him. They were full of dismay at both these facts: his recalcitrance, her treachery. And it was unclear as to who was really at fault.

'She even rains on him, quite badly, but he doesn't listen,' Balram mamaji said.

'She shouldn't rain on him so much. One has to stand by one's husband.'

'But what can she do? It appears he has become like a child.'

'Poor praji.'

'And poor Savita bhabhiji.'

'They would have been better off had one of their children stayed with them.'

'Just doesn't happen these days. Sons go away for jobs, daughters to their in-laws.'

'One of them should call them over to stay with them.'

'But who cares, in the days of now? Everybody is rapt in their own existence.'

'It was not so in the old times.'

On this everybody agreed.

One of the particular reasons that Vipul liked being in Delhi was that he could watch television there. Television in his mind had the same associations as the Qutab Minar or foreign cars: an exotic vision, a blossom of technology, something that he could recount to an agog audience when he returned to Khajoori, where he would hold briefly the status Nini and Kuku held here in Delhi.

Television was broadcast in black-and-white, and was received on television sets, whose manufacture was still in its corrective stages, in grey-and-light-grey or bluish-and-cream. Images were indistinct, as though everything had been shot through obscuring clouds of mist. Crowds of small electric sparks flew about the screen. And on the screen the images did strange acrobatic things: they rolled up or down or sideways, the same image plucked and supplied inexhaustibly from an infinite reel at one end of the screen; or they shifted to one side, leaving half the screen blank; or they split up into two identical smaller images, like replicating bacteria. They flickered; they went and came; very often they vanished, and a notice appeared on the screen, handwritten and tortured, 'Regrets for the Interruption'. It required concentration and stamina to watch television. It was not a way to relax: it was like reading a newspaper with microscopic print – a hastily, carelessly written newspaper with smudged microscopic print.

Vipul's grandfather was a strong man and he could concentrate, as he did when he cooked meat, or read clean through a James Hadley Chase book. If the television programmes were to start at six in the evening, papaji would switch the set on at a quarter to six. During this time he would listen to the signature tune, a maudlin set of notes serenading a happy logo of geometric patterns and uncertain significance that included, in a corner, the face of a clock counting down to six. From this time until the close of the telecast, at eleven, when the screen went suddenly bright and the loudspeaker hissed and sizzled frenziedly, as though the machine had suffered a rabid fit, papaji would see each programme faithfully through, sitting in a nylon-stringed chair at a cosy distance, inhaling his filterless cigarettes. He was like a parent watching a child perform, periodically nodding his approval and encouragement, periodically shaking his head in mild rebuke, or simply marvelling, open-mouthed, at the prodigy that the child was turning out to be.

And with unflagging interest he watched programmes that dealt with the particularities of existence, such as the elaborate, half-technical tips on agricultural methods, or documentaries, sonorous and bleak, on dams recently put up; and programmes that engaged the fancy: song sequences from Hindi films, travelogues imported from American companies, tribal dances recreated on clumsy, allegorical sets.

Late one evening, when everybody else had gone out and only Vipul had stayed on with papaji to listen to his stories, there started a programme – the last programme of the day – on the International Film Festival that was being held in Delhi. In the first part of the programme there were interviews with film directors and actors, and abstruse panel discussions on abstruse films.

Then for the second part it was announced that a clip would be shown from one of the festival films. The name of the film appeared on the screen, a jungle of inextricable consonants, beneath which it said: '(Czechoslovakia)'. The clip started with the vision of two distant human figures silhouetted on a dreamy meadowy horizon. The figures walked towards the watcher. One became a woman and the other a man. Both were young. The man wore shabby jeans, a large-collared shirt, long hair. The woman wore a short flared frock, floral, whose hem rose and fell as she walked. She had loose fair hair down to her shoulder blades. They walked hand in hand. They were silent, their eyes cast down in thought. They approached, then loomed large over, and then passed by, the watcher. For a second the screen was replete with the woman's breasts. When the watcher turned to follow them, their backs were seen receding into a sparse wood.

There, among the trees, the two stopped. They held each other by the waist, and kissed with their lips. After a while they disentangled, except to continue to hold hands. They walked on, their steps lighter. The watcher saw them now from the front, now from the back, now from the side. Again they stopped. This time they engaged their lips in an agitated moulding and remoulding, moved their mouths about, glued themselves to each other over the rest of their bodies. Then again they disentangled, and walked hand in hand a little longer. They were silent still, their steps lighter still.

When next they stopped the man stared into the woman's eyes, questioning, proposing. Then he let himself down on his knees. Bending, he grasped the woman's calves. He kissed her shins and her knees. The woman, standing stiff, looked up at the branches of a tree. The man moved his hands and his face upward. There he rubbed her thighs, moved his mouth over them. Vipul saw that a woman's thighs are soft: the man's lips and hands sank into spongy tissue.

Papaji continued to look at the screen, forgetting his filterless cigarette for a while. Vipul picked up a magazine just in case he needed to pretend to be elsewhere engrossed.

The man spent some time on the thighs of the woman. He seemed to mull upon them in examination. The woman seemed to be suffering no awkwardness, and the man no qualms. He moved still further up her thighs, slowly, tantalizingly. The inevitable, the unimaginable, happened. His face went underneath the flare of her short frock in front, his hands underneath it at the back. The surface of the frock moved this way and that. He seemed to be searching for something in the darkness there. Then a small lacy garment fell along the woman's legs and rested on her ankles. The woman looked down at the man's neck. Her hands hung at her sides. They were inert, paralysed by the moment. A flower fell from somewhere above her and came to rest on her shoulder. The man spent an unsettlingly long time in that position.

Vipul glanced at papaji. Papaji stared unflinchingly on. Did papaji, Vipul thought, feel the same consternation as he? Was he paralysed by this vision just as the woman was by the actions of the man? Did papaji also think, giddily and wordlessly: Who are this man and woman? Are they husband and wife? Even so! Where is their shame? Where is the *woman's* shame? Does she not have parents who might be seeing this now, or brothers or sisters? Would she have this done to her by anybody at all, and be watched by the whole world thus? The temerity, the audacity, the abandon of it!

Now the man's face and hands resurfaced – and continued upward. On the way he kissed the woman's belly and her breasts and her neck. His lips reached hers again. Then he put one hand on a breast, and brought the other down to the woman's hips. Both hands moved exploringly, coaxingly, reminding Vipul of the way papaji's hands moved when ushering the masala into the meat.

There they remained, this anonymous man and woman in this improbable arrangement, among the trees and long grass and flowers; all of these, and the woman's probably colourful frock and her probably colourful lacy garment about her ankles, watched in unconfiding black-and-white; the man and woman still as placid as the trees among them and the grass below; the only sound the crackles of the white electric sparks that shot about the screen.

The clip ended. Immediately a Doordarshan announcer announced, quite baldly, as though nothing out of the ordinary whatsoever had happened over the last few minutes, or at any rate as though she hadn't herself witnessed any such errantry (What an actress! Vipul thought), that it was time for closing down, that they would meet again early next morning, and till then she supplicated their leave, her hands in a namaste; following which the screen was washed white and the speaker erupted into its fitful retiring noise.

Papaji rose from his chair and equally baldly switched the television off and said to Vipul that if he was sleepy he should go to bed now;

and Vipul said yes he would, though he was certain that he would not, and that he would lie awake some way into the night considering the shamelessness, so much more flagrant than Sushma didi's, of the people of Czechoslovakia.

And so Vipul learnt his first stark and enlightening lesson on the motions of sex, in the mute, stupefied company of himself and his grandfather; and he thought he had some idea now of what purpose there might be to the venereal hair that Father Rocqueforte had once, effulgently, mentioned.

A WINTER MEMORABILE

In and around Delhi, there lived many other relatives of Vipul's, on both his mother's side and his father's. Often the family would go about on their own, visiting them. They would hire an auto-ricksha, which was also known as a three-wheeler (making it seem uniquely possessed of this trait). Autos, for Vipul, were to Delhi's soul as elemental as television, foreign cars, and second-hand books on the hurricane-lamped pavements. They reminded him of the severed heads of dragonflies. At front they had the same roundly convex shape, and rearward they were likewise abrupt and flat. Low down at the front of the autos, there was a small mudguard, and underneath that a small tyre, always busy and nibbling, like a dragonfly's mouthparts. The autos, moreover, moved in the same erratic way: one could never tell when and to which direction they would sharply turn, and they involved themselves in a large fraction of Delhi's road accidents.

These roads were host also to multitudes of another instrument of transport that Khajoori's roads had not yet had the privilege to host: the motor scooter, also called the two-wheeler (making it seem uniquely possessed of *this* trait). This machine had neither the dignity of a motorcycle nor the balance of a three-wheeler, and it was uncouth and excitable. If the auto was a dragonfly, then the scooter was a bee, rushing about with precipitate accelerations and retardations, adamant in getting its way, squeezing through other traffic like noodles snaking through a colander. And what a horn it had. You would place the sound that it made somewhere between the caw of a crow and the bleat of a goat, except that it was more raucous than the former and more importunate than the latter, belligerently beggarly.

In the autos they visited near and distant relatives, and relatives who lived in near and distant colonies. They visited the families of Vipul's father's brothers and sisters; they visited Vipul's mother's cousins and their families, and cousin-aunts, and cousin-uncles. There were all kinds of relatives, galactic in their variety: relatives who fussed over them all; relatives who were level-headed and even somewhat cool; relatives to whom they did not feel very close but who, unnervingly, waxed intimate towards them; relatives who would not be content until they had overfed them to enteric giddiness; relatives who were too poor to offer 'cold drinks' like Fanta and Coca-Cola and who made for them corrosive squashes instead; relatives who were so rich that they offered fresh fruit juice; relatives who invited them to stay; relatives, far-removed, who threatened to visit them uninvited in Khajoori.

When the holidays were half over, they, along with the families of all of Vipul's father's brothers and sisters, moved on to Punjab, to the town of Barnala, where Vipul's paternal grandparents lived.

The composition of the cousins on Vipul's father's side was unimodal. Some genetic implausibility had brought itself to bear upon the reproductive processes in all the couples – so that all the brothers had imposed maleness, alone, upon their wives' ova, and all the sisters' ova had accepted maleness, alone, from their husbands – and so all the cousins were boys.

The bus went through the countrysides of Haryana and Punjab, where short patches of farmland alternated with numerous small towns and cities. In Punjab, the towns had a dusty, afternoonish look about them. Their skylines were coarsely ragged, and profusely, irregularly openworked with plexuses of television antennae. Vipul had never seen so many antennae in so little space before, not even in Delhi. They suggested that the people of Punjab had lately changed from rustic and agrarian to technical and informed. But the people themselves, on the streets of the towns and cities, belied this impression. They moved in still-rustic ways: on bicycles, cycle-rickshas, tractors, perhaps mopeds and scooters; there were very few auto-rickshas or cars. The men had about them a pre-urban warlike look, not simply because they were built massively and dressed in kurtas and lungis and turbans, and were fiercely moustached and bearded, but because many of them carried, slung on their backs, rifles as carelessly as one might carry a comb in one's pocket. And the language that they spoke was fertile with earthy, often ingenious abuse, and if you were at a bus stop and overheard a conversation between two ten-year-old boys you blanched, feeling untutored, callow.

Vipul compared these, the locals of the Punjab, with the reclusive and enervated species around Khajoori, and felt that if, following the example of the USA and the USSR, the maps of Punjab and Bihar were ever to rise to battle, the latter must in a minute be torn to shreds and scattered about in the oceans, making there a forlorn archipelago.

At the bus stops, vendors climbed into the buses to sell things of all kinds. They sold churan, a sour powdery mixture of herbs and spices that could be taken only a pinch at a time and could make your stomach rumble if you over-pinched; they sold rat poison; they sold vitalizing tablets in bottles which carried labels bearing pictures of bow-limbed wrestlers; they sold sweets – Punjabi sweets, most of them stony and brittle, composed of a base of unrefined jaggery and impregnated with puffed rice or groundnuts or sesame seeds, very different from the fleshy, soft sweets of the rest of northern India; they sold fountain pens: the newest ones had transparent fuselages in which the ink shook and slid and shone; they sold lime- and sandalwood-scented combs that, after a brush or two with well-oiled hair, started to reek fetidly; they sold bottles of a locally made aerated drink, each having an unexplained sphere of glass, coloured indigo, floating in it; they sold peacock feathers for students to place in textbooks, for luck. At the bus stops the bus became a market inverted: here the shoppers sat in their seats, while the goods travelled up and down, hunting custom. If you sat in a bus for half an hour at a major stop, such as that in Ludhiana, you could do your weekly shopping there.

The hawkers were possessed of an unpunctuated, snowballing loquacity. They harangued from the time they got on the bus until the time they got off, pitching their goods with high passion. But before and after this, on the roads, they could be seen walking in stark, sullen silence; the world outside a bus was too loud for them, and there they could not compete; and there their goods, it would seem, turned spitefully mediocre.

The man who hawked churan said:

'My brothers and sisters, and dear children, give me just a minute of your time. First I'll tell you who I am. My name is Satnam, of village Nijjaran, district Jullunder. Now look at what I have in my hand. On the surface, it's just an ordinary bottle. But inside, there is sheer magic. Prem Teer churan. The one in a thousand churan. Of course you may all be eating churan every day. You will rightly ask me what is special about this one. So listen. One, it's better than the others. Two. It's cheaper than the others. Three. It's tastier than the others. Now let me tell you the price. For this entire bottle of fifty grams, one rupee. Just *one rupee*, my dear brothers and sisters. Now in the shops the churan is available for no less than one and a half rupees. Even the label on the bottle says that price. To believe me, you must look at it. Here, papaji (he said to an elderly man sitting near him); here, behenji (to a 'sister' further down in the bus), look at it, satisfy yourself. Of course you may wonder how I make a living by buying churan for one and a half rupees and selling it for one. Dear folk, let some secrets remain secrets. Now the second point. I told you that this churan is better than the others. Try it, taste it with your own tongues. Take a pinch. You will find clearly the taste of anaar seeds, a great cure for indigestion. There are dozens of other ingredients which I can't reveal. Now most other churans in fact make your indigestion worse. That is because they are made by amateurs, for quick profit. But Prem Teer churan is made by Vaid Hukum Chandji. Moga's world-famous Vaid Hukum Chandji, brothers and sisters, who knows all there is to know about the human body. Yes, yes, behenji, taste it, there's no charge for tasting it.

'Prem Teer churan, brothers and sisters, cheap as cheap should be, tasty as tasty should be, effective as effective should be. Banish indigestion, sleep restfully at night, dream nice dreams, live well, eat as much ghee and butter and pickle as you wish, without fear – Prem Teer churan is there to digest everything for you, from vegetable to stone.'

They reached Barnala early evening. They identified half the heavy luggage on the roof of the bus as theirs, and hired ten cycle-rickshas to carry them and their luggage home.

Barnala was a village on the verge of, but for some years vacillating on, passing into a town. There were buildings enough in it for the appearance of a town, but the odour that garnished its breezes gave it away, for instead of petrol smoke you smelled dung: camel and horse and mule dung; wood-wheeled carts were still the mode of freight. And the smell of dung was there off the streets too, and it gave away the houses, for although they looked in their construction, their solidity, like town houses, people kept cattle in them, just as they would in a village.

For this reason Barnala seemed to Vipul a place planted firmly in the native soil. Khajoori and its surrounding colliery area, with its coal-blown, mined look, gave you the impression of being a part of the mineral underground, while Delhi, with its big-city variousness and its mess of concerns, was simply elsewhere, a place apart from the land.

Vipul's grandparent's house was a townhouse of the village type. It was too spacious for the two of them, so they had rented out some of the ground floor, at the back, to a family that sent froth-fresh milk up to them at five-thirty every morning. It was built to the same plan as the house in Delhi: hollow in the middle, courtyards everywhere, the rooms occupying fractional space. But it was much more solid, the paint stuck tight on to its walls and ceilings, and there were no ill-grounded structures at strategic points that would collapse under your weight.

Barnala was colder than Delhi. In the mornings, when they woke, everybody moved to the kitchen. There was no other place warm enough. Group by group they went there, shivering, after brushing their teeth, and warmed themselves before the coal fire and had breakfast there. Vipul's holiday breakfast here was cornflakes in hot milk, in a long brass tumbler. The flakes, as soon as they touched the milk, squirmed and folded, like the rainy-season millipedes when lynched by Vipul with pebbles, then lost their crinkles and swelled, and congealed with each other to form a pulpy yellow suspension in the milk. This Vipul half ate, half drank.

Bibiji, his grandmother, sat on a pattra, a wooden plinth a couple of inches high, and in front of her, she rolled perfectly round chapatis for lunch. It is not impossible to roll a perfectly round chapati if you are given sufficient time and freedom of movement to do so; but to roll it without once lifting the roller from the slab, in a few unmeditated instants, is a feat. Bibiji could do this with every chapati. The ball of wheat dough under her roller acquired a volition of its own, for as she rolled, it kept rotating even as it kept flattening, so that it seemed to waltz itself into a roundness with the same inanimate aestheticism which gets scattered iron filings to arrange themselves about a magnet into perfect symmetrical arcs.

Bibiji enjoyed being teased. One of the boys would ask her, 'Bibiji, are you in love with Dharmendra?'

Bibiji, who never saw films, but knew about the heroes in them, would ease herself into a laugh, and all her flesh-rich rounded parts would shake a little.

But she laughed the most when Sameer asked her, 'Bibiji, tell us about all the boyfriends you had as a girl.'

Then there was no controlling her.

'Boyfriends!' she said. 'Boyfriends!' The words made her breathless and coughy with laughter. Her hilarity was such that you would have thought she was laughing at another, for who could laugh so unmindfully at oneself? Now her body heaved and fell and heaved and fell massively with each puff of laughter, and if her flesh could have made sounds, it would have creaked and jangled.

'Boyfriends!' she kept repeating, as though she had never been young and unpockmarked; as though she had been born as she was now, toothless and gnarled and called 'bibiji', and had taken immediately to her function in life, casting her spell on the self-rolling, self-circling chapatis. It seemed then to Vipul that even to try to think of her as a girl was an affront to her seasoned grace and mirth.

In the afternoons, after lunch, everyone drifted into the courtyard, where a number of cots were laid out. Here they all sat and reclined, each moulding themselves to their idea of greatest comfort, so that at any instant the family would have looked like a gallery of sculptures depicting the convolutional possibilities of the human form. Some sat stiff, as though on a straight chair. One sat cross-legged. One sat with one leg indrawn and the other extended. One reclined, her torso raised on an elbow. One lay flat as a corpse, on her back, palms joined under her head. One sat with his legs forming a hairpin, angled over to one side, the kind of posture girls are meant to adopt when modesty is to prevail.

The winter sun, considerately distant, quietly warm, shone equally on them. It bathed the courtyard white, and it tinged each skin with an underglow of light, so that brown became sepia, sepia cream, and cream bleached, whitening.

They involved themselves in the pleasures of the mundane. Some of the boys took up long shoots of sugar cane that were stacked against the wall in a corner of the courtyard. After washing them, they started trying to strip them with knives, starting at the top, ineptly and ineffectively.

Vipul's father said, 'Come here, let me show you how to tackle sugar cane. You don't need a knife.'

Taking a shoot, he inserted one end deep into one side of his mouth, underneath his molars. His lips thinned and moved to that side, exposing his gums and teeth in an alarming snarl. His eyes narrowed like those of a newborn, partly through concentration and effort, and partly to prevent the sugar cane's juice, when he had breached its defence, from shooting into them. Holding the cane in his hands like a gigantic flute, he worked his teeth on it until, with a great jerk of his head, his hair flying aloft, he tore off a cube of the flesh along with a small length of the bark. The excised part looked, and he held and chewed upon it, like a toothbrush. He drank noisily the juice that emerged.

'Did you see?' he said, squelching his words through the cane and the juice and a grin of triumph. And then, with great verve and finality, he spat out the juiced cane, which lay there on the courtyard pulped and flattened.

The boys straightaway essayed the technique. With their snarls and narrow eyes, and jaws clamped fiercely, they looked like a pack of dogs gnawing at long bones. When finally a toothbrush of flesh detached itself, Vipul's mouth was filled with the unmodulated sweetness of sugar cane – no trace of tanginess here, nor of bitterness nor sourness; just the elemental sweetness of sugar. His tongue, alive to the taste, flicked about with snakelike darts inside his mouth.

While they mastered this art, his bhua, his father's sister, taught her son how best to eat a segment of orange: how to incise and open the skin, revealing the hairs of flesh, glistening rows of soft orange spindles. Her husband, sitting hunched on a bed, used a pair of moustache scissors to pare limitlessly the corns on the joints of his toes, and filed his toenails until they were perfectly arced and smooth. Vipul's mother oiled her sister-in-law's hair so that it became lush with shine and scent. Bauji and bibiji, too old to keep their eyes open in the face of the narcotic persuasion of the weather, went to sleep with strangely querulous looks on their faces, as though unhappy to have the family there – to have their quiet home turned into a humming familistery again – or perhaps ruffled by the dreams that cavorted uninvited inside their minds.

And thus an afternoon passed in which absolutely nothing got done. And it was not that the family had lapsed into a vacuum of thought and activity; rather they had knowingly, wilfully, created this emptiness, so that on this afternoon, as on several others that ensued, they did not affect the working of the world and the world did not meddle with their immaterial ways; a kind of polite standing off by mutual consent, until after the holidays the intrusions and the rebuffals would again commence on both sides.

*

In the late afternoons, the cousins went up on the roof to fly kites. The winter sky in Barnala was a theatre. Here kite designs, kite colours, kite skills, kite acrobatics, kite battles – everything to do with kites – were on show.

Most kites were peaceable creatures, content to flutter and bob on their own in a small volume of space, content just to be there at a reasonable altitude and look down surveyingly at the earth. But some kites, sailing higher and ever higher, reduced themselves to imaginary points in the sky, lost to gravity. Many kites were there just for a frivolous saunter, parading their splendid ribbons, a ribbon at the tail, ribbons at the ears, ribbons on top, craving attention. And there were the raw kites who were just learning to fly: how they started and stopped, rose and fell, sputtered about in a frenzy of failure, until they tore themselves in the paper.

But the ones to watch were the kites that were out for battle. They went swaggering into the sky, and did not find rest in any one spot; they climbed up and down, and went to this side and that, not fitfully, but with a gentle restlessness, ranging the sky, wanting to be its Queen.

If you kept watching, within a few minutes a challenger would waft up. It would announce its intent by executing the same swaggering flutters as the self-proclaimed Queen. And the first would notice this, and acknowledge the contender by floating still for a moment. Then, hostilities commenced, it would bristle and glower.

At first the battle looked like an act of clumsy lovemaking, as the kites touched and parted, twined and instantly untwined, kissed shyly and recoiled. Mere appearances. They would soon be clashing head on, like bulls, battering each other's ribs, inflicting wounds here and there, rustling invective.

But the real war was fought between the twines by which they flew. It was the twines who finally entangled in a ravelled knot, and tried each to sever the other with the help of their sawteeth of crushed glass with which they had been coated. Then when one was decapitated, its kite took to the breeze, in a gentle long journey earthward, while the twine, unanchored in the sky, instantly shrank into a twist of limp wavelets.

Vipul's family – his immediate family – went one day to pay their respects to his mother's uncle – the one who had the mysterious falling disease. For their visit, Vipul's grandfather arranged for a car and a driver, and so they went, in an Ambassador driven by a rash young man, to the town of Jullunder, where again Vipul saw the skyline thrown into dishevelment by television aerials, and the roads deluged in cycles and cycle-rickshas and mopeds, on which cars had no prerogative of way and which drove the young driver, who was used to the clear roads of Barnala, into a rage of declutching and gear-changing and engine-roaring.

Vipul's mother had written the address on an orphaned piece of paper, which after an unsystematic and flurried search she retrieved from the quarry-like, catholic interior of her handbag, and she now read out, 'New Market', 'Near BMC Chowk', and so on. After an hour of slow, predatory, and blind meandering, python-like, through the town of Jullunder, which alternately relaxed airy and colonial and cantonment-like, and contracted old and muffasil, thin-laned and populous with smells and sounds and traffic, they finally reached, in the heart of the old part of town, the address. It was one of the narrow lanes that were just wide enough for a car, but rendered unusable by the charpais, chairs, scooters, cycles and heaps of rubble that lay howsoever about. The house was some way down the lane and they walked to it, past a shop that sold only ice and smelt of sawdust and damp sackcloth, and past a narrow-doored clinic whose board advertised, in red letters both lurid and sympathetic, the fact that the doctor inside specialized in confidential diseases. And there were miscellaneous shops here and there, housed in cupboards built into the outer walls of the buildings – of watch repairers, jewellery workers, 'electricals'.

They came upon the doorway of the house. It was open. There was no bell, no knocker. A curtain, worn and sometime green, made the entrance. A voice came from inside; it was a radio voice; it read the News at Slow Speed in Punjabi, the rendition sapping the language of its sinew, rendering it mopey. Vipul's mother drew aside the curtain with an intruder's stealth. Inside, the room was in a gauzy green darkness, like that in the depth of a well. In the far right corner, by the cabinet from which the news issued, an old man, pulpy and spectacled, filled up an armchair. Close in front, with her back to them, sat a thin shadow of a woman, erect in a study chair.

They had been surprised to see Vipul's mother; it was almost as though they had failed to recognize her – but they were just having trouble accepting the fact that she was there, standing on this side of the curtain, a relative who they had assumed had quite forgotten them, as the rest of the world had.

'What's the name of the place you live in, Indu, again?' praji was saying now, still gazing at her with no belief in her presence.

'Khajoori, praji.'

'Right, right, right,' he said, and inspected the air with a false memory in his eyes, as though he had seen the place. 'Khajoori. I've heard you live in a big bungla.'

'Big enough for us, praji.'

'With many servants given by the company.'

'There are enough for us.'

'And are you never going to invite us there?'

Vipul's mother said, in an offended way, 'Do I need to call you there, praji? Isn't my house the same as yours? Don't you think you can just come and stay?'

'Right, right, right,' praji said, pleased with her vehemence. Then he turned to Vipul's father. 'What are you earning, Jagdish?'

'Enough to make things work out, praji.'

'Of course, of course, I can see that,' praji said, looking at him a little more attentively to assess this, perhaps from the quality of his clothes. 'Two and a half thousand? Three?'

'Something like that.'

'And living in a bungla, with company facilities, company servants, garden vegetables. You must be saving most of the salary.'

'Everyone has expenses, praji. The boys have to be taught, and we have to drive twenty kilometres to the markets…'

'Right, right, right,' praji said, rubbing his ears, as if his disbelief had shifted from his eyes to his ears. 'Ah, the children. What are the names? Bittu, Bitty?'

'Right, praji, right. You have such a good memory,' Vipul's mother said.

'This is Bitty?' He pointed at Vipul. 'Come here.' Vipul walked up to him with a mixture of awe and dread, hands half folded. 'Which class is he in?'

'I've passed the seventh,' Vipul said.

'He's remained small. Why don't you grow? Ha?' And praji slapped him. He perhaps intended to pat him on the cheek, but his hand landed harder than intended, and elsewhere: Vipul received a ringing blow on his ear.

'I'm trying, mamaji.'

And praji laughed, pleased to have scared Vipul.

Vipul's mother said, 'Praji, are Neena and Babbu and Pappi all right?' – referring to his children.

'Must be. I suppose they must be.'

'Why do you say it like that?'

'Because I can only suppose they must be.'

Savita bhabhiji, who had gone in, re-entered with a plate bearing an assortment of biscuits – Gluco-D, Marie, Krackjack, Monaco. She began to offer them around.

Praji heaved in his chair, pushed himself up with enormous effort.

'Give it here,' he was saying, 'I'll serve them the biscuits with my own hands. They have come after years.' And immediately he fell.

They all lifted him back into his chair.

Savita bhabhiji said, 'What's the need for you to get up? Can't you just keep sitting for two minutes?'

'Let him be, bhabhiji,' Vipul's mother said, 'he's a little excited.'

'Excited maybe, but he should know his limits. He just refuses to see sense. Keeps getting up, keeps falling down, keeps hurting himself. Every time he does that he gets bedridden for a week. More and more work for me.'

'She's making a fuss over nothing, I'm absolutely all right,' praji said, gathering his breath. 'Just get dizzy now and then. Nothing wrong. Happens to everybody.'

After praji had been reinstalled Vipul's mother said, 'You should go and live with your children, bhabhiji.'

'One of them has to call us first,' bhabhiji said. 'Nobody seems of a mind to do that. But what about his brothers and sisters? What are they for? One of you could call him to yourselves.'

'He can come whenever he wants, bhabhiji,' Vipul's mother said. 'I've already told him that, and you too. But naturally children have a greater right to look after their parents, and Neena and Bablu and Pappi would feel bad if I took you away, wouldn't they.'

'Indu, you're talking about rights. They seem to have forgotten even their sense of duty.'

Evenings in Barnala came early, and on a note of deep northern gloom. To dispel it, people left their homes at dusk and took off for walks.

Babuji was a habituated walker; he and a friend of his who owned a drapery, and another who owned a cinema (in which the boys were treated, once every winter vacation, to a free show from the 'box', a high and aggrandizing enclosure, reserved normally for the appeasement of Very Important Persons), and a third friend who practised an abstracted version of the trade of medicine – all these friends, bald and balding, with few and with false teeth, with bowed and bowing legs, shuffling and, childlike, waddling, went each evening for a long amble alongside the railway track that skirted the village-town; they sauntered through the fields into which it passed, and inhaled there the seasonal exhalations of the flowering mustard, the sugar cane, the cauliflower, and the spinach, peppered once in a while by the reassuring industrial exhausts of a passing steam locomotive and its train.

The boys, too, went with this company – and they were the only boys out for a walk. Barnala's own boys seemed to have better things to do, perhaps readying up for another kite-flying day. The boys' parents and grandmother went elsewhere; they went marketing, even though they intended to buy nothing, even though Barnala had really no marketing to offer.

As he walked beside the track, with darkness gathering over the fields and eroding outlines, Vipul liked to watch trains come along and pass by, their shrieking headlights placed high on their engines, making them look like miners with their cap lamps on; and he liked to feel the earth throb to the thunder of the train, to the cadence of its clatter. And the trains, viewed at the altitude of the track's embankment, passing within touching distance, looked no longer the obliging machines they were born to be, carrying belatedly the grateful multitudes from their origins to their destinations, or back, but like vehicles of depredation, peopled inside with marauding regiments. Often one of the boys would place a sacrificial, affordable coin on the rail, and let the train go over it; afterwards, the coin would still, miraculously, be there, and be miraculously entire, but flattened and smeared over the rail into a foil.

Vipul would let it cool, then peel it off, and, upon returning home, put it into a suitcase to take it with him, this exceptional winter memorabile of Barnala, back to Khajoori.

From Barnala Vipul returned to Delhi, and after a few days there, prepared to leave for Khajoori.

Vipul was glad the holidays were getting over. He longed to be back in Khajoori. He felt cramped staying in houses without grounds, without gardens; at Khajoori, in the bungalow, he had become used to amusing himself with doings in which space was an equal participant; whether he played marbles against himself, or walked about listening to the BBC, or played cricket with Sameer and the Bull and the boys from the 'quarters', he did not have to look for space; his movements were free. In Delhi and Barnala, he experienced the charm and the annoyance of a hemmed-in existence: the charm, the sense of community, in sharing the same square yards with several other claimants; the annoyance of never being able to find a place or a period of unchecked peace; of languorous thoughts being never allowed to reach their fantastic, logical ends.

And he felt he had exhausted the possibilities that the ancestral places offered. Delhi and Barnala had their respective uses – Delhi for shopping and Barnala for dawdling in dung-imbued air – but each place had outlived its particular use in less than a fortnight's time, and nothing special remained to hold Vipul back to either. As for relatives, barring a few exceptions, it was more than adequate to meet them for a few days once a year, for beyond that interval the appeal of it began to age, then very quickly to stale.

EPILOGUE

When they returned to Khajoori they were told that Rover, during their absence, had died. Nobody knew how. It just happened one night, they were told, as such things do.

Vipul felt betrayed. There had been no reason for Rover to die.

He said to Sameer, 'I think someone has poisoned Rover.'

Sameer said, 'Who?'

'I *think*,' said Vipul, 'I don't know. Because he was absolutely fine when we left.'

'I don't see why anyone should poison him. I think he had a heart attack.'

'Can dogs have heart attacks?'

'Who knows? Otherwise why should he die? Anyway, let's give him a proper burial.'

'But they have burnt his body.'

'We can have a substitute for his body. The main thing is to give him a proper farewell. Otherwise his soul will feel unhonoured and will haunt us. After all, he was a very good dog.'

So the following day they went to the riverside equipped with a bundle of rags that was to stand in for Rover, a cross made from two ragged strips of wood, and a white square of cloth for a flag. They dug a pit in the sand, and put in it the bundle of rags. Then they sanded the pit over. They anchored in it the cross, and on the cross they tied the white flag. Why they put the cross there or why the flag they did not know; but it seemed decent and dramatic and ordained to do so.

Sameer said, 'We'll say our prayers.'

So they stood by the grave with folded hands and closed eyes, and for a minute or two prayed for Rover in heaven, or for him to be admitted there. And while he prayed Vipul remembered the time that Rover had bitten him on the head because Vipul had insisted on sitting on him (which had made Vipul look at him askance for days), and how sometimes he gave a most fearsome snarl when Vipul tried to take away his food, and how he extended a limp foreleg and folded down his ears when he pleaded for something.

Then Sameer took a twig and inscribed the sand at the side of the grave, in big letters, in English:

> Here Lies Rover the Alsatian Dog
> Thirteen Years Old
> May His Soul RIP

'Now he'll never forget us,' Vipul said.

They left their composition, their salute to the heaven-gone Rover, to its anchorless devices, to be claimed by the waters of the Damodar or to be blown over by its sand.

A few days later, at lunch, their father said, 'We'll soon have to shift from this house, and from Khajoori.'

Their mother said, 'So you've got the letter?'

'It came today,' their father said.

Vipul said, 'Shift where?' There was anger in his voice, and the raw-banana curry that he had been in the middle of enjoying turned tasteless.

His father said, 'I don't know, but somewhere across the river.'
'But I don't want to shift,' said Vipul.
'It's not in your hands, son,' said his father.
'Then whose? Do *you* want to shift?' Vipul said.
'Bitty, papa has been *transferred*,' his mother said.
'But why did he *agree* to being transferred?' Vipul said.
'There's no agree-disagree in these matters. We'll have to go.'
'Isn't there any way we can stay on?'
His father said, 'Don't be childish, Bitty. Things keep changing. You have to face them.'
'But there's been no change so far.'
His father laughed. 'Bitty, you should start reading the newspapers.'
Then his father and mother ignored him and started talking of concrete details; of the packing that would have to be done, and of how to manage it, how to schedule it, how to prevent theft while it went on; what they would take along and what leave behind, depending on the size of the house they would have to move to.

Indeed Vipul had not taught himself to look at newspapers with any seriousness, and news of many important things that were happening in the world around him passed him by – although, owing to the BBC, he was alert to several things of dubious importance happening elsewhere.

India's coal mining industry was to be nationalized, and the Imperial Coal Company, along with other private companies, would soon be reduced to just a name, and what was now just a name on the government's planning paper, the Indian Public Coal Company Limited, would become then the extractor of the coal. And his father was to leave the ICC and join the IPCCL; he, like the coal mines, was to be 'taken over'.

The transition turned out to be vague and seamless; for some time, he was as much a part of the overtakers as of the overtaken.

The IPCCL assigned to him the task of overseeing the taking-over of a belt of mines in West Bengal, before deciding on his posting.

So for a few months, the boys and their mother continued to be in Khajoori while their father worked in West Bengal. On weekends they would visit him. The journeys, when they were not made on the coruscatingly named Black Diamond Express, were made by a company car, an Ambassador provided by the IPCCL, eastward on the Grant Trunk Road from Jadugoda, in a direction opposite to the one they had taken when they had gone, with Veena masi and Neha, to see the pandit by the temple. In this new direction, in which lay West Bengal and the heart of India's communist sentiment, the Grand Trunk Road was being resuscitated after a period of severe neglect in the course of which it had become cadaverous and unnegotiable. There were many low-lying causeways which overflowing monsoon waters had entirely swallowed up, and only trucks had the throttled power and the strength of suspension to surge, in mighty joint-wrenching seiches, over them. At every such site a bridge was being built, turning causeway into culvert; and during the construction, the car had to take what was baldly called a 'diversion', a looping makeshift track of yet greater axle-maiming potential.

The house in which they lived in Disergarh was a bungalow turned into a guest house; a special bungalow, the kind in which Thapa would have very much liked to work, for it had housed, until recently, an Englishman named Mr Cooper. Mr Cooper had converted the greater part of the grounds into a park, a dot of a jungle, where he kept chital and sambar and antlered swamp deer and boar, and let snakes and other miscellany multiply. There was also a tribe of peacock and peahen, which produced shockingly harsh shrieks in the evenings. And beside the house there was an oblong pool adjoined by a kennel in which an otter, named Catkin but not called by this name by anybody ever since Mr Cooper left, swam and slept and ate his daily ration of fish, the kind-hearted provision of which was a logistical and financial annoyance which the IPCCL had not yet developed the lack of heart to discontinue.

It was the kind of bungalow in which Vipul, too, would have liked to live. But of course it was no longer a bungalow in the inhabitable sense; it was a guest house. There was talk of greater change to come: all the bungalows in the coalfields were to be partitioned, cut up like cake into several smaller pieces; and their grounds were to be used to capacity, with blocks of flats staked into them. So the house to which Vipul would soon move might be just one of those pieces of bungalow, or an aerial flat; the space allotted to his existence was to constrict, and he to somehow accommodate to it.

Vipul spent hours feeding sandwiches to the sambar, the only animal in the park that was neither too skittish nor too snappish for hand-feeding, and spent hours watching the otter perform. Catkin swam and endlessly swam the short length of his pool in an obsessed stereotypy; to see him roll over and reverse direction at each end was the bewitching thing.

Vipul wished that the peacocks, too, would perform, but they were adamant; not until the sky was cloud-black with promise of rain would they hold aloft their compound-eyed, all-seeing, oil-film fans.

And then, of course, the fan's moist colours would murmur the very words, seasonal and apt at the time:

Naache man mora,
Magan tikk-da-dheegi-dheegi;
Badara ghir aaye,
Rut hai bheegi-bheegi

And the peacock's soul, iridescent in his shimmering green-blue-indigo breast, would be ecstatic with song.

ACKNOWLEDGEMENTS

This novel has been resurrected, miraculously almost, after lying in a state of limbo for more than a quarter of a century. Grateful thanks for its fresh lease on life are due to Amit Chaudhuri and Pankaj Mishra, who very kindly steered it into propitious channels.

My thanks go out in addition to Amit, and to Saikat Majumdar and Sumana Roy, for their continual championing of the novel and of my writing, which at various stages helped keep *Speck* alive while it lay dormant.

I'm deeply grateful also:

– To my parents who, placed by happenstance into the far-flung Indian coalfields, made possible the sort of childhood I've tried to recreate here; and to my brother Naveen, co-partaker of the wilds.

– To De Nobili School, Digwadih, and the Jesuits and teachers who kept it going in the face of forbidding odds. They put together a fine schooling where, so easily, none might have existed. To my schoolmates, Vivek Sahay, Asim Agarwala, NK (you are sorely missed, Bala!), Dev Surya and Rajat Bhatia, who, by assuring me that the novel rekindled their schooldays for them, kept the flame alive.

– To Jatin Nayak, Dr Nagraj Huilgol, Adil Jussawalla, Neeraja Balachander, Arundhathi Subramaniam and Varsha Dutta, for their much-fortifying encouragement along the way.

– To Rahul Soni at HarperCollins, for his conviction that this novel merited a reincarnation. Also for his unflagging, affable patience at all stages, and his astonishing acuity at detecting ambiguities, inconsistencies and plain bloomers, helping me set them right.

– To, above all and in immense measure, Shivani. Helpmate, cherished friend, bulwark against vicissitudes. Inexhaustible fount of good cheer besides – and the staunchest believer I could have hoped for in the possibilities of my writing.

ABOUT THE AUTHOR

ROHIT MANCHANDA spent his childhood in the coalfields of Jharkhand and did his doctorate from the University of Oxford. He is a professor at IIT Bombay where he researches computational neurophysiology and, in a parallel world, writes fiction. His first novel was published as *In the Light of the Black Sun* in 1996, and is being republished titled *A Speck of Coal Dust* simultaneously with a new novel, *The Enclave*. He has also authored *Monastery, Sanctuary, Laboratory*, a history of IIT Bombay. Manchanda has won several awards for his teaching, including an INSA Teachers Award, and for his writing a Betty Trask Award and a Tibor Jones South Asia Prize.

HarperCollins *Publishers* India

At HarperCollins India, we believe in telling the best stories and finding the widest readership for our books in every format possible. We started publishing in 1992; a great deal has changed since then, but what has remained constant is the passion with which our authors write their books, the love with which readers receive them, and the sheer joy and excitement that we as publishers feel in being a part of the publishing process.

Over the years, we've had the pleasure of publishing some of the finest writing from the subcontinent and around the world, including several award-winning titles and some of the biggest bestsellers in India's publishing history. But nothing has meant more to us than the fact that millions of people have read the books we published, and that somewhere, a book of ours might have made a difference.

As we look to the future, we go back to that one word—a word which has been a driving force for us all these years.

Read.